FOR OLD TIME'S SAKE

"Brad, there are some things a woman likes to put behind her." Arlisa paused. "The past is one of them."

Brad was alerted to the inherent dangers of the situation, attempting to pick up from where they'd left off. Yet he couldn't help himself. He didn't deserve a clear berth where she was concerned, but the thought of parting on a kiss suddenly seemed appealing.

Odd sets of words immediately passed from his lips. "Sometimes the past can be your future."

Arlisa hesitated. "This is where I say good-bye, Brad."

He leaned across to her, so close, Arlisa felt his glare on her. "Where are you going?" The rawness of his voice sent Arlisa's pulses accelerating.

"Away from you," Arlisa pounced, discovering that he was staring at her mouth.

"Wait." Brad's fingers touched the bottom of her lip.

"Brad, you're getting dangerous," she resisted.

"Maybe," he agreed. "But for the sake of what we've been to one another, I want us to part on . . ." He dared say it ". . . a farewell kiss."

"Brad . . ." Her voice died in her throat. His hands had crept up to her arms.

"Not even for old time's sake?" came the hoarse, arousing tone.

Arlisa was aware of this man standing in front of her, where she could feel the heat of his body growing even closer. And then the hard angles of his face slowly became absorbed into hers.

**BOOK YOUR PLACE ON OUR WEBSITE
AND MAKE THE ARABESQUE
ROMANCE CONNECTION!**

We've created a customized website just for our very special
Arabesque readers, where you can get the inside scoop on
everything that's going on with Arabesque romance novels.

When you come online, you'll have the exciting opportunity
to:

- View covers of upcoming books

- Learn about our future publishing schedule (listed by
  publication month and author)

- Find out when your favorite authors will be visiting a
  city near you

- Search for and order backlist books

- Check out author bios and background information

- Send e-mail to your favorite authors

- Join us in weekly chats with authors, readers and other
  guests

- Get writing guidelines

- AND MUCH MORE!

Visit our website at
http://www.arabesquebooks.com

VIOLETS ARE BLUE

Sonia Icilyn

ARABESQUE
★BET
BOOKS

BET Publications, LLC
www.msbet.com
www.arabesquebooks.com

ARABESQUE BOOKS are published by

BET Publications, LLC
c/o BET BOOKS
One BET Plaza
1900 W Place NE
Washington, D.C. 20018-1211

First Printing: December, 1999

10 9 8 7 6 5 4 3 2 1

Printed in the United States of America

One

"I'm keeping an eye on you," Erica Belleville-Brown warned arrogantly, while she did precisely that, her squirrel-brown gaze boring directly into the younger woman whom she considered was attempting to cause trouble. "I want you to stay away from my brother."

"I'm not interested in Brad," Arlisa Davenport declared, resenting the steely persona she suddenly found herself up against. She'd come to *La Casa de la Salsa,* where the ultrarich who had a penchant for the Afro-Cuban dance scene were known to frequent, hoping to have a quiet night. The last thing she expected on such a cool night in mid-August, where a mild chill had left her in a bad mood, was to be confronted with anyone from her past. Least of all the sister of an old flame.

The after-work champagne drinkers had already given way to the Harare Henries crowd, the famed nickname given to the jet-set Nigerian men who she could see from where she sat at her stool by the bar in the popular West End club in London. And Generation X hormones were racing with a vengeance as her inquiring fawn-brown gaze quickly swept the room in annoyance, bypassing Erica's rigid frame beside her, to decidedly check out what was on offer.

Two bar stools to her right revealed a shapely woman

in skintight leather rubbing her chest up and down a man's arm like she was attempting to remove a stubborn stain. On a bar stool to her left sat a sorry figure of a man with a receding hairline and alert hazel-brown eyes that looked riddled with guilt, as though he'd been shamefully caught in the act of doing something.

Burnt out, Arlisa thought to herself astutely, recognizing that once a man had been with enough women, made enough children, frequented enough parties and smoked enough *ganja,* he was the type to be found propping up a bar stool with guilt laden across his smoldering features.

He was not the type she was looking for tonight. She, on the other hand, was waiting to catch a glimpse of Earl Vani, the man who had recently tackled the Jamaican government single-handed about what he described as their appalling lack of support for one of the island's growing industries: fashion. As a member from the small brigade of men who'd helped commercialize ghetto life into a multi-dollar industry, he'd made it one of his prolonged and personal crusades to pressure government to help finance his global endeavors. So what did she now want with Brad Belleville? Arlisa had convinced herself a long time ago that he was small dimes and loose change compared to Earl Vani. Nothing bankable in her opinion.

"You haven't changed, have you?" Erica mouthed with distaste, aware that she hadn't seen Arlisa Davenport in nearly two years. "That's why my brother needs protection against women like you, who are only out for what they can get. In fact, isn't that why you're here?"

Arlisa looked away, thinking to hide the wistful display of guilt in her brown eyes. A woman now intensely private about her personal life and intensely personal about her public life, Arlisa knew that she had not only become a doyenne of her time, but that her social butterfly lifestyle had inevitably earned her some enemies. Saved by earlier mistakes, many of which had involved men, she now considered herself a *Hypermega,* her own invention and phraseology for describing a woman who possessed a highly developed sense of her own perfection.

And as a child, she'd always told herself that such perfection would one day wed her into a fortune, which was why she was now one of the many immaculately coiffed women endlessly plotting on how to bag a millionaire. Arlisa wasn't remotely embarrassed by her avarice, either. Over the years she had taught herself some bizarre facts about life. Money counts. And what she deserved was a rich mate.

Self-acquired knowledge had taught her that there were four types to choose from, too. The self-made rich mate who always married quick, which was precisely why she had a keen interest in Earl Vani. Then there was the novelty-seeking rich mate who always attracted talent. She was neither a singer, dancer, model or actress, so that ruled him out completely. The outcast rich mate sought to shock his family. There was nothing scandalous about her past, except that she'd once gambled away one hundred and fifty thousand dollars at a casino in Monte Carlo, and had nearly lost the inheritance of the family newspaper her father had founded. But she'd matured a lot since then. And then there was the guilty rich mate who liked a woman who was struggling in a way he admired. Arlisa's only struggle presently was the debate in her head on what she should wear when she next visited the club.

Yet something in what Erica had said hit a raw nerve, and Arlisa detested her for it, too. Erica was a woman never seen in a state of less than total serenity, who often spent her days cruising the auction circuits to acquire the latest African artifacts and whose white antique open-topped sports car, a gift from her lawyer husband, was often spotted outside the best designer boutiques in London. This woman, who was always so judgmental of her, so watchful of her every move, had succeeded in allowing her composure to slip a notch. But Arlisa was quick in pulling herself together.

"Since when have you been qualified to give an opinion about me?" she asked flatly, disliking the satisfied expression Erica's face suddenly adopted.

"The moment I decided that you're a tramp," Erica tossed back in her cultured English dulcet tones, which still held a hint of her Barbadian accent.

"A tramp?" Arlisa laughed, telling herself not to pamper to Erica Belleville-Brown's choice of words, and more precisely to her snobbish manner. "I think you meant to say vamp. I'm very particular about what people call me these days."

"I'm sure you are," Erica agreed knowingly, her claw-like fingernails brushing back a strand of long, curly black hair styled in her usual trademark of careful dishevelment. "What with all those men I've heard you were seen sporting around town with, it's little wonder how my brother ever kept up with you."

"So I'm a scarlet woman, a harlot, Miss Jezebel in your book, right?" Arlisa rebutted loudly against the buzz of a Bronx beat rhythm, her tone laced with ice. "And you and your brother are—"

"Too noble for you," Erica finished sarcastically.

Arlisa adopted a challenging position on her bar stool, her patience now worn to a frazzle. "Noble women bore the brains out of me," she told Erica arrogantly, enjoying the way she saw the woman stiffen at the gesture beneath the red glare of flashing neon lights. "Maybe it's time you took your noble behind out of my face before I forget I was raised with any manners."

Arlisa received a headstrong glare. "You'll be wise not to make an enemy out of me," Erica threatened, her tone deadly in its menace as it eclipsed an eerie piano note echoing from the music.

"Especially now that we've established our mutual affection for one another," Arlisa responded, decidedly turning to the bartender. "Tequila Sunrise," she ordered, ignoring Erica entirely. Only when she detected that the older woman had diligently walked away to join the ever-growing crowd of late entries into the club, and she'd paid for her drink, did Arlisa return her attention to the room.

A vivacious Latin couple full of fire and energy immediately brushed their way past her, totally engrossed, their faces excited that the room had become full of life as the music style originally called *el son,* emerging in Cuba around the turn of the twentieth century, filled every corner of the club. Congas and timbals provided the spicy African beat and Arlisa could feel her spirit lift slightly as her feet began to tap the foot of the bar stool to the vigorous beat.

Her gaze stayed lingered on the same Latin couple as she watched the male lead sidestep around his beautiful accomplice, his arms forming around her in an overhead hand sweep that allowed his partner to swivel easily into them, where he pulled her into a wrap and gave her an intimate cuddle. Arlisa watched reminiscently as he repeated the pattern, this time performed with personal sensual signatures that the lead employed to coax his partner to do her best hook turns and free-spin techniques.

Earl Vani had moved her around exactly like that, but he'd not yet arrived and she could feel the impatience to dance rise up within her. Her gaze briefly diverted to the salsa groovers shaking the dance floor with their practiced techniques and intricate pattern combinations derived from the foundation of a basic three-step variation. *A modest man and a true capitalist,* she reminded herself, taking her mind back to the subject of Earl Vani. She began to slowly down the Tequila Sunrise, thinking of when they'd last spoken. *A practicing Rastafarian and at aged forty-six is renowned not only for his wealth, but for the fact that he always wears black in winter and white in summer.*

Knowing that mid-August still constituted an English summer, Arlisa was expecting to see him fully decked out in white, just like the picture she'd seen of Earl Vani on billboards in Brixton Market, promoting his line of shops and designer wear. *Let me see.* She thought back quickly to the statistics she'd compiled on the man. A numbers game she'd often played in her head as a young adolescent began making the quick calculations. *Two shops in Paris, one in Amsterdam, three in London, four in New York . . .*

"Do you have the time?" The weary voice of Mr. Burnt Out on the next bar stool sounded above the fast-paced salsa rhythm pumping from three strategically placed monitors overhead. Arlisa glared at him in annoyance for protruding into her bored but scheming thoughts. *No fine line in chat or a degree in charm,* she told herself, before glancing at her Rolex, a birthday present from her brother-in-law to commemorate her twenty-sixth birthday.

"Eleven-twenty-two," she answered firmly, her thoughts instantly rushing back to Earl Vani. *Big on sums, even bigger on small talk. Has a great camera profile, earns five hundred and sixty thousand dollars a year, but is worth millions. Has melting brown eyes, a sharp line in suits, adores food, style and . . .*

"I'm the owner of this club," her intrusive, burnt-out

friend declared concisely. "Would you like me to get you another drink?"

Arlisa turned her weary head again in annoyance toward the man whose slight Guyana accent was as pronounced as his enthusiasm: dull. "No, thank you. I'm waiting for someone," she answered politely. She was aware that Earl Vani always entered *La Casa de la Salsa* at the stroke of midnight with his retailing mafia, and with an unshakable stature that always seemed to set a battalion of adoring females' hearts aquiver. She didn't want to miss the entrance of this man she'd waited five weeks to see again, whose cherubic smile and average frame easily camouflaged the energetic heartbeats of his dance style, which he'd demonstrated to full advantage when he'd twirled her around the room in passionate time to the fast-changing rhythm of the salsa.

"I've been watching you," Mr. Burnt Out declared persistently. "All dressed in white, you're easy to notice. I think we're beginning to bond."

"Really?" Arlisa offered sardonically, noting his approval of her taste in clothes. Having an aesthetic sense which was often wounded by the sight of, say, red shoes with a yellow dress, Arlisa always made sure she creatively monitored herself with the greatest of care. Her selection that night was an offensively expensive fifteen hundred pounds blatant color-coordinated gesture to directly bait Earl Vani's attention again. Only *his* attention, she reminded herself cautiously.

And so she felt noticeably weary when she eyed Mr. Burnt Out, reaching into his jacket pocket from where he produced a small compact disc in a transparent case. Deftly handing it over to her as a gift, he said, "I'd like you to have this."

"What is it?" she asked, uninterested, regarding him over the rim of her glass.

"It's some music I've recorded." The Guyana accent thickened loudly. "When you listen to it, you'll get to know my soul and when you know my soul, you'll know Khadija."

"Who's Khadija?" Arlisa felt confused.

"Khadija is the name of my heart," the bar stool stranger declared.

"I don't think I should take this," Arlisa smiled uneasily, her head shaking her refusal of the CD he was firmly planting into the palm of her hand. "It seems some woman named Khadija has hurt you pretty badly and I don't want you to pass that judgment on me."

"I insist that you have it." The man's tone deepened aggressively above the blare of music that had quickened its pace rather steadily. "I know you golddiggers would rather I was a twenty-four carat, even though I'm a nice person," he laughed ironically. "But there's only scrap metal in this club tonight, Baby. Gold tainted at that."

Don't I know it, Arlisa mused in dissatisfaction, adding absently, "With a lot of rusty bits and more than a few screws loose upstairs."

She hadn't expected Mr. Burnt Out to take her remark personally. "Now, wait a minute," he rasped, offended. "This club ain't no goldmine. You can forget about striking it lucky here, Baby. I've seen your type before, thinking you can mess around with a man's soul. Well, before you—"

"Before you can find your soul mate," Arlisa interrupted, refusing to flinch as she coolly jumped up from her bar stool, intent on removing herself from this menacing intruder, "you have to find your soul. Seems you lost yours when you lost Khadija."

Replacing her glass on the bar, she pivoted regally on her three-inch white heels, ready to leave the bar. But a strong, clammy hand gripped her wrist harshly. Pain shot up her arm and made contact with her shoulder as she felt her body propelled against the wooden bar. A smothered scream of anticipation left her throat only to be dimmed beneath the loud, fresh new Puerto Rican rhythm that filled the room.

"Take that back!" Mr. Burnt Out bellowed, having left his own bar stool and was now standing to his imposing six-foot height, a good four inches above Arlisa. "I said—"

Arlisa didn't allow him to finish. Before she knew what she was doing, she reached for her drink and threw the rest of its contents directly at her bar stool adversary. She felt a sense of satisfaction rush through her body when her fawn gaze took in the red and yellow stain making its way into the fabric of the pale green, linen suit jacket. She had expected to immobilize the man, but his grip on her wrist only became firmer.

"Let the lady go," another voice suddenly intruded sternly.

Arlisa immediately felt the hold on her wrist loosen, and turned to eye her savior with mitigating relief. The face that held steadfast with her bar stool adversary was instantly familiar as their gazes briefly met. It was the way in which the newcomer's hardened honey-brown eyes narrowed astutely, the way his olive-brown hands clenched into fists, and the oval face contorting arrogantly that suddenly brought back a rush of memories.

"Show me the devil so I can spit in his eye," Arlisa wavered in disbelief. "Brad?"

"Still rattling the cages of men?" Brad Belleville announced, before turning his attention to dispelling away with her intrusive stranger.

"Do you know her?" Mr. Burnt Out instantly relented, pulling a soiled handkerchief from his jacket pocket, which he began to use to blot out the stain in his jacket.

"She's with me," Brad assured him sternly. "And she can be a feisty old gal when her blood's fired up."

"Man, you've got problems," Mr. Burnt Out derided knowingly, tipping his head in an easterly direction to where a clutter of women were standing patiently. "Your girl's looking to rival Fort Knox. Her and the six others over there, all waiting to get a piece of Earl Vani, no doubt. Well, I'm telling her the same thing I told them. He isn't in tonight. He's been barred."

Arlisa stared mutely at Mr. Burnt Out, feeling the red hot rush of embarrassment taint her tawny brown complexion. Her gaze veered toward Brad Belleville. They flashed cynical at the sneer as she studied the man who had flown to her rescue. She hardly recognized Brad's hard-boned masculinity, the straight nose and full pink lips set in an oval face, where his olive-brown complexion spoke of his biracial origins.

At first she was sharply aware of her fast mental arithmetic in deducting him to be a man now aged twenty-nine, three years older than herself. But she hadn't expected the short black curly hair trimmed close to his scalp, which was in perfect contrast to the shadow of a moustache that graced his upper lip. Nor did she expect the formal nature of his tailored Atlantic-blue colored suit, beneath which a casual open-necked shirt perfectly bespoke of that time of year where the late summer blooms were already dipping their heads to greet the arrival of a fresh new season. The last time they'd seen each other, he was clothed in jeans and a sweatshirt, hardly seeming so mature.

Outwardly, Arlisa was immediately aware of her cool disdain toward him, while inwardly she knew she was panicking wildly. For in the fullness of Brad's presence, where there was no doubting the devastating attraction he still possessed, her senses reluctantly screamed to her every nerve endings a poignant warning that this man still had a strong pull on her.

"I was trying to let him down diplomatically," she voiced haughtily, her panic easing slightly as she detected Mr. Burnt Out sensibly walking away. "I don't know why he reacted the way he did."

"Well I've noticed that you radiate something when you're about to crack on to a guy," Brad voiced disapprovingly, "and I can see those same vibes coming from you now. You have the devil's luck that he was in a good mood tonight," he warned her carefully.

"I wasn't interested in *him*," Arlisa hit back.

"No. It was Earl Vani, right?" Brad couldn't resist aiming the jibe, his eyes charting Arlisa carefully. "What else do you do nowadays besides still collecting boyfriends?"

"I . . . I . . ."

"And what was all that about Jerome Morrison?"

Arlisa was dumbstruck. Never being a person who could answer two questions at once, she said sharply, "That was last year. All water under the bridge now."

"Whose bridge exactly?" Brad sounded peeved. "Todd Scott's, Jarvis Townsend's, Cory Robinson's . . ."

Arlisa shook her head in shock. Of course these were all men Brad knew in one way or another from his childhood or teenage days. "You're still so judgmental of me, just like your sister," she taunted, aware of the irony. "Ten minutes ago she was on a roll, too, or should I say she was one big avalanche when it came to deriding my ethical standards."

"The only roll I know about is yours," Brad commented smoothly. "The Rolling Dice casino, in fact. And if I'm to be more specific, a little matter of one hundred and fifty thousand dollars."

Arlisa's eyes flickered in culpable shame. She suddenly found herself in a struggle to keep them from sliding nervously away from Brad's satisfied expression, appalled that he had noted her sigh of anxiety. "That was also a year ago," she confessed gravely, deciding not to inquire how he came by the information. She knew that Erica was always amazingly well-informed—knowing the *best* club in town, *best* hotels abroad, *best* species of winter rose, and was always at the heart of high society gossip. "We sorted it all out mutually."

"Kendra, right?" Brad surmised accurately.

Arlisa was used to her butterfly intelligence being dismissed as inconsequential when marked in comparison to that of her elder sister, but she nodded nonetheless to Brad's summarization.

"How is she, by the way?" he asked, his hard, almost brutal face softening at the mention of her sister's well-being. Though Brad had never met Kendra, Arlisa recalled that she had once spoken highly of her to him.

"Kendra got into a very united state with Shay Brentwood," she admitted ruefully, rubbed raw that his casual inquiry did not extend to asking how she had been. "And now she's the regular Mrs. Enterprise to her husband, who is joint heir to the Brentwood Communications Group in New York."

"I see," Brad nodded in surprise. "That big wedding last Christmas?" he added absently. "It seems that Mr. Brentwood knew that there was more to your sister than merely crude, physical attraction," he said in admiration. "Sounds like she always knew where her ethics lay."

"And as far as you're concerned, I'm somewhere between evildoer and sinner," Arlisa hissed, fuelled with angry dismay as she threw her head back challengingly. "Why don't you just admit it, Brad, and be done, okay? You don't like me."

Two thick, dark brows arched arrogantly. "I prefer a woman with old-fashioned values like honesty and faithfulness," Brad ejected sternly. "Whatever potent attraction that existed between you and I could never have survived your . . . should I say, those frequent occasions I've heard about when you like to display your pulling power on men."

"What?" Arlisa gasped, surprised, knowing that he had heard far too much gossip. "You're misplacing the truth and you know it. Whatever we had was destined to remain unfulfilled because of Erica, your interfering sister."

Brad's eyes darkened as he studied her again. Arlisa sensed that he liked the way she looked in her short, flimsy white dress and high heels, and the way she'd kept her makeup to a minimum; just enough to add a spark of life to her glowing tawny-brown complexion, where a hint of Revlon to her rounded cheekbones, salon-plucked eyebrows and fully endowed lips gave her that certain visual air of confidence that, mentally, she was grasping at right now.

"Erica's very protective of me," she heard him explain. "She always has been. She wouldn't want me to be with someone who wanders aimlessly from bed to bed. Fast love like that is just one big merry-go-round where every player takes a ride to enjoy a little surface satisfaction. The capacity for loving is never explored and we Bellevilles have principles—"

"That were rammed down my throat ever since I was a kid," Arlisa finished almost flippantly in her defense. "I remember the things you and Erica said about me and my father when he was dirt poor. You only took an interest the moment my father's newspaper began to make him some real money and we moved to a part of London that fit your standards."

The urge to agree was almost overwhelming, Brad realized. As a boy, he recalled his adolescent arrogance toward the young Arlisa Davenport. She was the girl with the neatly braided hair and simple pinafore dress, moccasins, and clean but cheap socks. A skinny little thing that he'd thought he could vent his frustrations on. At the time they'd first met, his parents' marriage had already fallen apart, as much because his father was unambitious as through any character weakness on his part. And his English mother had remarried into influential wealth, where he and Erica had become impediments to her newfound status. They were sent to live with their grandfather, Otis Belleville, who had raised them in a manner that was as old as his homeland, Barbados itself.

But he had often resented his mother for her rejection of him and his sister, and his lips twisted when he thought back to how he'd tried to take what arrogance he had held within out on the young, shy Arlisa Davenport. As childish as they both were, she had exhibited that same kind of attitude he'd recognized in his mother. She was a female always wanting to touch and take his things and seemed devoid of any affection whatsoever. As an adult, he'd interpreted that girls like her grew to be women who judged "love" to be something that was probably more available to the highest bidder, for he still remembered Arlisa's reaction when Cory Robinson had given her a friendship ring at his sister's eighteenth birthday party. He and Erica never received pocket money from their stingy grandfather. So how was he to buy her anything back then?

All his life, while the old man had ruled his every action and his mother had kept her safe distance, he'd harbored a certain attitude toward women. It wasn't intentional; more protective, if anything. And in his opinion, Arlisa Davenport, though beautiful as she was, had grown into something no different from the rest he'd met. Money creates taste. Wasn't that what his mother always said on the rare occasions she'd visited him and his sister?

Before Brad knew it, he'd muttered those same immortal words. "Money creates taste," he told a startled Arlisa.

There was real anger in Arlisa's face now and a regret that whipped under her defenses. She'd heard Brad voice those words once before, when she was nine years old and had gone with her father to visit Otis Belleville. Her father had planned to discuss the advertising of Otis's first restaurant in Streatham, South London, and had been excited about doing a feature in his newspaper, the *Nubian Chronicle*. She was to meet Erica in the playroom that she shared with her younger brother Brad. Otis had taken her up there to play, while he kept the meeting with her father downstairs in the lounge. But Otis's two grandchildren were the most spoiled brats she'd ever had occasion to meet in her young life.

They'd both bragged about their piano classes and horse riding lessons, and while Erica dallied in ballet, Brad dallied in the local soccer team. They both also made it plain to her that she was too poor to be their friend, and so she'd been promptly turned out of the playroom to dutifully sit at the top of the stairs until her father had finished his meeting with their grandfather in the lounge.

She was not to meet Brad again until she had been invited to Erica's eighteenth birthday party. It was obviously the social event of the year and every person of consequence had their children attend it, though she remembered that Kendra had been vacationing with their cousin Nellie at the time. She was but a teenager of fourteen when she found herself confronted with the seventeen-year-old Brad Belleville.

He'd been the first boy she ever kissed and Arlisa still remembered the moment. It was inside the dark cupboard beneath the stairs where she'd experienced her first flurry of excited anticipation. It was also to be the place where she'd experienced her first moment of embarrassment, too. Otis Belleville had caught them there. In retrospect, his timing could not have been put better. Brad had been biting into her neck while telling her that wise virgins lost their virginity as a strategic move, and he'd been trying to convince her that if she were to make out with him that day, he'd give her the diamond studded ring he wore on his right middle finger as a tangible promise to marry her.

But when Otis had found them, he'd simply smiled and ordered that they return to mingle with the throng of young girls and boys who were but mere acquaintances to Erica and her brother. Her heart had been filled with foolish adoration for Brad then, until she'd overheard the godawful things he'd said about her and her father.

She'd been in the kitchen, getting a piece of Erica's birthday cake when she saw Brad through the open window, talking with his sister. *"I've just kissed Arlisa Davenport,"* he'd bragged. *"She tasted like wet rubber. I thought I was kissing a fish. It's just like Momma said. Money creates taste. If you haven't got money, you can't do anything. And her father is so poor . . ."* She did not want to recall anymore.

"Still behaving like the Almighty, are we?" Arlisa dismissed in arrogance, pulling her thoughts back to the present as she picked up the compact disc, which Mr. Burnt Out had given her, from the bar and began slipping it into the haven of her white handbag, preparatory to leaving. "You know, I've never told you or your sister this," she admitted rather candidly, tucking her bag beneath her arm. "But if there's a shred of conscience in either yours or Erica's head that makes you wonder why I'm the kind of woman I am today, I'd say it was entirely appropriate. The way you both have treated me has shaped my whole view about life. Neither of you have any real understanding about what you do to people. Maybe one day, someone will have the guts to tell you."

Brad's mouth fell agape as he took hold of Arlisa's arm. "I don't think—"

"Remove your hand from my person," Arlisa seethed. "Or I'll chew it off at the wrist."

She knew her curt, almost acid words hit home the moment she saw the remorse cross Brad's honey-brown eyes. Yet despite the many things she'd remembered him saying about her, which should have been enough to extinguish the soft spot she'd always held in her heart for Brad as a teenager, Arlisa couldn't deny the attraction she still felt for him now. The fire had never died. Even presently, she discovered that she was trembling, her legs oddly weak, her fingers feeling clammy from the smoldering heat building up within, caused by the brief contact he'd made with her arm.

She told herself it was the shock of seeing him and Erica again, but in her heart of hearts, she knew it was a lot more than that. The reason for her familiar and involuntary weakness lay directly with the man looking at her so contemptuously.

"Just tell me one thing," Brad demanded hotly, aware that he was feeling unsettled, even fidgety at the sight of seeing this formidable, beautiful woman standing in front of him once more. Arlisa Davenport always had that affect of making him feel nervous and edgy. "Why did you have one of your brief encounters with me after your mother died? If I've been detrimental to you, as you say, why the affair?"

I wanted you! Arlisa's mind screamed in response, as her body suddenly became awakened to the short, but torrid one night they'd shared when she was twenty-four years old, before Brad abandoned her for his video shoot in the Bahamas. "I wanted you to know that this slippery fish didn't still taste like wet rubber," she rebounded, seeing the flicker of recognition cross Brad's face. She felt her body surge in warm triumph, knowing that she'd rendered him silent. "Yes, I overheard you tell Erica," she admitted, allowing the fierce menace of disclosure to dance in her eyes. "Just like I overheard you in your playroom when I was nine years old, calling me a poor freeloader."

"I see," came Brad's simple, impassive reply, his tone filled with shameful guilt. Though he felt buoyed by Arlisa's presence and gall to stand up to him, as his mind recounted the incidents she'd pinpointed for him so well, he'd also come to discover that he liked that touch of mettle in her, too. The last time they'd met, she was so mild mannered, almost fragile that he couldn't help being drawn into the sensual vulnerability she'd eluded then. He had himself to blame for not seeing her again. He realized now he'd led Arlisa to believe that they were not in the same league and how could he have ever thought that, seeing Arlisa now? She was a strong, desirable woman. Simply put, he could never have forgotten her. It was evident, however, that she'd forgotten him.

"Is that all you can say?" Arlisa was alarmed to find that her voice was trembling pathetically. If she was failing to remain calm at that precise moment, it was because every part of her body was in reminder of how expertly Brad had made love to her, bringing her to the pinnacle of ecstasy.

"Whatever I have to say isn't going to stop you from pursuing men and money with equal determination," Brad's voice stated tersely, masking his feelings from Arlisa by closing off the tremors his own tone was betraying. Right now, he didn't know what the hell to do or say to Arlisa Davenport except kiss her senseless. That was a feat in itself because he imagined that she would still make him feel uncertain of his moves, uncertain of what buttons to push, as she'd done the last time they'd met. Only instinct had guided him then. Suddenly, he felt just as she'd made him feel at seventeen, very much a beginner, learning about the world of women.

"I'm not burning myself in the middle and at both ends, if that's what you're thinking," Arlisa winced angrily.

"I think we should end this conversation before we say things we'll both regret," Brad decided suddenly on a whim, in an attempt at diplomacy. He'd come to realize that Arlisa was gravely hurt by his characterization of her, and he didn't want to deepen the topic any further.

But something like regret and a twinge of grief were already working their way through Arlisa's mind. It was only when Brad turned on his heels and was about to march away from her when, to her chagrin, Arlisa felt herself tug at his arm. "Don't you dare walk away from me," she admonished madly, a bravado totally familiar to her surfacing to hit back at his cool, casual appraisal. "I can't apologize for my past; it's gotten me this far, and I've learned lessons from all my mistakes," she blinked defensively. "And I'm at a point in my life where I now want to try and do things right. I know where you're going with this cruel assessment of me and I really don't appreciate that kind of jaded interest. I'm allergic to one-night stands, resent being referred to something out of the devil's handbook, and if we were to draw parallels between you and

I, I could just as easily accuse you of donating your trouser zipper to the Smithsonian Institute."

"My private life has always been tastefully discreet." Brad's reflexes in his neck muscles tightened noticeably.

"Yeah, top secret, hush-hush, undercover operations, where the hard edge of ethics meets the soft edge of fun," Arlisa surmised knowingly. "Well, in my experience, those tasting life's sweet marrow covertly are lovers who have something to lose, someone to protect or something to hide."

"Coy or lewd as that may be," Brad voiced, now feeling himself to be on the defensive, too. "I have never personally operated that way."

"But you've made assumptions about me," Arlisa hit back. "In fact, you really don't know anything about me at all. Your sister made sure of that."

"Erica?"

"Oh, what's the point of explaining," Arlisa dismissed, hurtful that this man could be so cold-blooded. "You're not going to believe anything I say anyway."

"Believe what?"

"Brad, there you are." It was Erica's loud-pitched voice that made the timely intrusion, deliberately aborting their heated conversation. Ignoring Arlisa, Erica possessively linked her hand through her brother's arm before asking sweetly, "Have you seen your fiancée?"

"Fiancée?" Arlisa was quickly emboldened to ask, her mind trying to recover from the shock of hearing the suggestion.

"Brad and Bernadetta Crossland of course," came Erica's satisfying reply. "Judge Crossland's daughter."

"Erica!" Brad flinched.

Arlisa could hardly contain the gasp that was about to burst free from her throat. But she knew that she'd heard correctly. "Con-congratulations," she muffled, too over-awed with shock to say anything more. Instead she was almost blinded with the image of Bernadetta, her arch rival in love, that woman who'd stolen Jerome Morrison from beneath her very clutches and had now evidently tossed him aside for Brad Belleville. The bitter smile came fast, but felt hard on her lips as she recalled Bernadetta Crossland's latent sense of masochism. Why hadn't Brad mentioned something about his engagement to her earlier? Why wait for Erica to embarrass her? Anger forbade her to risk looking him in the eyes, especially as their potent conversation was still playing on her mind, and his very presence on her heartstrings. "I hope you both will be very happy," she lied.

"I'm sure they will be," Erica's cold voice penetrated harshly, her squirrel-colored eyes darkening in triumph as she watched Arlisa walk away.

The sultry tune of *Dark Latin Groove* was echoing in its rhythmic Latin reggae beat as Arlisa's swift feet took her out of the club and into the night air, where she tried but failed to hold onto her composure. As she closed off to her mind the sound of her favorite group, every part of her troubled at seeing Brad again, two men made their careful study of her. Mr. Burnt Out regarded her rather luridly, but Erica's brother felt as though he'd been knocked clean off his feet.

Two

"I want Bernadetta Crossland's engagement to Brad Belleville plastered all over this week's edition of the *Nubian Chronicle*," Arlisa admonished scathingly to her elder sister two weeks later. "On the news page, along with the hookers and homicides. That's where she belongs." She quickly knocked back the small glass of sherry she'd been given, hardly paying attention to where she was going.

"Now where have I heard about her before?" Kendra smiled easily as she directed Arlisa along the corridor of the Yaa Asantewaa Art Gallery toward the main area where they were expected, to see the oil paintings of its latest exhibit. "Wasn't she the one you told me about who was having an affair with Jerome Morrison, the barrister?"

"The hateful rat," Arlisa spat out.

"Yes, I remembered you calling him that, too," her sister recollected with a wry grin. "She was Ms. Thang I believe? The woman whom you told me must be mad to think she could ever tame Jerome?"

Arlisa absorbed her sister's cool, collected expression rather grudgingly. "This isn't funny."

"Arlisa, I swear I can't keep up with you," Kendra confessed, her mink-colored, almond-shaped eyes clearly puzzled. "Wasn't he one of those sugar daddies you had? Brad . . . whatshisname who was shooting a video in the Bahamas?"

"Yes . . . I mean no," Arlisa quickly grasped her thoughts together to explain. "He wasn't a sugar daddy exactly," she clarified in irritation. "He's Otis Belleville's grandson. You remember Otis? The *Belleville Lagoon* restauranteur?"

"Goodness, yes," Kendra gasped in awe. "He was one of Daddy's first clients to advertise in the *Nubian Chronicle,*" Kendra paused in amazement. "Did you know he was invested last year by the Queen with a Member of the British Empire insignia? We did an article—"

"I don't want to talk about that man's MBE," Arlisa interrupted candidly. Her fawn gaze wavered briefly as she and her sister entered the gallery's main exhibition hall, noting the few familiar faces present, before she took up the conversation again with her sister. "Kendra, I'm not happy about this engagement," she finally confessed, her voice filled with the self-loathing of having admitted it. "I thought me and Brad . . ." Her voice trailed.

"Aren't you dating Morris Walker, the representative for the Jamaican High Commission?" Kendra began seriously, her own voice filled with concern that her sister should appear so dejected.

"He's yesterday's news," Arlisa declared a little sheepishly. "Brad's today's edition. And when I saw the headlines on him two weeks ago, I just wanted to stop the press."

"He's Bernadetta Crossland's hard copy now," Kendra clarified, sympathetically. "And from what you've been telling me, she's made a hot bulletin item out of him."

"Exactly," Arlisa agreed, pulling back her long, saloon-styled braided hair. "I was so embarrassed when Erica told me about Brad's engagement to that old relic."

"Erica?" Kendra asked.

"His sister."

"Right."

"Just seeing him again, after all this time . . ." Arlisa said wistfully, unable to stop the tremor in her limbs as she recollected the amorous touch of Brad's tutored fingers.

"Nearly two years," Kendra tossed in.

"Eighteen months," Arlisa clarified. "It felt awful," she continued forlornly, reluctantly dismissing the rush of sensation that ran through her. "There's so much I wanted to say and . . . it's just awful not being able to explain why things went wrong with . . ."

"With all those sugar daddies," Kendra contradicted absently.

"Kendra!" Arlisa directed a needle-sharp stare, thinking with an inward groan that her sister suspected she was sounding like some sour-faced old dowager.

"Sissy, you're a . . . free spirit," Kendra dashed into the fray with a grin, before taking a sip from her own glass of sherry. "You always bounce back with another guy. Let me see. Before Morris Walker, there was Prince Emeka Obeng-Amoo. And before him there was that filthy rich French guy called Raymond who you met in Monte Carlo. I never did know what became of him."

"He returned to the Grand Prix circuit for Mercedes Benz," Arlisa divulged, again rather sheepishly. "And like the others, they've all been just friends."

"Well, he obviously had no backbone," Kendra added with candor, of the Tobago-born native who now lived in France. "Considering that it was because of him why you embezzled one hundred and fifty thousand dollars from the Black Press Charity Fund and the Association of Black Journalists. Only a wimp could have left you alone like that to deal with it by yourself."

"You're just like Brad," Arlisa flinched inwardly. "Even he had to refer to that indiscretion."

"How did he know?" Kendra's voice grew alarmed. "That little matter was settled between me, you and Shay. I don't think my husband ever told Mrs. Adina, the company secretary, that you'd forged her signature and embezzled the money. His replacing it easily dispensed away with all the rumors."

"I don't know how Brad knew and I don't care," Arlisa exploded loudly, shameful that her past could have been so dysfunctional. It was only when her voice echoed with a hollow din across the room did she realize that they'd briskly entered the center of the gallery's main exhibit hall. Looking vividly embarrassed as the few people present zoomed their speculative gazes on her, Arlisa smiled weakly and faced her sister head-on. "I'm sorry," she muttered, a little bedazzled. Thinking on changing the subject, she added quickly, "I forgot to ask, how is Shay?"

"Mr. Corporate is back in New York," Kendra began affectionately, her mink-colored eyes instantly warming at the mention of her husband's name. "J.B. wants him to oversee the news team for their cable station. They're supposed to be flying out to Cuba today."

"Oh, that Fidel Castro thing," Arlisa broached in comprehension. "I don't know why Washington has to make such a fuss. The man was probably rushed into the hospital because he was suffering a little angina or trapped wind."

"That bearded revolutionary you're so loosely referring to is at the helm of Marxism's last stronghold," Kendra assayed smoothly. "If his condition worsens, Cuba may be forced into a national state of emergency."

"Castro's last stand," Arlisa scoffed, not wishing to debate the argument. She'd long since considered that since Kendra's eight-month marriage to Shay Brentwood, her sister had become more Americanized in her thoughts. "I'm sure he'll get his usual scoop," she backed down gingerly, "and be back in time to see you give birth to that baby." She tapped Kendra's pregnant stomach.

"He'd better be," Kendra laughed, just as they were approached by two heavyset women. "I'm not happy that he spent his birthday in New York."

"Hello Kendra. Arlisa," the wife of the former Secretary of Defense for Uganda greeted them, her quiet demeanor revealing her to be a woman of exceptional tact, who gave fantastic dinner parties for twenty or more guests and still found time to read a five-hundred-page biography about Winnie Mandela. "How nice to see you both again."

"Likewise," Arlisa answered, smiling amicably, though her fawn-brown eyes blinked blankly over her coquettish shoulder, clad exquisitely in one of her more regal suits in an attempt to disguise her acute sense of boredom. She hadn't wanted to come to the opening of the Yaa Asantewaa Art Gallery, but she'd felt obligated to accompany her sister, who'd promised them a decent feature in the *Nubian Chronicle.*

Lady Mandika Deboga smiled a perfect set of teeth, appearing the elegant cross between an African grandee and a British aristocrat, having acquired much of her education in England. "I'd like you to meet the First Lady of Ghana." She introduced the petite-looking political socialite who stood quietly by her side. "Her government was kind enough to partly fund the refurbishment of this gallery. Without their help we could never have achieved our aim."

"How nice to meet you," Arlisa acknowledged the introduction before adding, "My sister is the one interested in art. I'll be right back. I'm just going to get myself another drink."

"Of course," Lady Mandika said quite dubiously, her cultured African dialect quickly launching into a discussion with Kendra. Swathing her tall, slender body past her sister, Arlisa left the three women to wax lyrical about the art gallery and made toward the cocktail table.

She could feel a yawn coming on as her metal-tipped heels crossed the polished wood floor to a corner of the gallery, where a waitress as brown as a Tuscan sausage offered her another glass of sherry. Sipping it slowly, Arlisa's gaze swept the main hall more carefully, noting Penelope Palmer, the renowned Caribbean art dealer. Her mind relayed that no good social function would be complete without her because Penelope was often the loudest person in the room. She saw Kitty Lee, too, an old acquaintance, who brought a familiar smile to her weary face.

"Kitty!" Arlisa beckoned the woman with a nod of her head, watching as her friend came over.

"Arlisa." Kitty offered a warm smile on their meeting. "How are you?"

"I'm fine. You?"

"Couldn't be better. We eloped."

"You what?"

"Me and that Nigerian who owned the chalet in Gstaad." Kitty Lee offered the information full of giggles. "We eloped."

"You're kidding me," Arlisa gasped, knowing that Kitty Lee was the type to possess passionate tendencies, one of which was to wear matching colors: pink on pink, blue on blue and suchlike.

"Yes," Kitty continued, also a woman who contrived to look better than women who can. "Two months now. And things are great."

"Arlisa!" Another woman suddenly appeared, her voice

cracked and husky, a constant reminder to Arlisa that Ester McEwan smoked far too many French cigarettes, often giving her slight laryngitis. "What are you doing here?"

"Kendra had the nerve to drag me along," Arlisa insisted truthfully.

"I don't know what I'm doing here when there's Wilesden Green," Ester began, sporting her trademark Panama hat. "I do love my dawn raids there. I wanted to rush down this morning to pick up some Egyptian birthday cards, but instead found myself high-tailing it across town to this little shindig."

"That's so like you," Arlisa laughed, aware that Ester would much rather be scouting around the Afrikan market at Wilesden Green, talking with the sculptors and craft vendors whose artistic stalls sold wares that offered a real slice of old-fashioned Africa.

"I expected to see Erica Belleville-Brown here," Ester suddenly voiced, her tone braced for gossip. "She owes me an apology for that dreadful fuss she made when I bought Aubusson carpets for my house in Chelsea."

"She said you were copying her," Kitty suddenly agreed in recollection.

"And when I won my bid for those two enchanting little African doggies that I picked up at Sotheby's—you know, the ones with the sweet faces that I thought would look nice in my bathroom—she had to go and do one of her breathing exercises."

Arlisa mused as her friends chuckled profusely. Ester always had the wit for swooping on subjects and disemboweling them before swiftly moving on to the next one. Which was just as well, considering that she'd wanted to forget that fateful weekend when she'd seen Erica and her brother last.

"How's your sister?" Ester asked. "She looks well."

"Seven months pregnant, and loving every minute of it," Arlisa smiled, before suddenly feeling nauseous. Her alarmed gaze was quick to detect the party that had entered the exhibition hall.

The timing seemed almost too fortuitous for it to be coincidental, that Erica should be entering at that precise moment with Brad Belleville. Her smile vanished almost instantly and Arlisa felt herself begin to marshal her scattered thoughts into place as her gaze took in Brad's glamorous companion. It was none other than Bernadetta Crossland.

She watched with furious distrust as they began to ingratiate themselves into the classic set, charming their way in with all the dedicated tact and skill of social-climbers, where they were quickly welcomed with open-armed relief. But as the artistic herd closed ranks around them, Arlisa did not miss Brad's shadowy, restrained figure, which appeared on the fringes of her own state of boredom.

She was contemplating this when, from across the room, Brad's eyes swayed and instinctively locked with hers. A sweet eruption of heat quaked through Arlisa's body, leaving her weak and shaking at the knees. The lingering gaze was irresistible. Arlisa felt Brad's uninhibited exploration of her, drawing her into his possessive gaze where his slow, erotic appraisal of all her womanly features shocked her untutored senses. He didn't touch her with anything but his eyes, yet Arlisa felt her fingers clench around her white handbag, too overawed with the naked pleasure of his gaze. It felt almost as though she were locked in his arms.

When the gaze broke, something in Arlisa did, too. Her own eyes widened and became dark with the knowledge that something new and frightening had just happened to her. She sucked in a breath and licked her dry lips.

"Arlisa. Are you all right?" Kitty's concerned voice immediately inquired.

Arlisa's hesitation was easily registered. "I've . . . I've . . . just noticed Erica."

Her two friends' swift head turns were marked. "Talk of the devil," Ester cooed. "Excuse me. I'm out on a mission."

"If she's hell-bent on getting an apology," Kitty said coolly, watching as their friend made a beeline toward Erica Belleville-Brown, "Ester will be waiting forever."

Arlisa downed the last of her sherry and looked agonizingly at the empty glass. There hadn't been enough in there to still her nerves, she thought. What she needed was something much stronger. She recalled that there was a wine bar across the street, but she didn't dare leave Kendra all by herself, not when she was so heavily pregnant. Another glass of sherry seemed the only option.

She was almost afraid to scan the room, but she did so, this time noting the Jamaican High Commissioner talking with several art dealers she'd seen in passing whenever she'd joined her sister at functions such as this. "I'm just going to get another drink," she told Kitty, excusing herself to return in the direction of the cocktail table.

But before she got there, a familiar male voice halted her progress and Arlisa felt her body stiffen, unable to stop the tremor running through her loins in recognition of the person who had approached her from behind. "Can I talk to you outside?" he inquired casually.

Arlisa shivered as she turned on her heels to face Brad Belleville. Up close, he looked even more adorable than when she'd first glimpsed him from across the room. Though he was dressed this time in a manner she remembered: new stone-washed jeans, a shirt with a fine gray stripe running through its white background, and a dark blue jersey tied loosely around his shoulders, he looked the epitome of all that a man should be. But Arlisa side-stepped him, deciding to keep as much distance between them as possible. It was at a chance meeting almost precisely like this where Brad had expertly ensnared her the last time.

"This reaches me," she prevaricated weakly, turning her gaze to an oil painting hung on the wall of a sun-swept beach in the Caribbean where natives were playing by the water's edge. "I think it has a unified message."

"Personally, I think it goes off on a tangent," Brad temporized sharply, his own gaze following Arlisa's toward the picture. "Just like you. Didn't you hear what I just said?"

Arlisa shivered. Brad gently took her arm and forced her around to face him. Her senses were alert to his penetrating gaze as she tried to contemplate his offer to go outside against the knowledge of knowing who he had arrived with. Desperately, she tried to dredge up an answer, but she couldn't gird herself into logically thinking how she could best refuse to go with Brad, not when her mind had begun whirling over the way in which he was looking at her. And not when there was a history between them that had still not been reconciled.

But as Arlisa's body began to warm at the unexpected attention of receiving Brad's presence, she observed from across the room the cool, stolid expression reflected in Erica's steely squirrel-brown eyes. There had always been something dauntingly ferocious about Erica that Arlisa had simply surmised as being a peculiar quirk of her upper-class manner, which she knew only few would realize about her. She tried to force a social smile to her lips in the hope of bringing about a softening to Erica's features, but when the squirrel-brown eyes squinted and the mouth, painted in deadly red lipstick, twisted to a scowl, Arlisa decided against it.

For a woman who was a brilliant off-piste skier and a first-class shot—a definite favorite in the grouse butt—she felt some sadness that she and Erica had never been friends. Could she risk following Brad outside when such an unfriendly atmosphere was cascading around them?

Maintaining an air of spurious hauteur, Arlisa jibed, "What do you want with me outside, Brad? To whisper some more poison in my ear?"

"Don't be like that." Brad's voice sounded subdued. "I realize that I owe you an apology."

"What?" Arlisa chortled, just as a sudden hush swept the room. Pastor Dennis, whom she'd known was to re-open the gallery, seemed poised and ready to make a speech.

In her bedazzled mind, Arlisa recognized him instantly. He was a figurehead of the West Indian community, a man who spearheaded fund-raising and charity events, head of the Presbyterian church and whose agility and quick-stepped gait almost made him seem much younger than his sixty-nine years. He was also a much-requested visitor to Erica Belleville-Brown's dinner parties, which she knew were held frequently for the intellectual wing of the Caribbean jet-set.

A faint smile touched Brad's mouth. His lips parted to reveal even white teeth, and he used his tongue to decidedly lick his upper lip, to dampen a corner in his amused gesture. "You seem surprised," he remarked.

Arlisa inwardly flayed herself for finding his softening features disturbingly attractive. The dark eyebrows that accentuated the bone structure of his forehead, the absurdly long eyelashes that were unusual for a man, and the olive-brown of his complexion were beginning to send her senses racing; all took her back to the memories she cherished from when they'd spent one brief night together.

And she loathed herself for even cherishing them. Perhaps it was because he'd allowed her to release some of the trauma she'd suffered after her mother had died. Or perhaps it was because she'd simply wanted to hold onto an image that she'd carried from when she had been a child.

Whatever it was, all Arlisa knew was that when Brad extended his hand toward her and she recognized the same gold diamond studded ring on his right middle finger, that very hand that had once traced the line between her breasts and had discovered every curve of her body, tormenting messages flashed through her brain on how he'd just as easily abandoned her to do his work in the Caribbean.

You silly, foolish girl, she screamed inwardly, amazed that her housemaster at school should have described her as being "—sane and sensible—a well-rounded girl." Absurdly, that girl no longer existed when she thought of all the dysfunctional things she'd done. Because of losing her mother, and then losing Brad, she'd almost lost her entire stability.

And now, she could hardly believe this sudden act of vain shame and repentance. Arlisa felt certain not to give Brad any avenue to escape whatever guilt had caught up with him so many months later.

Refusing to accept his hand, she turned and tried to ignore the fact that her mind had gone into a tailspin merely by having received Brad's undivided attention. "Excuse me," she uttered, also refusing to make any contact with those devastating honey-brown eyes, hating the way her voice sounded hurtful, betraying that she was evidently troubled.

"Arlisa?" Brad's deep baritone inquired. His hand now

placed on her arm gave the impression that he was reluctant to let her go.

Arlisa wasn't aware that something inside her had snapped until the words tumbled out in a fast flurry of anger and frustration. "Look, I don't want any hint of scandal by leaving here with you," she voiced madly, noting the wide-eyed look of resentment she was receiving from Bernadetta Crossland, who watched passively from where she stood, locked in a handshake with the ambassador to Zaire. "I'm staying away from you. That's one decision I can make for myself."

"Why do you feel obliged to declare your independence?" Brad's tone was relaxed, almost conversational, but his eyes never left Arlisa's face, not once. They, at least, were very intense as they crawled around her angry features.

"Why do you feel obliged to be threatened by it?" Arlisa countered just as easily, though she emitted a sharp gasp of frustration when Brad's gaze made her grapple mentally with her emotions.

"I don't feel threatened."

"Then why mention it?" Arlisa debated caustically, her own anxiousness and female insecurity forcing her to straighten her back as though she were attempting to measure up to the muscular hardness of Brad's lean body and the six-feet-two inches that made up his tall, imposing frame.

"I was originally talking about taking you outside," Brad concluded finally, "to talk to you."

"Why?" Arlisa asked.

"Come with me and find out."

"What about Bernadetta?" Arlisa could still feel her arch rival's eyes burning into the side of her neck. But Brad didn't appear the least bit concerned.

"What about her?" he said evenly.

"Won't she be wondering where you are?" Arlisa pressed, rejecting the thinly veiled flippancy in his tone.

"Probably."

"Probably!" Arlisa repeated, endeavoring to keep her own tone equable. "Doesn't that bother you?"

"No."

Brad seemed so certain of himself, and there was something guarded in his eyes that made Arlisa hesitate before she blasted him. "What's that supposed to mean?" Her tone had risen slightly.

"I can exercise self-restraint," he goaded, lifting his hand to brush his knuckles against the proud angle of her chin, as though he were attempting to wipe the skeptical expression from her face.

Arlisa felt herself sinking deeper and deeper into the mire, though her anger never left her for a moment. But under the magic spell of his hypnotic touch, she could sense her foolhardy curiosity pressing against her mind. Brad was playing with her, she thought. He was subtly experimenting with the intrigue and she had to admit, she was thoroughly hooked.

Suddenly, she didn't much care for the scandalous consequences when she thought of the mystery that would circle around them if she were to leave with him now. It wasn't as though she was part of the animated crowd, who enjoyed delving into conversations about the hassles of stimulating the corrupt captains of industry to part with their profits for worthy causes such as ethnic art galleries.

There was more than a pang of adventure when Arlisa began to convince herself that she did not belong in this atmosphere of fund-raising discussion. She was bored, and she knew it. And as she looked into the honey-brown eyes that baited her own, feeling something tangible inside her weaken, the surprised acceptance came quickly and impulsively, as did the smile to Brad Belleville's face.

Three

"You've . . . blossomed, Arlisa," Brad remarked rather smoothly, his brooding honey-brown gaze surely darker, more intense than it had been earlier, the muscles in his throat oddly taut. Arlisa followed slowly behind him as they walked toward the parking lot, only yards away from the Yaa Asantewaa Art Gallery, knowing that she was controlling nearly two years of built-up anger beneath her controlled facade.

The midday sun was shining above them now, though the day itself was somewhat cool, which was typically British for late August, but it did not dissipate the odd rush of tension presently tormenting Arlisa's mood. She felt agitated and she knew it, as they took a steady pace along the quiet sidewalk where only a few early afternoon commuters were going about their daily chores. "That's what they all tell me," she responded with the protective flippancy she had developed over the years to hide her sensitivity.

"They?" Brad stiffened at once, potently aware that deep down, he had always been jealous of every guy who had ever been within Arlisa's field of vision.

"I'm not that naive little girl you left behind when you went to the Bahamas," she reminded him quickly.

"So I've heard," Brad agreed, his eyes turning hard.

"True effort was never wasted where you were concerned."

"What's that supposed to mean?" Arlisa jabbed, her rising anger providing a defense behind which she could shelter herself. But Brad wasn't daunted by her puerile display.

"I mean your conquests with men," he jibed.

"Here we go again," Arlisa mocked harshly. "Those who can, do. Those who can't, don't. That's what you're trying to summarize about me, isn't it? So, are you going to interrogate me out here or in the bedroom?"

"Arlisa?" Brad pulled a rueful face.

"Don't," Arlisa quipped, giving the first indication that she was feeling uncomfortable. "You're being judgmental again. What is it exactly that you're dying to know?"

"Nothing," Brad lied, his pace slowing a little.

"Oh come on," Arlisa said blithely, stopping in her tracks. "All this huffing and puffing. It's just an excuse for the real issue you're dying to blow down. Which is?"

"Tell me about you and Jerome," Brad finally admitted, reluctantly.

"Bull's eye," Arlisa scoffed arrogantly, her fingers trembling with newfound jealousy that he could possibly be referring to the very man whose woman was probably now wearing Brad's engagement ring. Arlisa felt the bruise to her ego. Or was it to her pride? She wasn't quite sure. Jerome had passed her over for Bernadetta Crossland, and now that same woman was with the man who she'd never been able to forget. But Arlisa quickly reminded herself that Brad had been able to forget her. To him, she'd been a one-night stand, and she felt maddened by the very idea of having to clarify anything to him at all. "You just can't leave it alone, can you?" she reproved in annoyance. "Well, I don't owe you an explanation for anything, so get lost."

Arlisa's strides resumed, heavy and hard on the concrete sidewalk back toward the art gallery. But as she did so, Brad turned and caught up with her, pulling at her arm until she was forced to stop and face him head-on.

"You're a hard nut to break," he broached just as harshly, his own jealousy that she could even have been with Jerome Morrison plaguing across his tormented mind. Erica had been more than specific with the truth about how they were seen together, parading the party scene, tom-catting and club-hopping after he'd taken her as his own. "Who are you two-timing now?" he accused Arlisa hotly.

"You slimy little . . . crocodile," Arlisa shrieked, her rage now at full boiling point, her senses wounded that Brad could even insinuate that she shared herself among lovers. "I don't sleep around."

"Liar."

"What's it to you anyway?" Arlisa pursued with reckless thunder, her limbs now shaking with more than just the terror of her anger. "I know what you're thinking. A man looks at me and I have to jump, right? Well I know that men don't care what's beneath all the packaging, but it took me a while to figure out that my integrity is under there, and I hate it to be bruised or scarred. You did that when you took off to the Bahamas and then refused all my calls. You just had to make sure you made love to me first, when I was at my most vulnerable, too."

"Oh, that's rich," Brad defended angrily, his hands now wide akimbo on the side of his hips. "You only called me when you needed money." The words were spat out with such harsh dislike, Arlisa was rendered to complete silence. "As for that night of wild, unrestrained passion, you wanted it and badly, too. I still have the scratches you left on my chest to prove it." His eyes held hers, and something intense grew between them. "You marked me, Girl," he added seductively, "and if you weren't so pretentious about this sudden rise of integrity you now possess, you'll admit to yourself that you want to mark me again."

Brad's tone deepened richly and so seductively that Arlisa was forced to be more than aware of the amorous undertones which lingered in every word. Her innate stubbornness began to fight the affect the very suggestion was having on her nervous system. A sharp sting of something intensely erotic pierced her heart and tugged at every feminine instinct within her control to return an equally combative, voracious remark.

But Arlisa loathed the very idea. This man couldn't just walk back into her life and expect to pull her. She gave a fine shudder, knowing that she could not allow herself, betray herself into that sort of emotional danger again. It would be far safer to erect some barriers, especially now that Brad was engaged to the one woman who'd given her so much grief in the past.

She flinched the moment Brad's expression shadowed and became unreadable, finding herself taking one step backward as he advanced a step forward. "I wouldn't want to leave my mark on you if you were the last man alive," she broached. "A man who wants two women wants neither enough."

It wasn't Arlisa's imagination to discover Brad flinching beneath his cool, sullen facade. "You . . . you don't understand about me and Bernadetta," he began evasively. Too evasive, Arlisa decided. "She's a close friend of . . ."

"I don't want to know the rest," Arlisa rebutted, intuition divulging to her that she wasn't going to get the truth anyway.

Men lied. There had never been a time when she'd received a straight, honest answer about anything she cared to ask. And it wasn't as though she were asking trick questions either. A born talker, fast on her feet, and a woman rarely lost for words unless several questions asked simultaneously threw her off guard in open debate, Arlisa could hold her own even in the throes of scandal. Men on the other hand were different, she realized. A direct question instantly brought forth a lie. The twinge of uncertainty, the note of ambiguity, the tweak of vagueness in Brad's tone when he spoke did not go unnoticed.

"You say that as though you're jealous." he intoned.

"Me?" Arlisa laughed. It was her turn to lie. "Hell no."

She risked looking at Brad to prove the point, but instead Arlisa was suddenly struck. That face which had never left her subconscious was right there in front of her to behold. Those melting honey-brown eyes that had always succeeded in penetrating right through her clothes to engage themselves with her heart, which was pumping ever so loudly presently, were still able to hold her captive to his will. She could hear her pulse drumming against her eardrums, keeping the ebb and flow of her heated blood flowing.

And Arlisa felt herself react, too. She was beginning to shift nervously where she stood, even stooping to itch her knee over the pantyhose which clad her leg, knowing that the simple action was enough to tell Brad that she was affected by him.

But luckily, Brad bypassed her nervous fussing and instead trained his gaze in the manner of a scholar attempting to understand the traits of someone's mind. "I believe you," he told Arlisa tersely, his gaze devoid of any emotion. For some strange reason—that bordered on the absurdity to him—the innocence of the boy-girl relationship that had filtered into the man-woman affair he'd once shared with Arlisa suddenly made sense in Brad's mind. "Our paths

have crossed from when we were children. I don't know
if that's a good thing or a bad thing. I do know that you
felt I wasn't there for you, in the way you wanted, after
your mother died."

Arlisa winced at the memory, which came flooding
back. She'd one day gone along to the same church where
her mother had been buried and did something quite out
of character for a *Hypermega*. Or maybe it was entirely
appropriate for someone raised by the kindhearted mother
she'd once had. There were candles burning around the
altar and every impulse in her body had propelled her to
rise up and light a candle of her own. She'd done so with
every humility of a sinner, trying to find her soul, and
placed it by the altar along with all the others, in a symbolic
gesture to God that she'd . . . humbled herself.

Then thoroughly shaken by the experience, she'd left
the church only to find herself walking straight into the
tall, indomitable frame of Brad Belleville. The last time
they'd met was at Erica's eighteenth birthday party when
he'd kissed her beneath the stairs. Maybe she had been
vulnerable at the time, or naive; Arlisa had never quite
decided. Infatuated perhaps. But whatever the reason,
she'd accepted Brad's invitation to dinner and then coffee
afterward at his apartment. She hadn't expected them to
spend the night together. For the first time in her life, she'd
tasted that sweet nectar from God she'd always dreamed
about, but had suspected was impossible to find. She'd
discovered that Brad was that piece of her which had suddenly slotted into place, and she was even able to forget
his proud and prejudicial judgments on her from when she
had been a child.

The following morning, he'd taken her back home and
within three days of having swept her off her feet, he was
gone. The devastation had been a hard blow against the

bereavement she'd been suffering. Trips to Monte Carlo, which first began as sabbaticals to escape the humiliation and argument she'd later had with Erica, quickly became gambling extravaganzas to ease the pain she felt within. Dating Jerome afterward had been a mistake, too. Had it not been for Shay Brentwood, her sister's husband, she would have found herself immersed in a scandal from which she knew she could never have recovered.

"You're absolutely right," Arlisa agreed, just as quickly dispelling the memory from her mind to attack Brad's guilty conscience with all the venom he deserved. "Good friendship is hard to come by."

Brad watched Arlisa lick her lips, the innocent eroticism of it sending a powerful jolt to his loins. He was more than aware that out of the selfsame mold as Delia came this formidable woman whom he'd hurt, but who had also captivated him in ways he couldn't begin to understand. To him she held a unique beauty that would make any man place her on a pedestal to be admired, and he loathed himself for ever mistreating her the way he had.

But when he'd left to visit the Bahamas, there were ghosts from his past which had to be dealt with. Ghosts from New York and his childhood. Arlisa had not been the only one in pain. There was the strain from his mother who had divorced her wealthy husband, Sir Paul Worthington of the Worthington publishing empire, which prompted the urge he'd always had to prove that he could never be as unambitious as his father. There had also been a sense of disappointment within him concerning women.

But he'd kept focused and determined because he'd never wanted to rely on his grandfather's inheritance, and he refused to accept any of his mother's handouts when she'd settled for the four hundred thousand pounds per annum her ex-husband had offered in alimony to keep her accustomed in the manner she'd grown used to.

The film industry was where he'd set his sights and in so doing, he now realized that he'd neglected the one thing that really mattered most. His lack of showing any form of respect toward Arlisa, or any other woman for that matter filled him with unease. In truth, Arlisa had been the first woman to make him feel alive, and he'd never forgotten her, or that night, though he bitterly resented her for forgetting him.

While he was in the Caribbean, she had paraded around in his mind to the point that he'd asked Erica to keep him abreast on what Arlisa was doing. He'd been more than dismayed to learn that she was dating every guy in town. Todd, Jarvis, Jerome . . . To him, the list seemed endless, finishing with some guy named Morris Walker. Even now, he felt his blood fire up, thinking that she could've mobilized herself that way. Brad blamed himself. If only he hadn't ended what they'd had, who knows what would've blossomed.

The matter was trailing on his mind when he asked, "Is that why you started dating Todd?"

"Todd! Dear Todd," Arlisa chortled, licking her lips again, unaware that the motion was causing Brad to suck in a ragged breath. "He was good, quiet therapy. The last time I saw Todd, he was contesting a family will for some Jamaican estate left to him in Montego Bay. He never had time for me. I don't know if he ever got it sorted."

Brad found himself exerting a breath of relief that Todd and Arlisa had never been lovers. "He got his estate," he advised her with a shallow smile, none too revealing of the mitigation that had washed over him. "He's living in Jamaica now."

"Oh," Arlisa rasped, nodding her head in approval. "That's good."

"And Jarvis?" Brad probed, unashamed at how deep he was delving.

Arlisa cackled at the barefaced invasion. "I don't know where you get off," she chided, tight-lipped, putting all her weight on one leg. "Jarvis happened to be a friend, a thinker, if you remember?" She desperately tried not to react to the predatory mask on Brad's face, revealing all the shrewd, animal intelligence she'd recognized in other men, where natural instinct told them when a woman longed to be kissed. "We wiled away the time talking about the philosophies of life, and according to him, we're all doomed. I got myself out of that one pretty quick."

She heard the light laughter that left Brad's lips. He knew both men, of course. They'd all gone to the same school, such was the small intimate circle of well-to-do Caribbeans that it was little wonder that everyone either knew each other or had heard enough information for a person's reputation to precede them before personal introductions ever came about.

"And Jerome?"

Arlisa felt the acute shift in her mood the instant Brad referred to the Nigerian barrister she once dated. She'd foolishly tried to enlist his help once, when her financial troubles had required she find one hundred and fifty thousand dollars for the Rolling Dice casino in Monte Carlo. They were demanding that the debt she'd amassed there be paid and so she needed money pretty urgently. Her whole life, at that point, was a mess.

Jerome was encyclopedic when it came to rules of law—law being the profession he practiced, and to which he earned a small fortune. She'd been wishful in thinking that he would rise to her rescue and help her climb out of the hole she'd dug herself into. But what Arlisa hadn't gambled on was him setting his sights on Judge Crossland's daughter.

When she'd caught them both red-handed in his bedroom—he forgetting that he'd given her a key to his penthouse apartment—every fibre that she'd ever possessed in her body about one day ever finding true love vanished with every humiliating minute she'd suffered, learning firsthand about Jerome and Bernadetta's torrid affair.

Now that she really thought about it, she recalled that Jerome had made his denial of offering her any help in front of Bernadetta, while he'd hugged that old relic in his bed. That was probably how Brad came by the knowledge that she'd gambled away one hundred and fifty thousand dollars, money she'd embezzled from the professional funds she'd once presided over as treasurer. Why Brad wanted to touch on the subject of Jerome was a mystery to Arlisa, considering that he was now engaged to that very same woman who had once been an intimate playmate of Jerome's.

"He narrowed down something cruel in that department," she assayed, hardly imagining that the hardships of her life or the pretense of it being all but glamorous in her pursuit to find a rich mate would be of any concern to Brad Belleville.

Countless times she'd backed off men in her brief, non-committal relationships, never allowing any one of them to get too close, or to plan anything that suggested a future because she was too frightened of getting hurt. As Brad had once hurt her. And many of them had possessed all the credentials she was looking for in a rich mate, too: a house in the country, a career that had the prerequisite six-figure earnings, an apartment in the city and a pet such as a dog, bird or cat, which were an indication to her that he knew how to love something. But she'd never been able to commit. And Arlisa knew why.

This fixation on Brad, when he'd played such a relatively small part in her life, had seemed to mar her every relationship. Was it something to do with the trauma of how he'd made her feel so dirt-poor as a child, or was it the very fact that he'd taken her heart away when he'd first kissed her at the tender age of fourteen, and had kept her heart ever since? And wasn't that why, when they'd made love that one time, it'd been stupendous? But while her love was there, his was not. Men were allergic to love, she thought. The awful truth was all too revealing. She'd been expendable.

It was with that thought implanted on her mind when she added, "Jerome let me down, as all men do. Love is never a consideration. I've now discovered that men are seldom useful unless they have money. Money counts, right?"

Arlisa did not miss the stiffening of Brad's neck muscles in the side of his nape closest to her. And when their eyes met, she felt overawed by the hardened despair and the flicker of pain and anger she saw within them. She'd seen that look once before when she had been nine years old and had tampered with one of Brad's toy soldiers in the playroom he shared with his sister. She remembered then how vulnerable she'd felt when he'd yanked the small item out of her little fingers, telling her she was never to touch or take his things. In that moment, Arlisa wondered whether it had been those old memories, reflections she ought to have dug out and cast away a long time ago, which were attributing to the feelings she'd harbored for Brad.

"Yeah, money is the exception to every rule." Even the tone of Brad's voice had changed, too, totally consistent to what Arlisa had seen in his eyes. "Woe betide any man who crosses you without a fortune to his name." Brad couldn't help aiming the remark. To him, Arlisa Davenport was . . . obsessed, just like his mother had been. She'd obviously learned from an early age that men could be useful to her. She was a man's woman: worldly, experienced, self-sufficient, as long as there was a male wallet picking up the tab. How he despised such women. He'd been close-up to one such woman before in New York who was totally caught up in this kind of idealism.

And what disappointed him was that, in the depths of his soul, he'd wanted Arlisa to be different. While he was filming in the Bahamas, editing in a studio where the temperatures were extreme, or monitoring shots under the glare of a hot sun, she was playing around with men. *And why shouldn't she have?* an inner voice subtly demanded. He hadn't promised her anything. Hell, he hadn't intended to see her again. In his mind, Arlisa Davenport could never have belonged to him.

"I don't read fairy tales," Arlisa rebutted, herself now catching the sharp edge of the arrow Brad had shot at her. "You weren't playing Romeo to my Juliet, so I'm conforming to the standards set out there by men, where beauty and money go hand in hand. I'm meeting the competition," she even dared to suggest. "And if you think Bernadetta Crossland is a throwback to the girls of your grandfather's generation, where love is the exception to every rule, think again. She's an absolute conformist to the corruption, boredom and casual hypocrisy that have set in stone all the rules within marriage that were meant to be broken long ago."

Arlisa was surprised to find that Brad suddenly became silent. There was no defense. No argument. She stole the opportunity to chart the maturity displayed in the hardened-bone structure of his features. He'd aged moderately to a rather more worldly, experienced version of the Brad she remembered. There was a deep sense of wisdom beneath the manly exterior that Brad eluded, too, which the much younger part of herself could never have been made aware.

He was thinking and then to her chagrin he suddenly asked, "Do you believe in marriage?"

For an instant, the question threw Arlisa. In the time they'd spent standing on the sidewalk, hardly paying attention to the commuters around them while her sister and his were appreciating the finer points of Caribbean art inside the Yaa Asantewaa gallery, it hadn't occurred to Arlisa that Brad would even steer the conversation toward anything that would be suggestive of her future. She almost felt the mechanical movement of her thoughts when she zeroed in on the most crucial issue of all: Brad obviously had popped that inevitable question to Bernadetta Crossland. Not to her.

He'd veered too close to a conflict of heartache and so swallowing her misgivings, she challenged in return, "For women, yes. For men, no."

Silence elapsed for short seconds, though it felt like an eternity to Arlisa. Finally, Brad threw out another simple question. "Why?"

Arlisa didn't wait to react. "Love sucks," she reproved. "Love perpetuates marriage, marriage perpetuates divorce, divorce perpetuates alimony. It's all about money in the end. And in my world, a woman has to always come out on top."

Brad's eyes lit up, something in what Arlisa had said reminding him of his mother. "You're still direct."

"Yeah, I come straight to the point, if you remember," she smiled.

"Funny," Brad's voice changed again. "I liked that

about you. It's that little part of you that fires up and then keeps running away that I find so intriguing. It makes me . . ."

"Brad." Arlisa was to recall that Bernadetta Crossland wasn't too far away. "There are some things a woman likes to put behind her. A one-night . . ." She paused and then made her amendment. "The past is one of them."

Brad knew Arlisa had steered pretty close to the precipice, and he was alerted to the inherent dangers of the situation, attempting to pick up from where they'd left off. Yet he couldn't help himself. She was so beautiful, the kind of woman who'll be able to pick and choose for years to come. He didn't deserve a clear berth where she was concerned, and though he'd now decided that she may never be within his grasp again, the thought of parting on a kiss suddenly seemed appealing.

An odd set of words immediately passed from his lips. "Sometimes the past can be your future."

Arlisa hesitated, a sadness surfacing her well-being. It was important to her at this juncture that she made it abundantly clear to Brad that, however foolish she may've behaved in the past, she was not going to repeat history now. "This is where I say good-bye, Brad."

He leaned across to her, so close, Arlisa felt his glare on her. "Where are you going?" The rawness of his voice sent Arlisa's pulses accelerating.

"Away from you," Arlisa pounced, discovering that he was staring at her mouth.

"Wait." Brad's fingers touched the bottom of her lip, his thumb lingering ever so slightly against the wet flesh.

Arlisa was surprised at how deeply she inhaled her breath, knowing how attractive Brad appeared at that precise moment. But she schooled her features magnificently to that of a woman who'd learned to disguise her emotions with well-practiced restraint. "Brad, you're getting dangerous," she resisted.

"Maybe," he agreed. "But for the sake of what we've been to one another and because I believe your nature will always care for me a little, I want us to part on . . ." He dared say it. ". . . a farewell kiss." His voice was rough and uneven, setting off a chain of reactions inside Arlisa's body.

"Brad . . ." Her voice died in her throat. It came out as a whisper hardly audible, that there was simply no denying Brad's strong, magnetic pull. His hands had crept up to her arms, and then delved provocatively into her jacket, where he swept away the lapels at each side to draw small, enticing circles against the flesh exposed above the loose, low-cut blouse she wore. Arlisa could feel her senses spinning, as though sweet poison was working its way throughout her nervous system, causing devastating havoc in its wake.

She blinked, her dry lips about to protest. But Brad's voice bounced against the very softness of those lips. "Why fight it when you know you really want it," he jibed.

As deadly sins go, Arlisa felt unable to fight this one. "I . . . I don't want this," she gasped helplessly, feeling that her lips had started to part, her eyes huge and dark as they reflected the shock of what he was doing to her.

"Not even for old time's sake?" came the hoarse, arousing tone.

Something in Brad's voice caught Arlisa's attention. *For old time's sake.* Absurdly, the phrase sounded like an apology, though common sense told Arlisa it was not. It was a coax. An amorous lure to goad her into Brad's kiss. And he was a good motivator, she had to admit. She was thoroughly provoked to sway into his arms and taste again that sweet nectar from God that had saturated her senses from the tender age of fourteen. But there was a part of her that felt dissuaded. This man had left her once before. He could well do so again. Could she risk being captivated by Brad's elicit hold? Beguiled to even give herself an answer, Arlisa found herself pulling back instead.

Very logical. Very realistic, she tried to tell herself, as she failed to dampen the rush of enraptured emotions Brad had induced. "There were no old times," she lied again, the dull aching pain that was the testing of her true feelings for Brad rolling around inside her like a ball.

"That one night we spent together was old times enough for me," Brad crooned, his thumb still resting against her mouth.

Arlisa blinked at the admission, disbelief making her almost unable to comprehend that Brad had spoken such words. Then his gaze met hers. Her mouth became so dry at the blatant sensuality of his thoughts that words failed to engage themselves in her mouth. She was only aware of this man standing in front of her, where she could feel the heat of his body growing ever closer. And then the hard angles of his face slowly became absorbed into hers.

Suddenly, she was that teenage girl again, tasting Brad's lips as though it were for the first time. Only now Brad was a man and she a woman; a woman who liked the smell of his male scent, who enjoyed the wild, raging way in which he claimed her, who reveled in giving back the sweet satisfaction that she herself was receiving. Different in many ways from the last time they'd kissed, when they'd been in his bedroom making love in his bed, the one re-sounding truth that was still present and acutely erotic to Arlisa was Brad's opened-mouth taking of her.

She'd liked to feel his tongue then as she did now. Wet, supple, languishing; skirting and pulsing along the inner flesh of her lips. As a mature woman, she could fully appreciate the way the churning mass of feelings within had trembled to astronomical proportions. The huge aching ball of pain inside her splintered into a million pieces and tore into her nervous system, tearing at her defenses and self-control so subtly, Arlisa was left emotionally vulnerable, so close to betraying tears that she could actually feel the hot sting of them burning in her eyes.

The sweet delight was wondrous, exhilarating, and caught up in the sensation, she felt about to whisper her own silky admission. But Arlisa could hardly focus on absorbing or partaking of such bliss, when tormenting images of Bernadetta Crossland stormed into her mind.

Just as abruptly as he'd taken her, Arlisa pulled away. "I never meant . . ." She took a long deep breath, and looked Brad directly between the eyes. "I don't want you to do that again," she raged untruthfully, wiping a shaking hand over her wet lips, hardly believing that the kiss had ever happened. "Just stay away from me. Stay out of my life."

"Just like that?" Brad accused, the honey-brown eyes firing up, almost angrily.

Arlisa was enraged. "You're engaged," she seethed, her limbs still trembling in the alter-shock of his kiss. "What are you expecting? To have us both? Does three-way love-making form part of your life these days?"

Brad's guarded expression revealed nothing, except that she'd infuriated him. "I'm not engaged to Bernadetta," he divulged.

"So, Erica was being humorous?" Arlisa bit back.

"Erica . . ." Brad decided to waver from giving an explanation. He knew his motives for wanting Arlisa right then were not strictly honorable. "Just do me a favor," he added instead. "The next time you're in dire straits and find yourself needing a man, don't—"

Brad wasn't allowed to finish. Walking directly toward them, her face flushing with immense dislike, came his sister, Erica Belleville-Brown. "How's the trout?" Erica's quick wit sarcasm was directed toward her brother. "Did you receive the full compliments of the fishmongers?"

"Erica," Brad warned. "Arlisa and I . . ."

"Ar . . . lisa," Erica interrupted coldly, her bleak eyes twisting with added scorn. "Such an unusual name. What does it stand for exactly?" She eyed Arlisa with distaste. "It sounds like a cure for snake bite to me."

Arlisa could hardly recoil from the passion that was stirring within her as she held Erica's stunned gaze. "It's the name given for the tongue of a viper," she rebelled, disliking the untimely intrusion. "And where I spit, no grass grows ever."

She sensed Brad's mouth quirk in amusement as Erica reared automatically, hesitating before her squirrel-brown gaze penetrated into her brother. "Bernadetta is waiting for you to drive her home," she informed him blithely. "I advised her not to follow you out here in fear that she may cause a scene." Her eyes rose as though in a plea, and Arlisa was surprised to find that Erica had tensed.

"You're right," Brad suddenly responded, backing down obediently.

To Arlisa, this turnabout was like a slap in the face, a betrayal of something, though what exactly, she couldn't quite fathom. "If I were you, I'd get a ring on your fiancée's finger," she ventured, her tone cynical. "Because a wife always believes that her husband's philandering, even one as colorful as yours, has nothing to do with her. And like I said, Bernadetta is a true conformist. Good-bye, Brad."

Erica faltered at last, but Arlisa didn't wait for the feisty rebuttal. Instead, she turned on her heels and left behind the two people who had dogged her childhood memories, and headed straight back toward the art gallery's main entrance. Brad watched her go, realizing that Arlisa was now the antitheses of Delia, a woman who had a general mistrust of men. And right now, her general mistrust was with him.

Four

Arlisa hardly had the energy to keep on rehashing in her head what had gone on the previous day between her and Brad Belleville. Instead, her mind was in a quandary as to where her sister had gotten to as she marched into the offices of the *Nubian Chronicle* the following morning. The newspaper had once belonged to her father, but Kendra and Shay owned it now, and Arlisa had been assigned to work on the entertainment pages, having raised her way up the ranks from mail room assistant to subeditor on Europe's number one black community newspaper.

It was 8:37 AM when she knocked frantically on the editor's door, the office that belonged to her sister, only to find no reply. She could hardly believe that Kendra had left the Yaa Asantewaa Art Gallery without her. When she'd returned to the main hall after her confrontation with Brad Belleville, hoping to fill her sister in on what she'd been up to in the parking lot outside, it was Kitty who had approached her with a wary smile, telling her that Kendra had left with a man.

"She didn't look well. Morning sickness I expect," Kitty had explained in a concerned manner. "I think he took her home."

She felt herself ridden with guilt that she could have left her pregnant sister alone with mere strangers to keep her company. Perhaps Kendra had thought that she'd made her way home, too, but Arlisa couldn't be sure of that either because she'd not been able to get Kendra at her Wimbledon home, and their father, Ramsey Davenport, hadn't seen her since yesterday morning.

Withdrawing from the editor's room, she entered her own office, her gaze roaming with a flicker of worry over the tastefully decorated room, all the soft, subdued colors especially chosen by herself to put nervous advertising clients at ease. The work was piled high atop her desk as she seated herself in the straight-backed wooden chair positioned close by the small window that afforded a glimpse of London's Fleet Street.

There was the Windrush Day idea that she'd been working on, in collaboration with the Association of London Local Government, who were supporting a proposal to create a new bank holiday to commemorate the arrival of five hundred pioneers from the Caribbean in 1948. They wanted the nearest day to June twenty-first, the day on which the ship *Empire Windrush* had arrived at London's Tilbury Docks, carrying the first generation of immigrants to contribute to rebuilding England after the Second World War, and meet the modern age.

And then there was the National Talent Search 2000, that was being sponsored by the *Nubian Chronicle.* It was her job to make sure that the ten finalists were selected for the grand finale, which was to be held at the Millennium Two Thousand nightclub owned by Milton Fraser, a close friend of her sister's husband.

But as Arlisa sat in her chair, she couldn't concentrate on either task. Normally, she loved the ambiance at the *Nubian Chronicle,* with its overwhelming male population, an unintentional selection criteria on her father's and Kendra's part. She'd found the men more fun to work with than women and often endured their leers of admiration.

Today, her mind bordered on worrying about her sister, though Brad Belleville occupied it, too.

She could hardly imagine that his union with Bernadetta Crossland was borne out of any primal outburst of passion. Knowing Bernadetta and perhaps Erica's careful, strategic involvement, it was more likely to be a treaty between two influential families: Judge Crossland's daughter and the grandson of Otis Belleville MBE, and restauranteur.

She felt her ego bruise just thinking of the mere joining of such power, though her other vital parts remained intact—the parts that had held her together, her integrity, pride and honor in oneself. She was a *Hypermega,* an inner voice reminded. That glamorous creature whose reflection had smiled rather weakly back at her when she'd applied her makeup early that mild sunny morning.

A touch of lipstick to her pink, parched lips, kohl pencil to dominate the color of her fawn-colored eyes, red blusher to her rounded cheekbones that padded out the structure of her square face; her clothes, the sixteen hundred pound bottle-green-colored suit she wore, a statement at the office of her newfound status. And as a *Hypermega,* she was not the kind to bear a grudge. If Brad wanted Bernadetta, he could have her, she mused. So why did her heart feel so pained at the very thought of Brad's impending marriage to Ms. Thang?

It was the rejection factor, Arlisa decided forlornly. She had come to realize that when she'd been with Brad, anything more complicated than a one-night stand would've gotten in the way of his master game plan. The last thing she remembered when he'd disappeared from her life was that he was on his way to becoming a famous film director.

Nevertheless, she loathed at how he'd used her. She'd never been into casual sex, even though her reputation did not support that ethic in the slightest. Arlisa liked the company of men. Her sexual peccadilloes, on the other hand, would never prove any misconduct on her part in the magnitude often speculated, even though she'd never lived a nun's life either.

She felt the flash of irritation mask her face when she thought of all the other times she'd been let down by men. She adored Raymond de Costa, the Formula One racing car driver who had showed her the nightlife of southern France. But like Kendra had said, he left her high and dry when she had gotten into financial trouble. Jerome was a lowlife, Prince Emeka Obeng-Amoo was a jerk, and she'd tried to go the full haul with Morris Walker, but he was a reminder of what Kendra had told her about Selwyn Owens, the Member of Parliament her sister had once dated. An absolute bore and such a stickler for protocol. All of them had been lacking in something.

In fact, none of the men she'd dated had ever measured up to the feelings she'd experienced when she'd been with Brad Belleville. He was the only one who'd made her feel like her entire existence had undergone some form of transformation whenever he put his mouth to hers. Even in the parking lot, she'd felt eternally blessed to taste again the little piece of paradise he'd wanted to give her.

But as grand passions go, neither one of them had felt able to discuss that one night when they'd made love to each other. Real or imagined, Arlisa felt jarred somewhat by Brad's sheer dismissal of it ever occurring. For a fleeting moment, she felt herself retreating into fantasy to be reminded again of just how good they'd been with one another.

A hot ache coursed through her body as she remembered how those honey-brown eyes had changed to the color of sun-warmed slate. And there was the erotic journey he had taken her on when the tips of his fingers began at the hollow of her throat, and brushed their way steadily down the invisible center line of her body, pausing at her navel, to move farther down again until he'd reached the one area that had left her weak with longing. When his mouth had claimed hers, hard and urgent like his body, each rustle and sigh that had left her throat, serving to encourage him to push her to her limit, had made her move ever closer toward him until he'd braced her legs apart and . . .

"Arlisa!" The office door shot open. Arlisa swallowed and shook herself completely, almost appearing too congenial for the frantic woman who rushed headlong into the room. The startled green eyes of Kendra's secretary looked stricken with shock as they met her curious fawn-brown gaze.

"What is it, Leola?" she croaked, her senses becoming quickly alert as she placed Brad Belleville, and all her heady thoughts, to a far part of her mind.

"An old woman with a cane just brought this in," Leola shrieked, alarmed, handing over to Arlisa a simple, white, opened envelope. "She said some man paid her fifty pounds to bring it on up here and give it to someone. It's a ransom note. Kendra's been kidnaped."

Arlisa's raised eyebrows and expression of disbelief spoke for themselves, it seemed. "That's impossible," she crooned, her voice quavering ever so slightly. "Kendra's at . . ." There was an unpleasant moment of silence as her voice trailed to dust. Kendra was not at home, nor was she in her office. She hadn't seen Kendra since yesterday.

Instant panic shot through Arlisa as she pulled from the envelope the solitary sheet of paper. It read: DO NOT WARN THE POLICE. WE HAVE THE MOTHER WITH CHILD. WE WILL EXCHANGE HER FOR THE LIST OF KNOWN ENEMIES AGAINST OUR BROTHERS AND THE HEROIC DISSIDENTS FIGHTING THE

CAUSE. YOU HAVE SEVEN DAYS TO COMPLY. It was signed "The People's Power Party" with a notation that she should refer to an Internet page, where she was to receive further instructions.

Arlisa's first reaction was a nauseating one. There was a certain air of déjà vu when the words *seven days* loomed up to haunt her. Immediately, she was plunged into memories and the numbers game that she had been trying hard to reject. Seven days had been the same time constraint Shay Brentwood had given to her sister to raise the one hundred and fifty thousand dollars she'd gambled away, or lose her family's newspaper to him instead. As destiny would have it, Kendra had ended up falling in love with and marrying that very adversary, and now it was her turn to be faced with a seven-day constraint to save her elder sister.

"Where's the old lady with the stick who gave you this?" she barked murderously at Leola.

"She left," Leola wavered weakly, close to tears, "after she gave me the letter."

"How could you just let her walk out of here?" Arlisa raged, the anxiety now realized in the vanguard of her bosom, almost making her lose her breath entirely. She was out of her chair in a shot and rushing down the flight of stairs, taking the steps two at a time until she reached the marbled lobby at the main entrance of the building she was in. No one was presently using the swivel doors she eyed from where she stood and Harry the security guard was sitting at his desk, engrossed in reading his morning newspaper.

The center bell of the twin elevators suddenly came to life, moments before each car door opened in turn. Frantically, she quickly scrutinized the few personnel who departed, but none of them fit the description of an old lady.

Feeling her anguish rise by the minute, Arlisa made a quick anticlockwise dash through the swivel doors, where a brief perusal of the rush hour human traffic around her dimmed any hopes of her finding the elusive elderly woman with a cane.

Her mood was one of sheer frantic anticipation when she found herself back in her office, punching out a series of numbers on her telephone handset. *Zero, one, eight, one.* Arlisa paused to gird herself, fighting the urge to calculate the phone numbers logically. Leola stood by the door, watchful of Arlisa's relentless actions, her expression tearful and her fingers clenching nervously.

"I don't want you to say a word to anyone," Arlisa stammered, bravely forcing the tears not to spill from her own eyes. She held a steadfast glare with Leola and the other woman nodded, wrenching her hands again.

Then Arlisa looked at the handset, scowling furiously as she unraveled the rest of the phone number in her head. She was trying to call Brad, though she knew not why. When a voice announced that the number she'd dialed was no longer in operation, she felt the insides of her stomach twist in agonizing terror and she slammed the receiver back into its cage.

He was the only person she could think of to help. Ramsey Davenport, her father, wouldn't be able to handle the strain. But Brad's phone number was dead. That meant he'd either changed it or moved. She hated not knowing which. And the treachery of her not knowing seemed almost too much to bear against the current situation that was tormenting her. She would go to his grandfather's home, Arlisa thought decisively. Otis Belleville must have some form of contact with his only grandson.

The impassioned plea she made to Leola to keep calm flashed through her mind as, ten minutes later, Arlisa found herself frantically hailing down a taxi. When she got in the back and took her seat, the ransom note safely placed in her handbag, she did not wait for the impact to sink in on what she would do when she found herself face to face with Brad Belleville again. All Arlisa knew was that he had to come to her rescue. She was in need of him once again.

She rang the doorbell four times, but there was no answer. Arlisa knocked until her knuckles felt sore, but no one came to the door. Her mind sagged with unease, and a general tension invaded her body when she stared mutely at the windows. The curtains were closed, indicating that no one was at home, but this had to be the right address, she convinced herself. How else was she to reach Brad Belleville?

She looked dismally at the dial face on her watch, which read 9:55 A.M. The taxi had traveled almost clean across the city to get there amidst the cutthroat early morning traffic, and knowing that she had to face the hectic return journey to the *Nubian Chronicle's* offices was enough to eventually bring the tears of frustration tumbling from Arlisa's eyes.

For nearly ten long minutes, she stood on the bleached white doorstep of the Holland Park, eight bed-roomed palatial mansion and cried away the anguish that had risen up within her. In that time, she'd planted resolutions in her head that the only other person who could come to her rescue was Shay Brentwood, Kendra's husband, and a man whom she trusted explicitly. But he was probably now heading his news team out in Cuba.

Perhaps if she called his brother Joel in New York, they could get a message to him on the socialist island. But in the midst of the United States' thirty-six year trade embargo against Cuba, which prohibited U.S. citizens from doing business or making direct contact there, and now with this rumor that Fidel Castro was on his last legs, Arlisa had grave misgivings of ever getting word to Shay Brentwood at all.

Her head dipped, hardly wondering where she should turn next, she failed to see the blue MG pull up outside the house, until she heard the car door slam shut. As her head shot up, Arlisa recoiled in shock when her wet gaze caught Brad making his way up the whitewashed steps.

"Arlisa!" Brad was the first to speak. He was not oblivious to the glazed look of tears in her dreary eyes.

"Can I talk to you, in private?" Arlisa asked weakly, fingering her long mane of braided hair and not daring to look at Brad, though she was every inch aware of how immaculate he appeared. He made her uncomfortably conscious of her slender, fragile frame as she took in his tall, imposing body making its way toward her.

"Of course." Brad twirled the car key around his vacant fingers, while his other hand occupied itself in opening the front door.

Arlisa followed him into the house. The long, carpeted corridor was the first thing she recognized as they walked toward the cluster of voices she could hear from the direction she remembered the garden to be located. Her eyes burned in annoyance when she just as quickly recognized the cupboard beneath the stairs. Still glazed in varnish to bring out the pine-effect wood, it would forever be the place that held the secret of two teenage dreams, of a time so long ago when she'd received her first kiss. The memory eased a little before her gaze took her through the lounge and along the lengthy garden path until Brad began sounding out introductions. "You remember my grandfather?" he implied toward Arlisa.

She blinked, hardly recognizing the gray-haired man

who stood in front of her. He seemed a little thinner though absurdly so, wider on the shoulders, and his chicory-brown eyes were sullen but still glistened with life. There was evidence of a sparse gray beard, too. And he was casually dressed to greet the mild morning weather, which he'd obviously decided was fine for working at potting plants.

His height, towering under the Trilby hat men of his generation still wore, made her recall him to be one the first of many from the West Indies to arrive in England after the advent of the Second World War. Arlisa could scarcely imagine that Otis would even remember the teenage girl he'd once told his story to of how difficult the nineteen fifties had been when he'd worked for the British Railway company before using his earnings to save and invest in the line of restaurants that were to become the best in Caribbean cuisine across London.

The *Belleville Lagoons* were now worth a small fortune, and was of much interest to her unmarried friends for the simple reason that the handsome heir apparent was still definitely unhitched. But Arlisa couldn't imagine Brad ultimately becoming a restauranteur. She'd always suspected that if he were to inherit any part of his grandfather's empire, he would doubtless have arranged for each restaurant to be put up for sale, before returning to the career he loved best.

"Hello, Mr. Belleville." She politely accepted the introduction before noting the two women perched delicately like doves in the garden chairs that were situated around a groomed rose garden, each possessing a certain air of grace about them as they threw her their brief smiles of acknowledgment of her arrival, before resuming to chatter among themselves. "I don't expect you remember me."

"Little Arlisa Davenport," Otis Belleville hollered loudly. "Honeychile, how have you been?"

"Very well," Arlisa lied, aware of her present state of euphoria.

"And Ramsey?"

"You have to speak up," Brad prompted discreetly. "Granddad and his companions over there don't hear so good. They're the local old biddies who like to keep grand-dad company."

"My father's fine, too," Arlisa intoned a little louder.

"Good. Good," Otis nodded. "You will stay for break-fast?" he invited. "Will sliced watermelon do?"

Arlisa felt a frisson of panic. "Actually, no," she dismissed, turning toward Brad. "I really can't stay—"

"You look kind of peaky chile," Otis continued. "Maybe you should sit down and have some coffee."

"Can I talk to you inside?" She stole the opportunity to ask Brad urgently with a tightening of her throat muscles.

Brad nodded and took her gingerly by the arm, leading the way back into the lounge. He'd heard the edge of anxiety in Arlisa's voice and decided on heading straight for the wine bar. "Drink?" he offered.

"Barcardi, straight. No ice."

Brad raised his dark brows and looked across at Arlisa, standing nervously in front of the open doors leading out into the garden. He twisted the cap off the bottle of Barcardi and poured liberal doses into two glasses. Steadily replacing the bottle, he crossed the room toward Arlisa, his gaze never leaving her anxious face until he'd deftly handed over one of the glasses in his hand. Arlisa immediately downed some of the white rum, then found herself ejecting a cough because of its unexpected strength.

She swallowed, and her fingers closed around the glass as if for reassurance. Eyeing Brad, she was made joltingly aware first of the broad chest beneath the white shirt—silk, she noted—and navy-blue jacket, the taut waist tapering to narrow haunches, down to well-formed male hips and finally beneath the gray pressed trousers he wore, a pair of long, powerful legs.

"Are you going to tell me what you're doing here?" he asked. Brad could hardly believe he was seeing Arlisa again, after what he'd thought was their final parting. She looked so elegant, too, dressed in the bottle-green suit that brought out the warm hues in her tawny-brown complexion. But her somber expression did not skip his attention.

"I need your help," Arlisa began in a flurry, immediately providing Brad with all the information he needed by the gross. "And I'm not allowed to call the police," she cautioned quickly, delving into the safe haven of her handbag to extract the letter Leola had given her. Handing it over to Brad with shaky fingers, she again took another sip from her glass.

He listened, spellbound, as she unrolled the whole nightmarish scenario, knowing that Arlisa was appealing to his common sense, to the idealism that he would help her because of the peculiar bonding that had been buried between them since childhood. But Brad felt resentful of her having the gall to ask him, after the things she'd told him the day before.

"Where's the old lady now?" he asked, appraising Arlisa with a look that bordered on the skeptical.

"I don't know," Arlisa admitted ruefully, intuition telling her that Brad did not believe a word she'd uttered. The blatant insolence in his voice pricked her on the raw, and she felt the burning blood beneath her skin suffuse the delicate complexion of her face. "I swear on my mother's—"

"You don't have a mother," Brad reminded. "She died,

didn't she? Or is that another one of those things that's slipped your mind?"

Arlisa knew that Brad was referring to the epic one-night love affair that they'd shared. But she didn't have the patience to appeal to his manhood now. Her priority at that moment was to find her sister, while there was still time to devise a plan. "If that chip on your shoulder gets any bigger," she began, "you won't be able to fit into your shirt. I need a favor. I need your help," she implored.

"You need a favor?" Brad repeated, seeming disinclined to realize the imperativeness of the situation. "What's in it for me?"

Arlisa's eyes widened, her stomach giving way to an unpleasant little lurch. Raising her eyes to Brad's face, she saw something in his expression—something fleetingly dark and dangerous that made her pulses flicker. Half with fear, yet half with a strange exhilaration. "I thought . . . being an old friend."

"Let me rephrase," Brad began again stiffly, irked and annoyed that if this ridiculous story were true, that had to mean Arlisa wasn't really interested in him. "What's in it for me."

Arlisa had a swift vision of being perched beside Brad on his mattress, her long, shapely brown legs folded around him in total surrender. Humiliation returned full force to goad her as she tossed from her mind that little cameo arrangement. Her stomach knotted and her eyes welled with hot tears. Brad was just trying to rile her, but she would not lower herself to be provoked. "What do you want, Brad? Total possession?" When he remained mute, she added with a haughty flick of her braided hair, "I thought you'd do this one thing for me, for old time's sake."

One look at Arlisa Davenport's teary face was all it took for Brad to see in his mind's eye what he wanted most.

"For old time's sake," he repeated, smothering a tremor of impatience, recalling that he himself had spoken those very words only the day before.

He looked at Arlisa and sucked in a soundless breath, as though a clenched fist had been rammed into his midriff. She looked gorgeous, even in her teary state. Here was the woman he'd first made up in his mind he'd wanted when he was a mere seventeen years old. Wasn't that why he'd ruthlessly offered to take her virginity in exchange for the ring his father had given him?

Brad looked down into Arlisa's vulnerable eyes, his lips curving slightly, though it was not a smile, and it came nowhere remotely near his eyes. It was an involuntary reaction his face often had when his mind was thinking and he didn't want to give in too easily. But at that precise moment, he made a decision that would allow him to spend more time with this woman who'd kept his dreams alive since first seeing her again at *La Casa de la Salsa.*

Nodding his head as though digesting the full meaning of what she'd said, Brad raised his glass toward her. By the time he took a slow, almost hesitant sip, his penetrating gaze never leaving Arlisa's face, the deal was set in stone. "Here's to the journey ahead," Brad conceded in acceptance, "and to wherever it may lead."

Five

The numbers game had started again. While Arlisa searched through the interior of her extensive wardrobe, figures ran through her head in a modified series of careful calculation. *One hundred and seventy-five pounds.* That was the value of the navy-blue velvet trousers that she quickly selected and slipped her long legs into. *Ninety-nine pounds and ninety-nine pence. I'll round that up to one hundred,* she thought, of the black kitten heeled boots that she placed over the knee-length pantyhose covering her newly washed feet.

Rushing over to her wardrobe, she selected the most expensive silk shirt hung in there—the jet black Versace that she'd recently paid two hundred and fifty pounds for. Quickly wrapping herself in it, knowing that Brad had agreed to pick her up from her father's London home at St John's wood at seven o'clock, Arlisa made a hurried calculation that she was currently dressed to the value of five hundred and twenty five pounds.

Knowing that she never left her father's home dressed in anything less than one thousand pound sterling, Arlisa made her way over to the jewelry box at her dressing table, seating herself to seek out a gold pendant with matching earrings. Momentarily pausing to mentally catch her breath at the prospect of sneaking back into the offices at the *Nubian Chronicle,* she applied the jewelry and made a further addition of two hundred and eighty pounds.

A fresh surge of anxiety raged through her as she thought of being with Brad Belleville again. He'd promised to help her access the Internet address outlined on the ransom note from the computer terminal in Kendra's office, and as she paused to rehearse in her head how she should treat him, nothing sprang to mind except the long lingering kiss Brad had given her on that fateful day they'd met at the Yaa Asantewaa Art Gallery.

On the Arlisa scale, Arlisa being ten of course, he'd earned a resounding seven marks, one digit above his original rating. That meant Brad had risen from an average fifty-six to a new top score of fifty-seven. And as a *Hypermega,* she never took any interest in a man who earned any less than fifty-five.

Let me see, Arlisa reminded herself of some of the ten criteria that were never compromised whenever she were to devise giving a man her undivided attention. *On his chat, Brad scored eight. On clothes, another eight.* Arlisa sat at her dressing table and began to apply red lipstick to her dry lips. *On his resources to earn money. Mmm, that was a six.* She'd based that on whether he would receive his grandfather's inheritance. *Looks. A definite ten.* She'd always thought Brad to be the most handsome man she'd ever met. *His intellect. A nine.* Brad was a thinker, and she liked that, too. *Reliability. Mmm. By his proving to help her, that had to be worth at least a nine.*

Her mind went into a tailspin when she thought again of how Brad had kissed her two weeks ago. *His kiss. A definite seven.* Then her body suddenly bolted in shock. Her seven-day deadline had now gone down to six, and she still had to find her sister Kendra. The trade secrets of a *Hypermega* would have to wait, she told herself, thrusting her thoughts forward to her present dilemma.

Pulling the long braids of her hair tightly back, she tied them loosely with a black velvet ribbon and then glanced judgmentally at her reflection in the mirror. She looked stressed. Arlisa could tell by the deep circles around her eyes, put there by her crying earlier that day when she'd gone to see Brad at his grandfather's home. And the way her cheeks looked sullen and sagged reminded her of how she'd fought and despaired to hold onto her composure while telling Brad of her predicament.

Number seven loomed up to haunt her again as she looked at the dial face of her watch. It read seven o'clock precisely. The August sky was still quite bright, and most of the office workers at the *Chronicle* would be making their way home. *That's good,* she told herself, hurtling from her dressing table. They'd be no prying questions. No prying eyes. And Daddy was not home either, so she hadn't risked him asking her anything about seeing Kendra that day.

But the thought of her sister having gone missing caused her another flurry of anxious anticipation as to exactly what the Internet page might say. Suddenly impatient with worry at the thought, Arlisa tried to still the sickly feeling in her stomach and rushed over to her bed to retrieve her small black handbag. *Eighty pounds,* her brain instantly made the addition. *That's eight hundred and eighty-five pounds.* She opened the catch and found the contents sparse. Two credit cards, forty-five pounds in cash. A napkin. Driver's license. Address book. Ransom note? She hadn't made the full transfer of items from her white bag to her black one.

Frowning at herself, Arlisa went in search of the other bag, finding it at the bottom of her bed. Two items fell from its upturned position, each falling on to the soft, flow-ered comforter that was slightly disheveled. The ransom note and the music CD that Mr. Burnt Out had given her at *La Casa de la Salsa* caught her frantic gaze. She frowned again, throwing the CD to one side, recalling how rude that odious man had been. *A real cockroach among men,* she told herself, placing the ransom note into her black bag.

The navy-blue leather jacket that she plucked from the inner haven of her wardrobe was the last item Arlisa re-quired before she left her bedroom and rushed downstairs, expectant of Brad's timely arrival. She didn't know whether he was the punctual type or not, or whether he would have any trouble finding her address. She'd scrib-bled it onto a piece of paper at his grandfather's home before she left, giving him full directions. He was to pro-ceed directly from the meeting he'd told her he was at-tending and would be at her home for the time they'd arranged.

The clock was striking seven when she entered the lounge and placed her jacket and handbag on a stool. She paced the floor nervously looking at her watch. It was five minutes fast. Brad should be arriving at any moment, so she had to remain calm. But overcoming the nervousness was a difficult business. Within seconds, Arlisa found her-self at the wine cabinet, pouring a liberal dose of whiskey into a glass. She began to down it in slow mouthfuls, im-mediately reminded of the last time she'd sipped whiskey so anxiously in that room.

She was with Kendra, deciding what she was going to tell their father about her gambling habit. How she had to raise one hundred and fifty thousand dollars, or lose the family newspaper to Shay Brentwood, son of her father's worst enemy. She couldn't help wondering how Benjamin

Brentwood, Shay's deceased father, would've reacted knowing what the present predicament of her life was currently. He was always a man so overpowering and so controlling of situations and events; he would've known exactly what was to be done, in his corrupt, devious manner.

But she didn't possess those attributes. That was why, deep down, Arlisa felt so fearful of Brad Belleville. While in that very room, she had also been burying her sorrows because Brad had cared more about the West Indian film he'd been working on than helping her to raise the money she'd badly needed. The letdown, and then the one she'd received from Jerome Morrison, who had betrayed her in front of Bernadetta Crossland, had triggered the cynical and embittered feelings she had developed against men. They were not worth her attention if money didn't talk, and to her, especially back then, men were seldom useful unless they had money.

Still, the avarice didn't bother her. In that respect, Arlisa suddenly remembered Earl Vani. Taking another sip from her glass, she felt bemused. Why had he been barred from *La Casa de la Salsa?* She felt resentful somewhat at not having seen him again, because she'd been looking forward to compiling further statistics on the man.

Another sip from her whiskey glass took her thoughts back to Kendra. They'd cried together in that room, too. She'd gambled away a fortune, but the only thing she could think about was their momma. Merle Davenport had been a beautiful woman until she suffered ill health. It had been tormenting to know that the strong and confident woman she'd known as a child was to suddenly become a person so frail, no longer in control of her faculties until she'd finally died of pneumonia.

The weariness of it all was still, even now, emotionally

exhausting for Arlisa, and had been since her father retired from the *Nubian Chronicle*. She could also still feel the raw guilt stick in her throat at the trouble she'd caused him then. But since working for Shay and Kendra at the newspaper, submerging herself in her work while retraining her immaculate exterior, and ensuring that she was still the indefatigable organizer, a trait many at the *Chronicle* saw her accomplish, she'd grown to be supporting to her father who had helped her sufficiently to reformulate her life. Everything was going just fine until . . .

The doorbell suddenly peeled loudly into her ears. The glass instantly dropped from Arlisa's hand to the floor and whiskey embedded into the carpet. She formed a self-condemnatory frown to her face. Her senses were jerky and her limbs weak when she realized that Brad had arrived. The clock read two minutes past seven, yet the amount of memories that had flooded into her mind while in the lounge had made Arlisa fretful with worry.

Picking up her jacket and handbag from the stool, she left the glass right there on the floor and hurried toward the door. The demons were chasing her with a fury when she turned the gold key in the white Chelsea-style door, pulling it open with full force. Her chest expanded as she exerted a breath, her gaze catching the full presence of Brad Belleville.

"You okay?" he asked quickly, charting her expression, concern leveled in his eyes.

"I'm . . . I'm just a little surprised, that's all," Arlisa breathed. "You're on time."

"You did say seven?" He seemed unsure. Their faces were close together, the honey-brown eyes looking straight into hers.

Arlisa nodded, the number revisited propelling her once more into an unhappy abyss. "We better hurry," she tried to think, knowing that the numbers game was replaying again, disturbing the rush of adrenalin which coursed through her body on seeing how handsome Brad appeared. The motion detector required its four digits to re-arm the security system that protected her father's home. Dazed, she kept the door ajar, trying to keep her eyes off Brad, while she punched in the relevant buttons on the wall key pad.

She felt the rush of anticipation as the fingers punching in the code became unsteady enough to slip, prompting her to curse a profanity in her heightened state of nervousness. It was because Arlisa found Brad devastatingly attractive. Desperately trying to take him off her mind, she closed the door shut and eyed Brad's car as they made their way toward it. Catching her breath, a sudden attack of nausea made her realize that she hadn't assessed the value of her jacket.

"Are you sure you're all right?" Brad asked again, this time in genuine worry. He spoke very mildly, his tone perfectly sympathetic, sending a little shoal of goose pimples up and down Arlisa's spine.

She fabricated a smile, making a fast mental addition of three hundred and forty-nine pounds and ninety-nine pence. It was all she could do to take her mind off this deep attraction that rattled her silly, cursing those dreaded retailer's who exercised a psychological pricing policy that often made things appear much cheaper than they really were. Nonetheless, she felt the slight measure of relief knowing that the value of her clothing had superseded the mark required of a *Hypermega*.

One thousand two hundred and thirty-five pounds flashed through her head, in a rounded number, providing the low level of calmness she desperately needed, though it did nothing for the hot blood pumping through her veins.

"I'm fine, really," Arlisa tried to reassure Brad, thinking maybe he could see the simmering overtures in her face. "I'll feel better when I find out what's on that Internet page."

"Then let's get going." Brad saw the urgency. "Time is of the essence."

"What was your meeting about, earlier today?" Arlisa asked to dissipate her nerves as the blue MG, with its traditional leather-trimmed steering wheel, ivory instrument dials and all the modern refinements of a British car, sped down the early evening London streets. She was suddenly gripped with curiosity to know if Brad had ever succeeded in his aims of forging out the career he'd always wanted.

Brad briefly charted Arlisa's expression, his eyes skimming over every facet of her features before he returned his gaze to the road. "I met with two British filmmakers a while back," he began rather huskily, "and formed a partnership with one of them to invest in a UK distribution company for independent films. I had some details to iron out with my partner today."

"Really?" Arlisa exclaimed, surprised, realizing that her voice was like barbed wire being dragged very slowly across glass. Something in the way Brad had looked at her made her feel like her senses were whirling.

"Kudos Entertainment will be launched in two months and we're planning to release six films every year," Brad voiced potently.

"That's wonderful." Arlisa was genuinely pleased. "What sort of films will you be doing?"

"To begin with, archives mostly," Brad explained, his tone constrained. "Old African-American classics that nobody never knew existed. My partner and I had quite a time digging a lot of them out. We're going to dust them off and present them for a new modern market."

Arlisa acknowledged the shadow of excitement in Brad's voice. She also noticed the faint sensual inflection that belied his every word. It made her admire him with the deepest of pride. She always knew that Brad would make his money. He'd always had ambition, but her younger self had been much too immature in character to have recognized the powerful traits that she could see in Brad now. "I'm proud of you," she mustered, looking across at Brad, for a moment jolted by the fact that she'd lost sight of her mission.

His chin came up in a characteristic gesture of haughty acceptance. "Thank you."

Arlisa did not miss the deep sense of warmth in Brad's eyes. She looked away, quickly, tension rising in her gut once more. "Do you know the way to Fleet Street?" she asked.

"Sure," Brad responded calmly.

"That's where we need to be," she advised. "We're on the fourteenth floor of the building on the corner, just as you come into Fleet Street."

Brad nodded again, sensing the strained tension of nervous anticipation and sensual longing that existed between them. He would not do or say anything about it now. There would be another time for that, he decided. Right now, he'd promised to help Arlisa find her sister, and with that thought firmly implanted in his mind, he pumped the engine smoothly and pursued the rest of the journey in comparative, but thoughtful silence.

Kendra's office was cold and empty when Arlisa gently closed the door behind her. Only Harry, the security guard in the lobby, had seen them arrive, though she did see a light under the door of Lynton's office on their arriving on the fourteenth floor, suggesting that the financial director might still be in there at work.

She flicked on the light switch at Kendra's desk and placed her handbag by the telephone, throwing a brief glance toward Brad, who'd stationed himself by the computer terminal next to her. Arlisa's limbs were shaking as she seated herself in Kendra's leather swivel chair. Two buttons automatically operated the computer monitor and tower drive and within minutes, she had accessed the Internet server for admittance onto the world wide web.

Brad warily drew up a chair and took a seat next to Arlisa. He was unsure what to expect, now that he found himself facing a computer screen. The whole mystery was something he still found hard to believe. Somehow—perhaps it was because he'd never met Kendra—it felt almost as though Arlisa was pulling a practical joke. He'd never known anyone in his life to be kidnapped. The absurdity of it was both unignorable and oddly intriguing in a suspenseful, rather than gut-wrenching sort of way.

But he could not deny the sense of unease that had begun to tease his system when his gaze became alert to Arlisa's unsteady hand. She'd selected the "find" option and astutely keyed in the page address, clicking the relevant prompter to engage the search. Seconds passed, and then the monitor became active. Suddenly Brad felt like he was flirting with the utterly implausible when words began to spring forth in front of his face. A part of his skittering mind began to think that both he and Arlisa were bordering on a larger conspiracy when the elaborately designed page came into full focus.

His first reaction was one of wide-eyed amazement, thinking that he had become privy to the workings of a shady cabal, the sort who drove around in black limousines and held top secret meetings in underground subways, or on top of high-rise apartment blocks. His second reaction was to keep his super-rationalizing cool. Arlisa was already appearing fretful. This was her sister they were trying to find, maybe even save. He would have to keep his faculties in check.

"What does it all mean?" Arlisa harangued, impatient, reading each line, each word carefully. It read:

WE APPEAL TO THE ONE WHO HAS THE POWER TO RESCUE OUR BROTHERS FROM CASTRO'S COMMUNIST TYRANNY. WE SUPPORT THE DISSIDENTS WHO ARE FIGHTING TO BRING DEMOCRACY TO CUBA. WITH YOU IS THE LIST OF "KNOWN ENEMIES" IN THE CUBAN GOVERNMENT WHO HAVE CONSPIRED WITH THE UNITED STATES TO KILL US AS WE STAND IN OUR PRIDE FOR NATIONAL SOLIDARITY. RESCUE US AND WE SHALL GIVE BACK TO YOU THE MOTHER WITH CHILD. GO TO THE WESTBOURNE GROVE CHURCH CENTER AT 17:00 HOURS ON 29 AUGUST AND SEE THE QUEEN OF PHARAOH.

The page was copyrighted to the People's Power Party, and Arlisa suspected a Florida source. She knew that most of the paramilitary style groups formed by the inheritors of the mantle carried by those failed exiles who took part in the defeat at The Bay of the Pigs in 1961 were based there. And in the new era of the *Periódo Especial*, "The Special Period" euphemism given to the post Soviet Union influence, she suspected that many were now challenging the omnipotence in Cuban political life now that Castro had been hospitalized.

But Arlisa could imagine Castro surviving for many years to come, chalking up yet another American president on his illustrious scoreboard. As to what his country's demise had to do with her, she couldn't even begin to guess.

"I don't know what all this means," she told Brad, helpless in trying to decipher the implications on what the Internet page was imparting. The only thing that seemed familiar was the date given: Monday, the twenty-ninth of August.

"Carnival," Brad immediately prompted. "The Notting Hill Carnival will be making its way down Westbourne Grove on the date and time they want you to meet the Queen of Pharaoh." Brad lapsed into thought for a few seconds while Arlisa simply glared at him, uncomprehending. "Maybe we need to be looking for someone in disguise. Someone who's going to be dressed like an Egyptian queen."

Arlisa's eyes widened in disbelief. The Notting Hill Carnival was the most visible and enduring contribution to Britain from its immigrant Caribbean population, and was currently the largest arts festival in Europe, taking place every August bank holiday. Up to two million people attended it annually to watch the procession of masquerade and musical satire, culminating in a mass of participants dressed in elaborate costumes who paraded through the streets of London along a well-marked route.

There would be many die-hard carnival traditionalists dressed like African queens, celebrating the cultural heritage of the Caribbean while they danced the night away to calypso, soca and the salsa rhythms popular to the fiesta. Since the Carnival began its first procession in 1965, the costumes had become more ominous in proportion, more stylish in design, and certainly more expensive in taste. Exactly how were they to pinpoint the correct queen?

"Brad, this is frightening." Arlisa's lips were trembling.

"Even if we were to find this Queen of Pharaoh, I haven't got whatever it is she wants."

"Maybe your sister has it, somewhere," Brad responded, refusing to accept the bleakest view. "Was Kendra working on a Cuban angle for a feature in the *Nubian Chronicle?*"

"Not that I know of," Arlisa exclaimed. "If there's anyone who has a vested interest in Cuba, it's me. I adore the salsa."

"Do you dance well?" Brad asked, trying to calm Arlisa a little.

"Of course," she swallowed weakly.

"I should dance with you sometime," Brad smiled.

Arlisa glanced at him meekly. "Maybe, after I find my sister."

"The Carnival is in five days' time," Brad said, returning to the matter most pressing on his mind. "Whatever it is that these people want, we'll have to find it by then."

"Shay, Kendra's husband is in Cuba," Arlisa suddenly recalled. "His news team are hoping to run something about Fidel Castro being hospitalized. I wonder if he has this list?"

"Can we contact him?" Brad asked, serious.

"I don't know." Arlisa was truthful. "I'll have to call Joel, his brother in New York."

"Do it now." Brad reached for the telephone handset on top of Kendra's desk. But as he did so, a scratching sound was heard at the door. "What was that?" The sound caught Brad's attention instantly.

Arlisa heard it, too. "It doesn't sound familiar to me," she wavered.

Brad slowly rose out of his chair. "Shut down the computer," he warned, taking small steps toward the door.

As Arlisa switched off the monitor and the tower drive, then put the ransom note back into her bag, Brad carefully inched his way closer to the door, aware that someone was on the other side. Nervously, Arlisa followed him, reaching the door just as Brad had placed his hand on the doorknob and was attempting to open it quietly.

A Spanish voice echoed to where they stood as Brad's eyes peered through the break in the door. Arlisa stood behind him in time to see two men, dressed thoroughly in black, making a routine prowl around the office. Her heart was pounding when she noted that they'd begun leafing their way through the papers on the reception desk, the work space which Leola occupied. When they found nothing of interest, one man stood guard while the other rummaged through the five-drawer file cabinets standing side by side against the rear wall, next to the row of windows that looked out onto the main road.

He broke the locks easily with a screwdriver and opened each drawer, throwing out typewritten documents, research folders and handwritten notations until the floor was covered with paper. He moved around easily, as though reading a treasure map, deciding to rifle through yet another set of drawers.

Lynton's office door was slightly ajar, enough for Brad to make out that a man was in there, in a chair, trussed around the knees and ankles with surgical tape. He wasn't going to wait around for himself and Arlisa to receive the same lousy treatment. "Come on." He took hold of Arlisa's wrist quickly, watchful as the man standing guard disappeared to ransack an office dangerously close to where they were presently.

"Who are they?" Arlisa whispered, panicked, allowing Brad to take the lead while she followed as they both rushed from the room.

"Whoever they are," Brad whispered in return, successfully slipping out of the reception area undetected and into

the block-long hallway running the full length of the fourteenth floor to an unmarked door, "I'd say they want to be
one step ahead of the game before we are."

Arlisa heaved a sickly breath on approaching the door
leading to the emergency exit. Brad tried, but they were
unable to get the door open, and the only alternative was
staring them both in the face: a window. But there was
only one problem. Arlisa was a woman who hated heights.

Six

"You have got to be kidding." Arlisa choked out the classic rejoinder, staring out of the fourteen-story window, knowing that it was their only route of escape. "You can't possibly expect me to go out there."

"Yes I do," Brad coaxed, slightly irritated. "Only until we reach the next window. The secret is not to look down."

"Aren't you forgetting that the next window may not be open?" Arlisa debated, peeved that Brad suggested she should even attempt such a risky maneuver as to climb out of a fourteen-story window, walk along the thin twelve-inch ledge that was characteristic of old English buildings, to emerge at another window farther along, where they could climb in and use the adjoining elevator.

"If it's locked, then we'll break our way in," Brad said, taking a firm hold of Arlisa's hand. "Come on." He wasn't going to wait until they were noticed. "You can go first. This is your show."

"My show!" Arlisa almost screamed, watching as Brad opened the window. She hadn't intended to live out an adventure with an old flame she almost despised. To find herself suddenly force-fed through the small opening, where she had to immediately use every form of instinct to hold onto her bearings as the incomparable gravity of the task facing her loomed up to slap her in the face made

Arlisa realize that this was one drama she hastily wanted to end.

Brad was being hateful, though she did realize that he took every measure to ensure that she was all right. The moment he had perched himself onto the same ledge where Arlisa precariously stood, silently holding on for dear life, Brad took hold of her wrist and brushed his fingers gently against the blue veins to reassure her that she was not alone. Whether he also knew that the very motion would also cause an unusual sense of warming to run along her body, Arlisa could not be sure.

The feeling was exquisite. Despite the fact that she suffered vertigo, that her head was spinning, which was why she'd already closed her eyes and dared not look down, Arlisa could not deny the churning emotions creating havoc within her body. She heaved a deep breath like a relieving gasp as a rush of memory flashed through her mind.

Her limbs began to tremble with the whirling effect. It was incredible that one familiar touch, strategic as it was, could have propelled her back to precisely when Brad had kissed her there, the first time they'd made love. She felt uncomfortably eager, every part of her wishing to return to that point in time, where she could experience such surreal, exciting, wondrous pleasure all over again. But the deep common sense present in her hazy daydream was to remind Arlisa that she'd meant nothing to Brad back then, and still meant nothing to him now.

The shocking truth forced her eyes wide open. Men like Brad never took women like her seriously. To him, she would always be someone who'd added to his sexual experience, who'd helped him gain insightful knowledge on the techniques he could apply in the bedroom to have a woman—any woman—submit to his will. And Brad could

always pull women, she was certain of that. He had the
looks, the intellect, the money. . . .

A number flashed through her mind: *ten.* Brad's lovemaking had notched a full score of ten in her little reck-
oning book. Of course. Why else would she still react the
way she did every time he came near, or even touched her?
Arlisa turned her head in shame and eyed Brad suspiciously. If she had made her calculations correctly, Brad
was a sixty-seven. *That's too high.* She tried to think, but
nothing sprang to her muddled, chaotic mind except the
danger in knowing that there were only two criteria left
that she had to work on to know whether Brad would reach
anywhere near the one-hundred mark scoring she'd devised in her head.

"Oh, God," she muttered, too nauseous to even contemplate whether Brad could dance, or even explore the concept of falling in love.

"Arlisa?"

The voice was heavy with concern, but to Arlisa, it propelled her into further confusion. "You're too high," she
murmured, overawed with the information still ticking in
her brain.

"We both are," Brad contradicted, not seeing the fullness of what Arlisa meant. "But if we keep our heads, and
take things steady, we'll be out of this in no time at all."

A look of fear dashed across Arlisa's face when the
noise of two police cars screamed down on the road below,
sirens bellowing, lights flashing, reminding her of exactly
where she was. Pulled back into her present dilemma, she
reached blindly behind and glued her palms to the wall,
erasing all thoughts of Brad's sweet touch from her mind.
"Brad, get me out of here," she cried, feeling a sudden
urge to faint. Against her will, the saliva began to dry from
her mouth and fear gripped her every nerve ending.

Brad looked doubtfully at Arlisa. "Don't do anything rash," he warned.

"Rash? Like what?" Arlisa screamed.

"Like fall out of my life," Brad informed with caution, steadily pulling Arlisa along the ledge—one step, two steps—inching his way down the thin strip of Yorkshire stone that felt hard and precarious beneath his feet.

"You fell out of my life long before either of us got into this ridiculous situation," Arlisa admonished madly, vertigo causing her to close her eyes again and allow Brad to gently pull her along.

"You'd think I was the only one not allowed to make a mistake," Brad objected, peeved at the remark.

"Did I understand that you just said you made a mistake?" Arlisa pounced instantly, opening her eyes. She pulled her hand away, the motion almost causing her to become unsteady on her feet. "I knew it. I was a mistake, wasn't I?"

"Arlisa?" Brad sounded like he'd been wounded. "There's no need for dramatics."

"Isn't there?" Arlisa jabbed. "I suppose Erica put you up to it. Her and that handy checkbook she always carries around. Things come easy to you both, doesn't it? Money, clothes, even wisecracks."

"Erica's always careful, especially with money," Brad defended.

"Really, and I'm not," Arlisa attacked, head-on. "I'm the gambler who'd lost a fortune, right? Well, money is so important to me now that spending it actually hurts. And when I do spend money, it's for self-improvement. What Erica does is habitual and for self-gratification. In fact, she derives pleasure from offering money to women like me to stay away from her dear, upstanding brother."

"Now what are you talking about?" Brad prodded, taking offense at what Arlisa was insinuating.

"I'm talking about Erica handing me a check for five thousand pounds to stay away from you," Arlisa crooned, staring at Brad, forcing the point home. "And like an idiot, I took it and ran away to Monte Carlo to lose myself." She scoffed, a part of her mind hating what she'd done, hating how low she'd felt when Erica confirmed that Brad was in the Bahamas. "I was glad when I lost it all on the roulette table, too. I never wanted to take it in the first place, but your sister's smug face . . ."

"Erica wouldn't—" Brad began, amazement forcing his eyes to widen.

"Erica would and did," Arlisa rebutted, the painful experience causing tears to form in her eyes. "If you didn't want to see me again, you only had to say. Instead you left a lousy message on your answering machine to say you'd gone, leaving only the phone number of your camp for me to go on. What were you? Some kind of wimp with no backbone?"

"Now, wait a minute," Brad blazed, his head thinking quickly, quite alarmed at what Arlisa had told him. "It wasn't like that. I was called away urgently. It was one of those twenty-four-hour things, where a contract just landed in my hands and I had to be on a plane. I would've been a fool not to take it, so I gave Erica a letter to give you to explain why—"

"What letter?" Arlisa gushed.

Something flickered in Brad's eyes that Arlisa couldn't quite decipher. "Erica didn't give you a letter?" he probed carefully.

"No," Arlisa said. "She gave me a check, which I blew in Monte Carlo. I came home and after two months called you. And you didn't want to speak to me," she added, her tone hurtful. "In fact, when I finally got you, you more or less threw Jerome Morrison's name into my face and told me you weren't going to help me. You've let me down twice."

"Twice! That's rich," Brad harangued, deciding to resume his way down the ledge. "What about you and Jerome?"

"Jerome!" Arlisa raged, pursuing Brad recklessly, not as careful for her own safety as her temper speeded her on a fast pace down the ledge. "We've been through all this before. What about you and Bernadetta?"

It was at this point when Arlisa tumbled and slipped. "Aaahh." Her breath flew from her mouth and bolted straight into Brad's lungs. His instant fear prompted him into immediate action as he crawled to his knees at the edge of the ledge and sought the hand Arlisa was using to hold on for dear life.

She was caught and saved within a whisker of her life when Brad reached for her left wrist, and with all his might, pulled her back onto the ledge. "That was the damndest thing," Brad wavered, pulling Arlisa into his trembling arms as they both sat, crouched on their knees. "You've just taken ten years off my life expectancy."

Arlisa snuggled into the safety of those arms, shivering with shock, and feeling herself to be in a safe haven, a place she did not wish to escape. She'd heard of blood running cold, but hers was positively frozen. She thought her heart had stopped. The near escape had evoked in her a sensation of the most helpless, hopeless, anguished despair she'd ever known. She heard herself scream the long agonizing cry of disbelieving supplication that came from within at being so perilously close to . . . "I'm sorry," she whimpered.

Brad held Arlisa tight and pressed her close to him,

making her fully aware of how hard his heart was beating. For a moment back there, he'd felt as though his world had ended. That he'd been propelled into some sort of haze that would admit no hope of Arlisa surviving. But there was no need for him to worry now. She was in his arms, where she belonged, and right now he had to find a way of getting them off that damned ledge.

"Come on." Brad quickly prompted them both into action.

"I can't." Arlisa was frozen.

"What?"

"I'm scared to move," she gasped, fear mirrored in her eyes.

She was appalled to find Brad to be unrealistically calm about the whole situation. "I can see an open window about three steps away," he encouraged, slowly removing his arms from around Arlisa. "We're both going to stand up together."

"No." Arlisa had never felt so scared in her life. "I can't." She held Brad's hand tightly, curling her fingers around the diamond-studded ring on his right middle finger, anxiety rushing through her by the barrelful.

"Yes, you can," Brad continued, gently pulling her up as he, too, stood to his feet.

Arlisa was reluctant to move, but Brad's firm grip and stern hold on her arm had her on her feet in an instant. "I can't look," she cried, placing a protective hand over her eyes. She could feel the tears of terror there wetting against her fingers, her hand still trembling and shaky from the experience she'd just been through. But she kept some semblance of thought to moving her feet along to Brad's easy pace, inching her way down the long ledge until they reached the point Brad had indicated.

"We're on the other side," he said absently, thinking that

he should double-check first that they were not going to position themselves anywhere near the culprits who had been in the offices at the *Nubian Chronicle*.

"I hope so," Arlisa whispered, awed with relief that their terrible ordeal might soon be over.

"Get inside," Brad ordered, shifting slightly to one side to facilitate Arlisa's body movement as she entered the building through the open window. Within seconds, he followed, and soon they were both positioned on their feet in a parallel corridor.

The sound of something slapping against the floor was the first thing to hit Arlisa's senses. *The cleaning lady,* she immediately thought, the normality of life suddenly washing over her, bathing her every nerve ending. The cleaning lady would be mopping the floor at this hour, she thought sensibly. That meant she'd already cleaned the offices at the *Nubian Chronicle* and therefore was not to know that it was currently being invaded by . . . spies. That one word hit Arlisa hard, arousing all her suspicions on the links the invasion might have to her sister's kidnapping.

"We have to find out what those men were looking for," she instantly chided, shaking herself into action, though the frissions of fear never left her body.

"No," Brad whispered, placing a cautionary hand on Arlisa's arm. "Whatever it is, they obviously think we've got it. We should be thinking through the options of what it could be."

"There's no time. My sister's life could be at stake."

"We have enough time to go back to my grandfather's house and rethink," Brad decided.

"I thought this was my show," Arlisa derided.

Brad sighed. "Do you ever wonder how we got together?" he asked, lacing his fingers through Arlisa's left hand.

Arlisa's sense of duty was immediately compounded by the delightful rush of pleasure she felt on knowing that Brad's fingers were closed around her own. "Sex," she rebounded.

"Sex." Brad raised a brow.

"And a little confusion along the way," Arlisa concluded. In a flash, she was transported to that moment in time when Brad led her to the cupboard beneath the stairs. It was the submissive nature deep within her character that felt all too familiar now.

The old, dormant, hidden emotions that were suddenly surfacing and which she couldn't hold down. Maybe Brad was feeling them, too.

It made Arlisa restless and impatient. The dire consequences of getting involved with Brad Belleville were all too predictable, she thought. His career came first. He was practically engaged to her enemy. His sister vetted personal parts of his life, which would prevent her from ever finding a niche there of her own. It was all so complicated. And now her sister's disappearance was sure to hamper any reconciliation, even a friendly one.

"Confusion." Brad wasn't certain of what she meant.

"You don't know who you want," Arlisa addressed personally. She scowled, and Brad scowled back. "And just because I had a close shave tonight doesn't make you in charge," she snapped ruefully, feeling angry at herself.

"And just because I'm being patient, as much as I know how, doesn't mean I like this little excursion you've thrown me into," Brad rebutted in kind, disliking the rejection.

"Fine," Arlisa spat out, snatching her hand away. "I can take it from here without you."

She turned on her heel and was about to march away, but Brad caught hold of her arm. "I can't just leave you here," he relented suddenly. "Who knows what might happen to you."

"A lot less than what's happening to me now," Arlisa snarled furiously.

Their eyes locked, and Brad charted Arlisa's face carefully. "What *is* happening to you?" he probed, gently.

Arlisa tugged her arm restlessly away from Brad's hold on her. It was far better to hold him at a distance, she resolved, than to risk the kind of danger she knew instinctively would come from accepting his offer of help. If only she was not in the predicament she was in, she would be in a much stronger position to deal with this unwanted emotional turbulence still surfacing to frighten and confuse her.

What was alarming wasn't so much the acknowledgment she'd made to herself that Brad was certainly affecting her, but the very fact that so many memories of how she'd felt for him as a teenager and when they'd made love were beginning to dog her every thought. There was that adolescent at fourteen, who was capable not of love but only of adoration. Hero worshiping. Infatuation. And then there was the woman who fell desperately in love with a man who could not love her equally in return.

As a teenager, she'd created an ideal in her mind about Brad Belleville. His was the picture in her imagination that filled her needs and longings. And now he was her knight in shining armor, helping her to find her sister. Somehow, her ideals about him had merged, making Arlisa intensely aware that she did not know the real Brad Belleville at all. Aside from the fact that he now worked in the film industry, she couldn't confess to really knowing anything further about him.

The truth startled Arlisa to the point that she was conditioned to answer in all honesty of her true feelings. "I'm beginning to see that we're really strangers. One night and childhood dreams don't make old times."

"I see," Brad nodded.

"I mean," Arlisa paused to clarify. "We know each other, but we don't *know* each other. Does that make any sense to you?"

Brad reared back for an instant, correlating his thoughts, his own judgment making him aware that Arlisa was right. She did not know his kindness, his compassion, his concerns. She had never seen the innate gentleness of his true nature. All through her childhood, Arlisa had only seen his hard, cold attitude, never knowing the real cause behind his arrogance. And as a young woman, he had given her access to him, had allowed her to share his bed, but had never truly reciprocated anything in return.

In all honesty, he wondered whether what existed between them then, and now, were left-over, lustful embers of a teenage crush that should have died years ago. So why, for some unfathomable reason, did he feel like the smoldering heat he had always felt with Arlisa had fanned into a white-hot flame? That had to mean something. It had to mean that something existed that couldn't be denied, that should be explored to its fullest potential, even to the physical intensity they'd once shared before.

"I know I accused you of a lot of things," Brad countered lightly. "You've only known harsh reality with me, and my prejudicial assumptions about you personally, about your ethics with men and your free and easy lifestyle."

"You're a man," Arlisa affirmed.

"I've been heartless, cold-blooded and unforgiving."

"Like I said," Arlisa temporized. "You're a man."

Brad smiled at the conjecture. "Point taken," he chirped, before schooling his words more seriously. "I'm a difficult person to get on with," he added, keeping his tone equable. "It's part and parcel of my upbringing. I'm old-fashioned, and there are not many guys out there like me today. I'm not one for that big merry-go-round I was telling you about. Whatever I enter into, I go in with good intentions."

"I'll try and remember that," Arlisa conceded, unconvinced.

"Well, I'm not going to force you to believe me," Brad taunted, glancing along the corridor. "For now, I vote that we hightail it out of here."

"I'm all for that," Arlisa agreed. "We must be in the offices of Lamboro and Co, the insurance brokers," she surmised, her own fawn-brown gaze searching the area astutely. "The exit must be over there."

"Let's go." Brad quickly led the way ahead, pulling the heavy fire doors open and allowing Arlisa to proceed, before he checked behind them to ensure no one was following.

They took the stairs in leaps and bounds, descending in a flurry filled with an unusual sense of pumped-up excitement. On reaching the bottom, Arlisa was forced to admit the veracity of that old saying about being careful what you wished for, in case you got it. Countless times she'd wished for Brad Belleville. Now that he was within her reach, she'd become decidedly fretful. Probably, it was just as well that she had other things on her mind to keep it preoccupied, like discovering the whereabouts of her sister.

Within minutes, she emerged with Brad into the dimly lit lobby to discover the security guard face down on the floor, blindfolded and gagged, his wrists taped crosshanded. "What the hell . . ." Brad began, instantly loosening the bonds from around the fifty-seven-year-old man.

"What happened?" he queried, as the startled eyes of the security guard widened.

"They rushed me," Harry explained, his newly released fingers reaching immediately for the unmanned switchboard, where he began to dial a series of numbers. "How did you guys get down here?"

"Window," Arlisa said, refraining from thinking about their ordeal. "And I think Lynton is still up there."

Harry Pestlow sought no further information. He cared not to discover the mastermind behind the break-in or what the men were searching for. His only concern was the safety of the building and the few resident staff still on the premises. "I'm calling the police," he alerted, his manner controlled. "It's probably best that you two wait outside until they arrive. The side entrance is open."

Brad wasn't waiting to be told twice. Lacing his fingers through Arlisa's right hand, he led the way past the main swivel doors to a smaller, obscure door farther along, which took them out onto the paved street.

"We should wait here," Arlisa said, her heart sinking heavily when she thought of the last time the *Nubian Chronicle* had been under siege. A virus had been planted into the computer network, shutting down everything that would expedite the general processing of the newspaper. Now, it seemed, someone else was in cahoots with Kendra's kidnappers to get to the information she required first. The sudden thought of telling her father finally tormented her mind. "I think I should call Daddy," she implored. Her voice weakened at the prospect.

Brad paused and looked at her. "You haven't told him that your sister's been kidnapped?"

"Not yet," Arlisa confessed, feeling renewed tears tug at her eyelids. "He'll want to go to the police, and you remember what the message said."

Brad nodded, releasing Arlisa's hand to reach for his car key. She felt the loss of warmth from the contact instantly, the break actually giving her a small, forlorn shiver as her body felt deprived of the comfort of his. "We should go to my apartment instead of my grandfather's house and think what to do," Brad advised.

"Why not Otis's house?" Arlisa's suspicions were roused.

"If there's the slightest chance that we're being followed, or even watched, I don't want to embroil him in anything."

Arlisa nodded, the curious aspects of the bizarre case beginning to weigh on her nerves in calculated kilograms. "Okay," she agreed, her vision blurred by the tears she was fighting hard not to let fall. "I'll go with you."

"Good," Brad breathed, walking toward his car, "because I think the first thing you should do is think back to what your sister did last."

If only Arlisa could think that far back. The only thing that stuck in her mind was the ever-growing longing she felt to be close to Brad Belleville. Something within craved to be in his presence, to have him at a close distance so she could just reach out and touch, and she shivered a little with guilt as she quickly followed him over to his car. Her thoughts should be elsewhere—with Kendra, her sister. Arlisa shivered again. She didn't feel particularly cold, but the evening air felt raw and damp, and the thought of Kendra's baby snuggled inside its mother's womb deflected her attention to where her mind should be.

She felt the stomach muscles in her gut tighten with tension and a tiny frown appeared between her eyebrows as they darkened with sisterly concern. "The last thing Kendra did at the *Nubian Chronicle,*" she told Brad, her mind alert, "was to talk to her husband on the phone before he left for America to see his brother about taking their news team to Cuba."

"Then we have to get hold of Shay Brentwood," Brad countered firmly, flicking open the car door. "Maybe he has the clue that we need."

Arlisa shivered again.

Seven

With her mind full of worry, the engine humming almost silently, the darkness of the night all around them, the confines of Brad's car forced an intimacy Arlisa would rather not have experienced. Although she tried not to give in to the temptation of thinking about visiting Brad's apartment once again—the place they'd first made love—she couldn't help but allow her thoughts to wonder in curiosity on whether she'd recognize it.

She swallowed the whimper of anguish burning in her throat as her body responded to the provocation of her own thoughts. The low ache deep inside her began to gather momentum and intensify with every passing second. Surely, such wild yearnings could not be present after the dangerous encounter they'd just been through, she thought. But they were, Arlisa realized and to her chagrin, she could feel her nipples swell and harden, to push against the soft fabric of her Versace blouse.

Out of the corner of her eye, Arlisa saw that Brad was looking at her. A hasty downward look at her own body reassured her immediately that he could not possibly see the hardened thrust of her breasts against the silky-textured fabric concealing them from him. Relieved, she returned Brad's stare. "Is something wrong?" she asked, alarmed that her voice sounded pained.

"I was wondering if you're all right," Brad questioned

slowly. "All this business with your sister, the office getting knocked off, the ransom note and Internet site, is just making me . . ."

"I'm fine," Arlisa quipped.

She received an inquisitive glare from Brad. "You don't look fine," he probed challengingly.

"I do have every right to worry about my sister," Arlisa relented in her immediate rebuttal.

"Of course you do," Brad offered sympathetically. "And I'm sure she's all right. I seem to remember that you told me she was a fighter."

Arlisa's mind went blank. "When did I tell you that?" she wavered, bemused.

"That night we . . ." Brad paused. "When we were talking in my bed," he amended. "Before . . ."

"Okay, you don't need to spell it out," Arlisa said, the sweet scenario forming itself in her head. That had been the first time she'd ever talked to anyone about her sister. Brad had been a good listener then. He'd understood her need to talk, to unburden some of the things lingering in her bosom. Like her mother dying, and her father losing his will to continue working at the *Nubian Chronicle*. It had been Kendra who'd held the family unit together. Her sister had always been the responsible one. "For a moment, I almost forgot I'd told you anything about her," she admitted softly. "You'd like her."

"You told me that, too," Brad smiled, steering the car smoothly down a side road. "You always spoke highly of Kendra. That's why I imagined it was the content of her character, rather than her physical attributes that her husband was attracted to. I try to pay attention to the behavior of others. It's all about character."

Arlisa nodded sensibly, trying to look at the mature angle of what he was implying. Brad had always been disciplined. She'd known that from when she was very young—seeing how organized he'd kept his toys—that he possessed a sense of order and management. She was still in awe of it, even now. "Is that why you decided to work in the film industry?" she asked, deflecting her mind from the real issues plaguing her well-being.

"Not initially," Brad confessed, pumping the engine to a steady forty miles an hour. "My first idea was to be an actor. Then I became unhappy with what I saw black actors do on the screen. They either tossed a spear, cooked somebody for dinner in the jungle, took a bullet, carried a plate, or played a piano, like Sam in *Casablanca*. I didn't want to have to kiss ass to play small parts like that."

"So you decided to become a filmmaker instead," Arlisa concluded thoughtfully.

"Yeah," Brad nodded with a smile. "But only when I heard rumors about those lost masterpieces I was telling you about. There were so many early pioneers in the black film industry who've gone unnoticed, like Oscar Micheaux. And there were so many films, too. *Harlem Rides the Range, Murder on Lenox Avenue, Chicago After Dark, Moon Over Harlem . . .*"

"So that film you made in the Bahamas," Arlisa intoned. "Was that beneficial to you?"

"I earned enough money to partly finance my latest movie," Brad clarified, his smile broadening at the achievement. *"The Price of Glory* comes out next year. It's my first picture. Not bad for an independent. I'll be going to the premiere in New York in the spring."

Arlisa's eyes widened at the revelation. "You made a movie?" she gasped, hardly imagining that she heard the truth.

"Yeah," Brad laughed, turning his eyes from the road for an instant to regard the look of sheer incredulity mirrored across Arlisa's face. He was smote by the look of longing in her eyes. "You sound surprised." He chuckled to take his mind off the throbbing in his groin.

"Yes I am," Arlisa admitted rather ruefully. "When I saw you last, you told me that was what you wanted to do. It never seemed quite real to me then."

"We told each other a lot of things that night." Brad's tone changed demurely. "What we found together . . . it was bad timing."

Arlisa moved uncomfortably in her seat, turning away from Brad, acknowledging that for some reckless reason, this action of his seemed to intensify all her aches and pains. "Your sister contributed a great deal," she pounced. "What is it with Erica anyway? Why is she so against me?"

"Cory Robinson should ring a bell," Brad reminded, a little crossly. "You took him away from Erica, remember?"

"No," Arlisa gushed, clearly shocked. "He never dated Erica."

"He did," Brad clarified. "Until he saw you at her eighteenth birthday party. Not long after that, she heard that you were dating him."

"I see," Arlisa nodded, amazed that Erica should resent her all these years later. She hadn't known that they'd been together. This was all news to Arlisa now, and if Erica was ever to know that she'd only seen Cory to try and make Brad jealous, she would perhaps have thought more kindly of her. Nonetheless, it was no reason for Erica to treat her with so much ill regard to the point of deliberately sabotaging whatever Arlisa had nurtured with her brother. "I only went on two dates with Cory to forget what you said about me," she said, prevaricating the truth. "And I got into so much trouble with my mother for it, too."

Brad brought the car to a sudden halt, not wanting to

think about Cory Robinson or the ring he'd seen him give
Arlisa back then, which she'd been so pleased to receive.

"This wasn't where you lived before," she immediately
responded, deliberately shifting the topic of conversation.
She noted that they had arrived at an apartment block at
Pimlico, in South London. Brad had pulled into an underground parking lot, into a reserved space that bore his
apartment number.

"I sold the other place," he explained. "This one's a
little bigger. I needed a studio room to cut film. You'll like
it."

"I'm sure I will," Arlisa agreed nervously, glancing at
her watch. It read 11:39 PM. Nearly another day gone, and
she was no closer to finding her sister. The horrible thought
infiltrated her mind the moment she departed Brad's car
and walked alongside him to the underground elevator.
"Can I call my father, just to make sure he's all right?"

"You'd be wise not to tell him anything just yet," Brad
advised carefully. "At least let's wait until we find out what
we can first."

"I know," Arlisa agreed, nodding her head. "I don't
want to worry him unduly."

"This way." Brad's strong, warm fingers clasped hers.
"Watch the step."

"Have you eaten?" Brad asked, kicking off his shoes to
pad socked-feet into the small kitchen inside his apartment. As Arlisa took refuge in the first available chair
situated adjacent to a huge television set, he flicked on the
electric kettle and sought two cups from the cupboard
overhead.

"I'm not hungry," Arlisa shouted toward the kitchen,
carefully surveying the room, illuminated by an elaborate

light display intricately designed with branches, appearing to be part of a tree. It looked beautiful set against the cream-colored wall overhead. And two large, cream, leather sofas and the chair she was seated in were coordinated to contrast the bare, polished wood floor that stretched the entire expanse of the room.

One wall shelf overburdened with videos and a hi-fi unit with three CDs sprawled on top of the cream leather stool nearby gave her a homey feeling. But the room was cold, too, and Arlisa realized that one of the two large windows facing her was slightly open to admit the gust of evening wind. She deposited her black handbag and blue leather jacket by her side in the chair and walked over to the window intent on closing them.

Only then did Arlisa realize that they were not windows at all, but sliding doors which led out onto a balcony, where shadows of pots of flowers and an old wooden wishing well met her inquiring attention. She turned to chart Brad's entrance into the room from the kitchen, knowing that she must have appeared surprised.

"Are you sure you're not hungry?" he said, making his own way toward the balcony, brushing his hand slightly across Arlisa's back before he switched on a wall light beside the sliding doors.

The brief contact was enough to trigger a whole new wealth of signals inside Arlisa as she stood and tried to look at the night sky. "I'm sure," she nodded, modulating her tone to disguise the rush of fire that shot through her body.

Suddenly, the balcony was lit up with light and Arlisa gasped in awe at the view. There was the street below and a little farther afield, she could see the river Thames from the vantage point where she stood, itself illuminated against the midnight sky.

"You have a beautiful view," she said incredulously.

"I know," Brad agreed. "It was one of the main attractions that made me buy the place." He threw Arlisa a curious gaze before his honey-brown eyes bypassed her and landed on his answering machine which was situated on the floor, close to the sliding doors. I really need a table or something for it, Brad thought, making his way over to the small machine, which was flashing its usual red light, indicating that messages were waiting.

His day had whirled by in an unrelenting battery of contacts and phone calls before it was packed with the intrigue Arlisa had provided. As a rule, he would be home by seven, have taken a shower and be sitting at the desk in his studio room, going over script ideas and budget costing accounts for the next project to take his fancy. And then there was the trip to Manhattan he was planning, to coincide with the premiere release of his latest film in the spring.

The red flash on his answering machine beaming at him on his approach was just another reminder to Brad that his life had become far too busy to indulge in Arlisa's predicament. In less than two years, his status had grown to controlling million-dollar budgets to gaining entrée to every dinner table from Paris to London. His infinite connections had also grown proportionately bordering on the impressive. And his next plan was very big league. He had ideas of taking Hollywood by storm. He simply hadn't the time to follow Arlisa like a lapdog on some wild goose chase to where neither knew would lead.

But some protective instinct warned Brad to stick around. And Brad trusted his instinct more than he trusted Arlisa. To him, she was still too needy, still so demanding of men, and a definite man hunter. So why had she been such a constant in his mind? Why, since seeing her again, had his every waking hour been filled with images of Arlisa Davenport? He questioned that against the unbidden recollection of a young woman he'd once known in New York, and a stab of pain rocked his heart.

Dismissing it quickly, he hovered by the answering machine and pressed the button that activated the tape to replay his messages. As Brad leaned his back against the frame of the sliding door and folded his arms against his chest, the first of nine messages began to unfold, echoing thinly across the room. Two networks in England were interested in his ideas for directing a documentary about inner-city ghetto life in London. His partner had called to finalize the date of their next meeting to clarify and tie up the loose ends for Kudos Entertainment. His mother had left a message reminding him that she would be flying to Vienna in the morning, another in the long line of her vacations abroad.

There was his regular barber reminding him that he was due for a trim, and the dentist rescheduling an appointment he'd failed to keep. He grimaced as the annoyed tone of the receptionist told him that they would be leveling a ten-pound charge. Lauryn Hill's manager also called about the possibility of him directing her next video, and the agency he'd signed up with in Los Angeles left word that they were sending over a script by international courier for him to take a look at. Erica's voice was the last to filter through, prompting Arlisa to immediately turn away from the view which had captivated her.

Brad grimaced again as she first went into her usual diatribe about him never being around when she needed to talk to him. Then came the threat levied at Arlisa. "I refuse to allow you to see that woman," she wallowed, "she's nothing more than a . . ." Mercifully the machine's tape cut out.

Predictably, Arlisa rose to the bait. "Honestly, that

woman should be part of the mafia," she admonished, heaving a sickly breath. "She'll be putting a price on my head next."

"Ignore her," Brad sighed wearily, pushing his tall frame from against the sliding door's frame.

"How can I ignore her," Arlisa cursed, "when she's conniving for you and Bernadetta to become a vital statistic? Your sister is not a delightful, unassuming, wonderful person. She'd like to skin me alive if she could get away with it."

"Calm down," Brad bristled, moving closer to Arlisa. "You're going to upset yourself more than you are already."

"I'd like to slap her," Arlisa smiled deviously, "just once, to put her right where she belongs. In the gutter."

"Arlisa," Brad stated sternly. "Don't . . ."

"Oh, I'm sorry," Arlisa spat out sarcastically. "I seemed to have forgotten that I'm referring to the woman who likes to choose the love of your life. I was the hit and run proposition, right?"

"Hit and what?" Brad laughed, squaring up against Arlisa, his hands dropping to rest on her shoulders. "What is this?"

"This is me finally admitting to myself that I've been used," Arlisa confirmed, staring headstrong into Brad's face. "In fact, I've put a word to it. Expendable. That's what I am to you."

"Arlisa, don't ever say that." Brad's voice sounded pained. "You were never that to me."

"No?"

"No," he remarked more firmly. "Our path simply crossed at a time when . . . when neither of us were ready to take things that little bit further. It wasn't your fault and it wasn't mine. And . . . well, I have a lot of things to sort out with Erica, especially where Bernadetta is concerned."

"I knew it," Arlisa responded, throwing Brad's hands off her shoulders, storming back into the lounge. "You and Bernadetta. Erica's idea, right?"

"She introduced us," Brad acknowledged.

"Why?" Arlisa's tone was accusatory. She threw herself back into the chair she'd been seated in earlier.

Brad followed her into the lounge, but chose to stand by the telephone. He stared at the woman looking hard at him, thinking there was little point in lying to her. It was always apparent to him from the outset that Bernadetta did not possess the attributes that he needed from a mate. They had different growth rates, different principles, and Bernadetta couldn't handle change. The circles he moved in, on the occasions when she'd joined him and Erica, seemed to intimidate her, too; he could see that she was suffering such agonies of insecurity whenever they were around people who were experienced jockies riding educational horses. Bernadetta's winning goals in life would always be attached to a successful husband who worked in an arena that was neither demanding nor pressurizing.

Arlisa, on the other hand, was a real power trooper who thrived on risk, was impulsive by nature, and could hold her own at any given function. It seemed the easiest thing in the world to now explain to her why he could never agree with his sister that he should date Bernadetta. But when Brad squared up to the fiery woman whose eyes were confronting him head on, somehow the task didn't seem as easy as he'd thought.

"Erica's husband has some law problems that Judge Crossland can help him with," Brad began in explanation. "Erica was thinking that if I got engaged to Bernadetta, the whole matter could be sorted out behind closed doors."

"It never hurts to have friends in high places," Arlisa derided, "or friends who have friends in high places, so the famous adage goes. Where are your morals and ethics now, Brad?"

"They're not misplaced," Brad began. "I did not agree with Erica."

"But one is apt to get tempted," Arlisa dismissed.

"And one is apt not to listen to the full facts of the case," Brad remarked just as quickly.

"Which are?" Arlisa demanded.

"Erica's husband might be struck off the bar for malpractice," Brad exclaimed. "Judge Crossland carries a lot of clout in this city. I promised Erica I would help."

Arlisa scoffed. "And there you were, accusing me of not being dogmatic when all the time you're a fraud. You and Erica both."

"You're not listening," Brad appealed, walking directly toward her. "I'm sorry if . . ." Brad's voice trailed. Deep down, he could feel the overpowering urge to tell Arlisa of his yearning for her, but he was also stuck with knowing that her mind was off gear to correlate the information. Right now, he was unsure what to do, except face all the pent-up fury reflected in Arlisa's face.

Arlisa could feel the color come and go under her skin as Brad inched closer. She risked looking at him and felt as though she'd entered forbidden territory. She felt stunned by what he'd just revealed to her. In her mind, Brad's willpower to stay true to his convictions had failed him, for he'd betrayed himself and everything he stood for.

Some sensation, some awareness of him as he finally stood over her, made her flinch. "You surprise me," she offered simply. "What am I supposed to do now? Commend you for your apology?"

"No," Brad admitted. "I don't expect that. Maybe I expect you to understand that Erica is my sister, and that she's the only true family that I have."

Something in his voice caught Arlisa's attention and she found herself suddenly paying attention to Brad. "What happened to your parents?" she probed curiously.

Brad heaved a deep, timorous breath, slowly moving out of Arlisa's reach. "Divorced," he spat out, as though the very word was obscene. "My mother remarried one of her own kind, an Englishman, when I was ten years old. That's why Erica and I went to live with our grandfather. Her new husband did not want any mixed-race children around."

He turned from her and began to pace the room, looking uncomfortable in his progress. "And Dad. Well, he was quite a character," he scoffed, embarrassed. "Reuben Belleville was always in debt."

"The bookies," Arlisa nodded knowingly of the horse betting pastime that was all too prominent among West Indian men of the older generation.

"The bookies," Brad jeered. "He must've lost an absolute fortune."

"Do you ever see him?" Arlisa pressed, aware that she'd become almost sympathetic to Brad's background, her anger disappearing almost as quickly as it came.

"He's been coming and going for years," Brad objected harshly, throwing himself bodily into one of the cream leather sofas, resting on his back to stare blankly at the ceiling. "In the early days, when a horse came in, he'd be 'round at granddad's house with presents galore, and bragging about the money he'd won. Then we wouldn't see him for months after, and so that meant he was on the losing track again."

Arlisa retook her seat. "You never got to know him properly?"

"No. In fact," Brad scoffed, "the only thing he ever gave me was this signet ring." He held up his hand to reveal the diamond-studded gold band on his right middle finger. Arlisa had seen it before, but now it triggered a memory. Brad had wanted to give her that ring when she was fourteen years old. On provision, of course, that she gave him her virginity in return. "It means a lot to me," she heard Brad add. "Because it's the only thing he's ever really given me."

"But you knew your granddad, Otis, right?" she asked, pulling her mind back to the present.

Brad chuckled slightly. "I was always kinda scared of him," he confessed. "He had so many rules for me and Erica to live by. The garbage had to be out by eight o'clock on Tuesdays, the paraffin had to be put in the heater by six."

"You remember paraffin heaters?" Arlisa gasped.

Brad turned his head slightly, gazing at Arlisa from across the room. "Yeah," he laughed. "And tin baths and coal fires. And those gas-controlled water heater things that went over the wash basin." His eyes warmed suddenly. "In the time granddad's been in that house, I've seen every known modern technology installed. Erica and I always joked about that house being as old as Buckingham Palace."

Arlisa giggled, for a while forgetting her own troubles. "This takes me back to the first house I remembered we ever lived in," she began. "The toilet was outside and we had a cellar where the coal was kept. And if I remember correctly," she said, throwing her mind back, "there was an old gramophone in there which Daddy chopped up for firewood after he went out and bought one of those blue spot radiograms that played the thirty-threes and forty-fives."

"That every good West Indian home should have if they were going to have friends over for a little Saturday night blues, dominoes, smokes and booty."

Arlisa laughed out loud. "Those were the days," she crooned. "Our parents' generation sure knew how to party."

"I thought that was your forte," Brad appended, diverting the subject.

Some of Arlisa's smile dropped from her face. "I like to dance," she corrected. "The salsa, if you must know. That's what I was up to when you saw me at La Casa de la Salsa."

"I thought you were waiting for Earl Vani," Brad returned, his eyes narrowing teasingly.

"He makes an excellent dancing partner," Arlisa prevaricated slowly. "But I don't expect you to understand what I mean. You either like the salsa or you don't."

Brad dissolved into silence for a few seconds, then jumped up from the sofa. "I have a salsa CD here somewhere," he began, kneeling to his feet to quickly browse through the selection scattered close to the hi-fi unit. Finding what he was looking for, he inserted it into the unit and turned up the volume until the soft, romantic music began to fill the room. "Care to dance?" he invited.

Arlisa glared at him. She couldn't summon the words to respond the moment she heard the drugging Latin beat. And seeing the deep, amorous bait in Brad's eyes, she could only nod her head, eventually saying thickly, "Do you know how to do the basic step?"

"Turns, swivels, and if you're lucky, even a dip," Brad smiled deeply. He marched across the room and took Arlisa's hand by the wrist, pulling her bodily from her chair. "And I've got a great floor for us to drum up some rhythm," he added, tapping one socked foot against the hard wood.

Arlisa could hardly reject the invitation. The Latin music was already working its sedating effect on her and to her chagrin, she found herself instantly slipping between Brad's arms, as smoothly and as easily as though she'd always belonged there. She placed one hand on his shoulder, and he held the other upright at shoulder length; when the correct piano note struck the opportune chord, Brad began to steer Arlisa across the room.

They moved in communion with each other, taking parallel steps where every risque beat fell, alert to every diversion in the music, which allowed them both to keep tune with the rhythmic Afro-Cuban melody. Arlisa automatically succumbed to the euphony she'd always felt while doing the salsa. This was her only avenue of freedom, where she could escape all the burdens of the world and truly feel at one with herself.

But this was no ordinary dance. She was dancing with Brad Belleville, and Arlisa was more than aware of the distinct sensual undertones that marred their every movement. Their hips adjoined, his forehead on occasion touching hers, she felt herself sinking deeper and deeper into the intimacy that the music demanded. The sounds of Miami always induced this effect in Arlisa, and she could almost feel herself moan in unison to the sweet dulcet tones that were as soothing and as pleasing to her ears as having the fullness of Brad's body pressed intimately against her own.

She was focused intensely on every aspect of the dance, to every delicate, swift movement that Brad instigated to divert her into the turns and spins that kept her feet busy skipping around the room. The sheer physical movement had her breath panting heavily, but she couldn't blame it

on just the salsa. Arlisa knew that whatever else was going
on with her was undermined by the insidious weakness
that flooded through her body, caused by Brad's familiar
blank expression. His gaze was dark with concentration,
yet in their dusky depth, Arlisa could see the triumphant,
smoldering recognition of his power over her. Brad knew
exactly what he was doing.

The dip came unexpectedly, as did the soft feel of his
warm hand as it slowly traveled down the side of her body,
landing on her hip. Their eyes locked, and the delicious
bone-melting pleasure that coursed through Arlisa's loins
merged with the music as primitive as an African drum's
echo in the Sahara desert. Then she was on her feet again,
exerting quick steps around the room: a spin, a turn, two
swivels and then another dip that brought their faces together.

Arlisa's passion was thoroughly reawakened the moment Brad placed his mouth fractionally close to her own.
They were both perspiring, unsuccessful in laboring their
breathing when their lips brushed, tasting each other's
flesh. The clean, salty tang of him filled Arlisa's nostrils,
creating a ravenous hunger that was lush and tempting.
Through a veil of dark lashes, she watched his gaze sink
down her half-reclining body, drifting into intimate territory as though searching for a flaw in the otherwise perfection of her brown skin. The silence between them
frizzled her senses.

Her lips parted as his gaze darted upward, spurred by
the pressure of his caressing fingers, which slowly moved
a band of braided hair from her perspiring face. It was like
being touched by a live wire. Arlisa's skin quivered and
she could feel the nipples that peaked her breasts spring
erect, telling of her arousal. But the dance was not over.
Within seconds, she was upright yet again, so pulled and

coerced around the furniture, her body directed to all parts of the room, that she seriously wondered whether she could keep up with Brad.

He was getting bolder by the minute, his every movement filled with teasing, inoffensive strokes and caresses, all of which were earth-shattering and volcanic to Arlisa's nerves. A definite pause in the music had her hesitating when Brad locked her to his rigid frame and she could feel his heart pumping as violently as her own. She could probably tell him the exact day she'd first experienced his heart beating so strong if she wanted to dwell on it. But Arlisa had now decided that both she and Brad were unsuspecting victims of fate.

She reminded herself that this shining knight of her dreams was utterly without honor, that she'd passionately been in love with the idea of love and was blinded by her own romantic idealism. So why did she feel as though she'd recaptured something quite precious, like something out of a fairy tale? Arlisa was bewildered when the music fell dead.

"That . . . that was exhausting," she smiled weakly, as she repositioned herself safely on her feet.

"And how did I rate?" Brad mocked, his honey-brown gaze scanning her intensely. "Any good?"

"Rate?" Arlisa was dumbfounded. "Quite . . . quite fine. Eight out of ten."

"An eight," Brad laughed, shrugging, not taking the score seriously. "I guess I can live with that." He turned his back and walked toward the kitchen. "I'm pooped. I'm going to make a sandwich. Sure you're not hungry?"

"No," Arlisa replied, her brain having already made its calculated diversion. *Sixty-seven, plus eight,* she thought. *Goodness, Brad was a seventy-five.*

"I have ham and cheese?" Brad's voice yelled from the kitchen.

"I said I'm not hungry," Arlisa yelled back.

She looked around nervously, feeling the sudden chill from the open sliding doors. Arlisa made her way there and closed them, eyeing the man on the street corner. He looked up at her and she looked down, only able to see a part of his face, as the rays from the street lamp bounced against his profile. He seemed sort of familiar, and Arlisa was always good with faces, but she dismissed him instantly and turned her body toward the kitchen, charting Brad's reentrance to the lounge.

He had a carton of milk in one hand and a huge sandwich in the other, consuming them both in the manner of a grown man with a healthy appetite. "You look like you haven't eaten all day," she observed, walking over to the cream chair where she deposited herself comfortably.

"I haven't," Brad confessed, striding toward her. "It's been all work and no play. And tonight . . . What a night."

Arlisa's present dilemma loomed up to haunt her once more. "Can I use the telephone to call my father?"

"There's a phone in the bedroom." Brad gestured toward a closed door. "Use that one. The handset on the phone in here isn't good."

Arlisa nodded and rose to her feet. Within minutes, she sat on Brad's king-sized bed, having turned on a bed lamp to seek out the phone by the bedside. A quick dial and the series of numbers immediately connected her to her father. Ramsey was tired and hadn't felt well all day. He inquired diligently of Kendra.

"She's at Nellie's," Arlisa lied, though she felt the stammer in her breath. "I took her there this morning. She says she's going to stay over for a few days."

"What about the office?" Ramsey sounded shocked, almost unconvinced.

"Lynton's there," Arlisa pressed, the vanguard of her bosom suddenly heaving sickly when she thought of what was going on at the *Nubian Chronicle* presently. "And I'm on top of things, too," she lied again. "Don't worry, Dad, I'll see you in the morning."

The pressure was almost too much to bear when she hastily concluded the call with her father and began to dial the number for the *Nubian Chronicle*. Harry answered the switchboard almost instantly and Arlisa felt the sigh of relief rush from her mouth. "Is everything all right there?" she asked, panicked.

"Yeah," Harry revealed. "I'm just giving the police a statement now. We didn't get the guys. They must've left through the same side entrance that they came in before you and your friend got to me."

"How is Lynton?" Arlisa probed further.

"He's a little shaken," Harry informed with concern.

"I see." Arlisa was concerned, too.

"Look," Harry divulged. "I'm gonna finish giving my statement to the police. I'll see you in the morning."

"Harry," Arlisa cautioned. "Don't leak anything to the press about this, okay? I want to try and figure out what's going on first."

"You're the boss," Harry returned.

Arlisa sighed again as she replaced the handset. She wasn't the boss; her sister was. And damn it, where in the hell was Kendra? Her gaze flickered toward the door, where Brad stood silently. Droplets of sweat were still above his brows from the dancing, and his gaze was narrowed curiously.

"Everything okay at home with your father?" he asked

quietly, venturing into the bedroom, taking slow strides toward her.

"If you mean is he suspicious; not yet," Arlisa admitted, the signs of worry quite evidently displayed across her face. Nervously fingering the long mane of her braided hair, she added, "I hope I don't have to give him . . . any bad news." Her voice was shaky and pathetically weak, but sheer stubbornness made Arlisa refuse to cry.

Brad was sitting by her side in an instant. "We'll find your sister," he insisted calmly.

Arlisa chewed at her lower lip. "You don't understand," she stammered. "He's been through so much these past couple of years. My mother dying, his retirement. And me," she scoffed, sardonic. "I was so reckless, I just don't know how he coped. I did a terrible thing, gambling away so much money, but at the time, doing it relieved me. I really couldn't see the insanity of what I was doing. If it hadn't been for Kendra and Shay . . ."

Brad's arm circled around Arlisa's shoulders. "You don't need to explain to me why you gambled," he explained. "What matters is that you found the strength to stop. Which is more than I can say for my father."

Arlisa's tear-glazed eyes met Brad's. "You can't forgive him, can you?"

"It's not the money, Arlisa," Brad breathed, his tone shaky with the revelation. "Being lied to hurts more than any money, and Reuben—that's how I refer to him—always lied to me."

Arlisa dipped her head and snuggled into Brad's chest. The comfort she felt there was as revitalizing as it was needful. "My father forgave me for what I did," she swallowed, trying to force down the lump in her throat. "My mother always said if you can't forgive, you can't forget. I was so thankful for it, because it helped me get my act together from being a wild party girl to that 'sensible, well-rounded girl,' as my teacher put it in my progress report at primary school."

Brad rubbed his hand across Arlisa's shoulders, coaxing her to snuggle into him even more. "How old were you then?" he breathed, bending his face closer so that the sweet scent of her perfume invigorated his senses.

"I don't know. Seven, probably," Arlisa drawled, her tone husky; her heart, she was chagrined to register, barely skipping a beat. "It was before I met you."

Brad chuckled, his free hand boldly taking hold of Arlisa's, where he proceeded to lace his fingers through hers. "You were nine when you met me, right?"

"You know I was," Arlisa wavered. She could feel the heat and dampness of Brad's chest through her Versace blouse, aware that his heart was beating as crazily as her own.

"I still remember what you were like," he proclaimed, his eyes darting sideways, back to the past. "A skinny little thing, very simply dressed. With a scowl."

"A scowl?" Arlisa challenged.

"And shy," Brad added, squeezing Arlisa's fingers, arresting her attention. "You were always touching my things, too. Picking things up from one place and putting them in another."

"Yes, I noticed even back then that you were quite an organizer," Arlisa countered. "What I didn't like was the way you and your sister treated me."

"Horribly," Brad admitted truthfully. "We were spoiled, but not in the way you think," he explained. "Otis gave me and Erica the best of everything, but he was essentially a stingy old man. To him, money was well spent if we learned something. Erica speaks fluent Spanish and I speak French."

"Really?" Arlisa was amazed.

"That's what he was like," Brad went on. "He ruled our lives completely. And whenever Mother came to see us, I used to feel like I had to live up to her wealth, up to the standards that she lived by. As a boy, I rebelled against it in the beginning, and I think I took a lot of that aggression out on you. Whatever I did back then, I'm sorry."

Arlisa stared at Brad, feeling intensely touched by his apology. She couldn't look away from the hypnotic black gaze that was all too familiar to her. "Do you remember when you first kissed me, underneath the stairs?" she said starkly, the memory thrust out of her throat before she could stop herself.

Brad felt a savage rush of pure adrenalin fire through his body. "I've always remembered it," he confessed, his voice thick, his cheek suddenly warm against Arlisa's. "Just like I remembered the first time we made love."

Arlisa turned her head completely, her mouth opening against the bottom of Brad's cheek. "I remember, too," she gasped.

Her hoarse, muffled whisper made Brad's head spin. "Can I remind you again?"

Arlisa met the gaze that bore deeply into hers. "Remind me again."

Eight

Arlisa's whisper made Brad's head spin. Whatever it was that existed between them, had ever existed between them, was suddenly heightened out of all proportion. It ignited and burned right there. And whatever it was that they were looking for, that was imperative to Arlisa finding her sister, no longer seemed important in the brief span of seconds that passed as his eyes met hers.

The important thing right then was that Arlisa's breath was moist and hot against his, her skin so warm and tender against his fingers that instinct propelled him forward to take her mouth into his. She made a deep, smothered sound in her chest and melted right into him.

Brad's sullen brown eyes which held that strange mixture of desire and uncertainty, with hints of his sultry male glare, thrilled Arlisa to her toes. This was the Brad she knew best. The Brad that made her blood swim hazily throughout her loins. As he angled her and lowered her to the bed, laying her easily on her back so that she had no option but to cling on to him, Arlisa's eyes fluttered shut, unable to cope with the sensual overload. She felt gloriously weak, almost faint, and the very emotion was exquisite.

Nothing existed in her world at that moment except the heat and tumultuous sensation Brad was putting her through, which intensified when she felt his hands drifting down her sides to her shapely hips, trembling beneath her velvet trousers.

And Brad's lips never left hers, throughout his provocative exploration. While his body lowered gently on top of hers, Brad's kiss deepened, his teeth deliberately grazing ever so slightly across her bottom lip. Arlisa could feel his hardness lodged tightly in the hollow of her groin as his fingertips slid under her black Versace silk shirt, their next casual journey delving beneath the lacy fabric of her lingerie, until he reached the peaking against the soft abrasion of her bra.

Arlisa's hand slid up into Brad's hair, gripping short, black curly strands and twisting them between her fingers as she waited in breathless agony for his touch to steal against the sensitive flesh of her nipples. But his fingers stayed inexplicably at the sides of her breasts, kneading the soft, tender skin he found there with almost painful thoroughness. Arlisa found herself panting with sheer excitement.

Fireworks went off in her head. Dynamite exploded. A combination of pleasure and desire washed over Arlisa completely, enveloping her senses, telling Brad that she was his. Her grip on the tiny curls of Brad's hair tightened, tingling his scalp so that he was forced to break free of her lips and look at her. Brad's eyes glowed with catlike satisfaction as he whispered his helpless fascination.

"Whatever you want," he told Arlisa, admitting to her that he was hers, to do with as she pleased.

His words were instantly smothered by Arlisa's urgent mouth, hot and hard and sweetly bold, as her lips slanted across his, her tongue smoothing inside the wet interior of his mouth, sucking at the pulsing flesh she found there. The darkness that demolished all thought came rushing up at her like the approach of night, sweeping away any semblance of reason or logic, taking her into the black hole of pure, unadulterated passion.

All concept of time vanished. The universe shrank at an alarming rate until it was composed of almost nothing, except the warm, human body of Brad Belleville. This was the man who had once been at the center of her universe, and even now still seemed to find his place there. But the blinding, erotic spell that Arlisa felt herself under was even more captivating and bewitching than she'd ever known before.

Brad dragged his mouth away from her, his fingers still moving delicately against her breasts. Arlisa almost screamed as every instinct in her body fought to savor the gravitational pull of their mutual desire, not wishing to depart from her secret cosmic circle where Brad was all but everything to her. "What are you doing?" she gasped, unable to prevent the little shudder of response his caresses produced within her.

"I shouldn't rush you into this," Brad whispered, already tracing his reluctant brief farewell across her breasts, resting his fingers against the black diamond-shaped buttons on her silk shirt.

Natural physical will had Arlisa instantly wriggling beneath him, eager to seductively persuade Brad again. "You're not rushing me," she responded, her gaze fixed and mischievous, vanquishing Brad's momentary uncertainty. Placing her fingers on the buttons of her shirt, Arlisa pulled it open and found herself laughing, a sound of pure female provocation, when Brad instinctively in return used his teeth to attack the lacy strap of her bra.

Such expert, lighthearted fun was just what she wanted. This was what she needed to forget her troubles. But to her chagrin, as easily as Brad had bitten into the strap of her bra, he just as quickly let it go, tossing Arlisa a subtle, respectful glance. "Arlisa." The reservation in his tone caught her attention. "I don't want to put you on that merry-go-round I was talking about."

Arlisa blinked hard, grateful for the dimly lit darkness of the room, appalled at the sudden break which had her senses dizzy in amazement. "What . . . what did you say?" she gasped, unsure.

Brad pulled himself up to a sitting position and ran an exasperated hand across the top of his head, trying desperately to curb the furious beating of his heart. "Fast love," Brad remarked, laboring the pace of his breath. "Right now, we're both just looking for a little surface satisfaction and . . ."

Comprehension attacked Arlisa like a megaton force. She felt the full flurry of red-hot blood rush into her face, knowingly aware that it was already a telling sign across her tawny-brown complexion, speaking of her embarrassment. "Are . . . are you suggesting that I'm taking a carousel ride right now?" she asked, hardly surprised that her voice had weakened dramatically.

Brad shook his head in denial. "I'm saying . . ." he began, ". . . that we once made love—"

"Made love," Arlisa interrupted, now pulling herself up on the bed, hastily refastening the buttons of her shirt as an icy thrill of erotic fear coursed its way down her spine. "So you know that there is a difference between that and having sex?" she scoffed, suddenly feeling deranged.

"Yes, there is," Brad answered simply. Calmly.

Too calm. Arlisa scrambled hastily to her feet, away from the temptation who in her mind seemed intent on hurting her again. "Why are you doing this?" she asked, confused. "Is . . . is this about your principles again? You preferring an old-fashioned woman. Because if it is, you're fooling yourself. I've never been noble to you. You and your sister made that judgment on me already. And this isn't about you wanting to explore, how did you say it?" She painfully took her mind back to when she'd first seen him again at La Casa de la Salsa. "The capacity for loving," Arlisa spat out. "Because you've already made your admission about the discreet intimate affairs that you've had." Her heart was aching as the truth hit home. "No. This is about Bernadetta Crossland," she said angrily.

"That's not true," Brad shot back. "I thought I explained to you about her."

Arlisa turned to keep him in her night-blurred sight, deciding to walk toward the bedroom window, though she could feel but not see his eyes boring into her, causing the tingling of her scalp that usually presaged a severe attack of nervous sexual tension. "Your explanation wasn't good enough," she jabbed, lifting her hand in a fierce warning-off gesture, words from her past sliding unbidden into her mind, which she'd never forgotten. *I'm the one he reaches for in the middle of the night, or did you think that was you?*

Bernadetta Crossland had thrown those very words harshly at her when she'd caught the woman with Jerome Morrison. In Arlisa's mind, they applied to her very situation with Brad Belleville now. He could never belong to her wholly because another woman had left her mark on him. And despite what he'd told her about Erica and her husband needing his help, Brad's refusal to make love to her simply heightened her suspicions, making her feel ugly and ineffectual. "I don't want to share you," she hastened to add, brushing back the curtains she saw hung around the window to peer out at the night street. Again she saw a man on the street corner, but she paid little attention.

All she wanted to know at that juncture was how much of her feelings had transported to Brad. In her mind's eye, the debate as to why he had rejected her was as tangible and as concrete as ever. Aside from refusing to believe Brad's feeble excuse about Erica wanting him to see Bernadetta Crossland, Arlisa sensibly told herself that to Brad Belleville, she was still not up to his standards.

And there was nothing more damaging or more harmful to a woman than the issue of questioning her own sexuality. Could she ever be woman enough for Brad? Did not the fact that she had a sense of her own perfection appeal to him in the slightest? Obviously not, Arlisa thought with frustration. To Brad, she would always be a woman pursuing money and men with equal determination. Though that had once been her intention, Arlisa began to realize that her motive for finding a rich mate suddenly held no importance. Surely what she needed more than any money was the deep level of respect that came with being loved.

This one thought protruded her mind as she heard Brad's voice infiltrate her troublesome thoughts. "That's an extraordinary thing to say," he remarked in answer to her earlier statement.

Arlisa slowly turned from the window to find Brad looking at her, almost in confusion, his mood positively benign. She tried to evaluate what it meant, logically listing the alternatives of how she should react, as though she were solving a business problem. It boiled down to two: She could either step back from the entire situation that any involvement with Brad would present, or she could continue to behave like a jealous schoolgirl who was suffering an acute case of infatuation.

"We're in extraordinary circumstances," she relented quietly, deciding that she would stem the tide and save face by pulling back, the only move that would protect her from emotional harm. "And we're both confused. Perhaps it's best that I try and find my sister, alone, and leave you to sort out your imaginary love life with that relic you've gotten yourself friendly with."

"Relic?" Brad felt tempted to laugh.

"Well, she is getting on a bit," Arlisa couldn't resist aiming the jibe. "How old is Bernadetta now? Thirty-nine? Forty? A good seven years older than you."

Brad seemed unreasonably irritated by her candor. "You'll be telling me that she's ancient next," he smiled luridly, raising himself up from the bed.

"Well I'm sure she can go down in history as a woman who . . ." Arlisa hesitated as a flash of memory flickered before her very eyes. The man she saw from the window. Shaking herself, she diverted her thoughts entirely. Yes. She had seen him before. He was Mr. Burnt Out from La Casa de la Salsa.

"Arlisa?" Brad was next to her in an instant, having detected her swift change in mood. "What is it?"

"That man from the salsa night club," she began in a flurry of excitement, catching Brad's attention as she stared into his eyes. "He's outside."

"What?" Brad shook his head in measured bewilderment. "The one who gave you a piece of his mind?"

Arlisa winced at the memory. "He gave me more than that," she recollected, steering the subject successfully. "He gave me the creeps, and now I think he's following me."

Brad pulled a curious face and stepped back to look through the window. His gaze scanned both sides of the street, seeing no one suspect. "Are you sure he's out here?" he asked, stretching his gaze widely.

"I never forget a face," Arlisa insisted, turning to join Brad at the window where she, too, glanced in either direction. The man she'd seen, or thought she'd seen had gone, and for a brief moment she found herself questioning whether she'd even seen him at all. "He was right there, by the lamppost," she insisted again.

"Maybe it was someone who looked like the guy," Brad remonstrated calmly, pulling back the curtain.

Arlisa shook her head, feeling quite confused by every facet that made up her life currently. She was going through too much, she decided. Life wasn't about the simplicities of finding a rich mate anymore. It had taken a large leap into the serious nature of dealing with danger, uncertainties, and emotional upheaval. It was peculiar at that moment that she should think that she had bordered on the verge of the twilight zone. Anything could happen. Within the last forty-eight hours, anything had. And it was getting more fast-paced by the minute.

What she needed was sleep. Things always looked better in the morning. She would go home, rethink everything, attempt to calm the jitters that were still creeping around her nervous system, and begin again the task of finding her sister. "I'm tired," she sighed heavily, dismally moving from the subject of Mr. Burnt Out. "With the kind of day I've had, maybe I'm not seeing straight anymore. Can you give me a ride home?"

Brad glared at her, his features oddly possessive. "Stay here," he immediately invited, his gaze warming as he caught sight of the tiredness in Arlisa's eyes.

There was a silence, several heartbeats long.

"You're asking me to share your bed?" Arlisa asked, in a distinctly edgy tone.

"No strings attached," Brad confirmed, holding her gaze, as though he had decided to suddenly bait her in challenge.

"And where would you be sleeping exactly?" Arlisa queried again.

"Next to you," Brad answered easily, adopting a warm smile, "to protect you from the bad guy outside."

Arlisa shook her head. "I don't quite know how to take you," she admitted warily. "You seem so . . . contradictory of your motives and actions."

"Look, Arlisa," Brad's tone became serious. "I want you to stay because I feel compelled to try and get to know you all over again. But there are so many things going on between us right now, like your sister being kidnapped and the break-in at your newspaper. The last thing I want is for you to accuse me again of taking advantage of you when you were at your most vulnerable."

"I see," Arlisa nodded, knowing that Brad made perfect sense. She had accused him and now he was being respectful. His sincere treatment of her had to mean that whatever she'd told him, he was taking it seriously. "In that case," she began, backing down, even forming a shallow smile to her face, "I'll stay. Then we can go to my father's house in the morning and call Shay Brentwood."

"Done," Brad agreed, snapping himself into action. "There's a shower cubicle in the corner over there," he said, pointing directly ahead with his index finger. "And there are some clean oversized T-shirts in the drawer over there. You can wear whichever one you want."

"Thank you," Arlisa said, smiling again.

"I'm just going to make some phone calls to my business partner and my agent," he remarked, now making his way back toward the bed, where he sat and pulled the telephone and its handset onto the mattress. "I shouldn't be long."

Arlisa nodded, acknowledging Brad's need to continue his work. "I'll take my shower now."

* * *

One hour later Arlisa emerged from the bathroom, feeling totally refreshed. The sweet haven of the shower cubicle was steamy and hot, giving her solace and a sense of peace where she'd been able to clear her thoughts and her mind. When she entered Brad's bedroom, she was to find him between the sheets, wearing a pair of spectacles and sifting through wads of paper, totally immersed in his work. The image somewhat surprised Arlisa. She hadn't seen this side of Brad before, and she certainly did not know that he wore glasses.

"What are you doing?" she asked, self-consciously walking toward the chair situated close by, where she began placing the clothes that were in her hands.

Brad did not look up from his work, but spoke while still engrossed. "I'm just checking the budget for this documentary I hope to do."

"Sounds interesting," Arlisa intoned lightly before perching her bottom on her side of the bed.

Only then did Brad distract himself from his work to observe Arlisa climbing between the sheets beside him. She was dressed in one of his T-shirts with her braided hair swept away from her face, and her makeup removed to reveal the soft, even-toned tawny-brown of her skin. To him, she was adorable. He had to catch his breath. "God, you're a sight for sore eyes," Brad breathed, unable to stop himself. "I always thought a woman looked most sexy when she blushes, when she's just had a shower, or after she's made love."

"Brad!" Arlisa exclaimed, feeling hot blood rush into her face.

"There." Brad inhaled, noting the telling sign on Arlisa's face, which had colored to a burnished reddish-brown. "Very sexy."

Arlisa knew that she could not deny the cross-currents

of pure chemistry that were mixing up inside her stomach, sending shock waves to various parts of her body. It was all too revealing across her face, much to the delight of Brad Belleville. Her only saving grace was to turn her back against Brad and plump up the feathers in her pillow. "Maybe we should place one of these in the middle," she swallowed, indicating the pillow, "to save us from temptation."

"Shouldn't that be 'lead us not into temptation'?" Brad chuckled, recalling a line from the Lord's Prayer.

"Whatever," Arlisa wavered, frowning as she put her head into the soft cotton-covered pillow. All her nerve endings were screaming at being so intimately close to Brad, but she fought off the heat by reminding herself that she had to get sleep, for there were lots of things to do in the morning. Going to her father's house to get changed, then to the office to call Shay Brentwood. And of course, she would have to find time to fit in whatever Brad had to do. She couldn't expect his world to stop, to accommodate her immediate tasks. Closing her eyes, she swallowed the last vestiges of her raging desire and muttered one throaty, guttural word. "Good night."

Brad's husky, dry chuckle, holding all the potency of her own, was the last thing Arlisa heard before she fell asleep.

The sound of water running woke Arlisa. A quick glance at her Rolex, which she wore twenty-four seven, told her that it was seventy-thirty in the morning. When she rolled over expecting to find Brad asleep in the king-sized bed, her expectant gaze found his side empty. Realizing that Brad had obviously gone to take a shower, Arlisa rolled over and returned to her comfortable position.

A whirl of thoughts instantly shot through her mind. Facing her father that morning was the first thing to worry her. She couldn't explain away Kendra's absence forever. Surely by now she should be calling the police and explaining to them about the ransom note and the Internet page, which had given her instructions to be at the Notting Hill Carnival. Would that be when whoever had Kendra would be giving her back? And exactly what was it that she had to give them? The worrying thought that she didn't have what they wanted suddenly brought tears to her eyes.

This was all too much for any woman to endure. She just didn't know what to do. Had she even done the right thing so far? The perilous escape that both she and Brad had to make from the high-rise building that housed the *Nubian Chronicle* told her that she had. Whoever was up there were dangerous people. Probably the same people who had Kendra. So she had to be careful. Involving the police right now could prove fatal to her sister.

That one word, *fatal,* forced the tears to run down her cheeks. She could be blamed if anything went wrong, and God knows she'd always made a mess out of everything. Only in the last six months had she gotten her life back on track, and that was a trial in itself. The image of Shay's face and her father's ran through her mind just as she heard Brad emerge from the bathroom. He just had to help her, her mind implored. Brad just had to help her find her sister. A feeling of panic took hold like a vise grip, prompting a sob to escape her throat.

"Arlisa, are you awake?" Brad asked, briskly padding with wet feet toward the bed, totally oblivious to Arlisa sobbing behind him. He sat down against the mattress and bent over to find her crying quietly to herself. "Arlisa?" Brad instantly pulled her toward him and crushed her to his hard, wet chest. "It'll be all right," he reassured her, rocking her gently to and fro. "I'm sure no harm has come to your sister."

"Oh Brad," Arlisa sobbed, grasping at the enormity of the suspense and intrigue she found herself thrust into. "How can you be sure?"

"Because somewhere, we have what those guys were looking for, and until they get it, they are not going to do anything to Kendra."

"Brad, I hope you're right," Arlisa whimpered, using the back of her hand to wipe the tears from her face. "This is one thing I really have to put right, but I don't know what it is they want."

"We'll find it," Brad encouraged warmly. "We just have to use our heads."

"Yes." Arlisa swallowed the emotional pain that throbbed in her throat, enjoying the communion that had built up between herself and Brad. "You're wet," she said absently, pulling herself away to look at him in an attempt to compose herself. The frisson that shot through her body on seeing his bare chest and the lower part of him simply covered with a pink towel was all too revealing of how quickly Brad could steer her feelings to one of blatant desire.

"I've just taken a shower," Brad admitted, leaning his back against the headboard.

"I wish I could've joined you," Arlisa countered lightly, hoping that she could assuage her mood.

Brad's honey-brown eyes ensnared hers like magic. "That can still be arranged," he ventured huskily, acting on pure instinct.

The realization that he was going to kiss her came too late for Arlisa to take evasive action. Her mouth opened slightly, and softened on a breathless gasp of disbelief when Brad's mouth suddenly claimed hers. Immediately, her brain was alerted to the belated dawning that this was a kiss of intense passion. She felt her lips swell eagerly as she returned the intimacy he was offering them, the intimacy to explore the outline of his mouth with her tongue-tip, to stroke its moistness and taste the tingling of his flesh, until Brad submitted to the shivering excitement of his arousal and thrust his tongue within the receptive moistness of her mouth.

It was a dream, totally unreal, an impossible fantasy coming true yet again, that she should find herself wanting Brad and him wanting her so badly. When Arlisa found the strength to open her dazed, desire-drugged eyes, her heart pounded madly as she absorbed the way Brad looked at her. God, she'd never thought that honey-brown eyes could look so hot, his filled with so much deep fascination, Arlisa almost thought she would burn beneath the heat.

"I want to taste your skin in my mouth," Brad whispered hoarsely, diverting his mouth to explore the delicate interior of Arlisa's ear. It was impossible for her to do anything but gasp at the wild jolt of sensation that racked her body while he licked and stroked the lobe as though it tasted sweet.

"Brad," Arlisa absently gasped again, feeling herself sink into some secret abyss, where only her secret fantasies existed.

Brad's flat hand slid up and down her T-shirt covered back, massaging her against his chest, his other hand finding hers and drawing it down between their bodies, pushing her fingers beneath the soft toweling covering his lower torso to the soft nest of hair hidden there. He groaned, racked by shudders as he curled her pliant fingers firmly around him, shaping her to his need until he arched his back and thrust graphically into her soft grasp. "Oh, God, Arlisa," he rasped on a heated breath.

Arlisa melted with liquid pleasure. This was so erotic, touching Brad so intimately, feeling him harden in the palm of her hand. He was so strong in his desire, yet so vulnerable in the way he nuzzled his head into her neck, as though he were seeking comfort, restitution, a belonging that moved her to the depths of her being. Brad needed her. He needed this. His behavior wasn't like what they'd shared before. There was tenderness mingled with the passion, and she felt a surge of the old recklessness that had yielded her to him the first time.

And she, too, needed to be free of the shackles of confusion and doubt that had frequented their every meeting. And whatever unwelcome adventure lurked ahead, at least she could make of this consummation an untainted memory to hold in her heart.

Her hand tightened around him and he moaned excitingly into her ear. She eased their bodies closer and began a slow rotation of their hips, replacing her stroking fingers as she caressed her hand back up his naked chest and over the strong column of his throat, sliding her fingers over his left shoulder before she again claimed his mouth to deepen the long, voluptuous kiss.

Her passionate response snapped Brad into full action, and within seconds he was on his feet by the side of the bed. "Come on," he urged, taking hold of Arlisa's right hand, gently pulling her from the bed. "The shower's nice and steamy. I want to touch you in there."

Arlisa flicked her tongue along her parted lips, savoring the delicious surprise as she hurtled herself from the bed, every fiber in her body eager to taste again that sweet nectar from God.

Her gush of breath was warm and spicy as she entered the shower cubicle next to Brad, every part of her shaking as he first removed the towel from around his waist and then the T-shirt that covered her naked body. When he closed the door and flicked on the shower spray, her senses immediately were filled with sweet delight as he coaxed her body into his. His broad, muscled shoulders, perfectly detailed biceps along his arms, and a narrow waistline that tapered smoothly into well-formed male hips joined with her.

The kiss Brad claimed was hot and sweltering, jarring all the dormant impulses inside Arlisa to rise to the surface. Their bodies merged as the water took heat, the driving force of each droplet against their skin provoking an impatience for the violent pleasure they both knew they could give.

She shook her head as the steaming downpour renewed her appetite, the water melting between the joining of their lips so that instinctively, they licked and stroked their tongues against each other, their thirst not for the water, but to release the wildness that was bursting to be free.

A pulse jolted briefly in Brad's left temple as his hands unconsciously dragged Arlisa's hips possessively against him so that she could feel the mounting hardness of his manhood. "Jesus," he murmured on a hoarse breath, allowing his hands to slide up Arlisa's thighs until they rested shakily on her waistline.

Arlisa held Brad suffocatingly tight around his neck, tipping her head forward with the devouring force of her hunger, kissing him on his neck with a savage eagerness that shattered all the boundaries of her self-restraint. Her hands relentlessly explored his slender back, massaging lower and lower until she reached his rounded buttocks, where they took refuge in the softness of his hairy skin.

And the smile she gave him was sultry and knowing. It told Brad everything he needed to know about the erotic pleasure Arlisa wanted to give him. As the water intensified to a needle spray, its very heat causing the shower cubicle to steam up to a devilish intensity, Brad's confidence exulted to a fierce sense of victory.

In his world, Arlisa Davenport belonged to him. In his fantasies, she'd always belonged to him. And she was no longer the same woman he'd last made love to when she was twenty-four, nor the innocent teenager he'd kissed at fourteen. Nor was she that little girl he'd once despised at nine years old who'd kept touching his things. Arlisa had not only blossomed, but had matured. Like vintage wine, she was sweet and ageless, leaving a tangy taste on his lips. This was the woman he would always want. His fingers moved provocatively, sliding down to smooth over the softly rounded cheeks of her bottom, and his heart pounded widely when he felt Arlisa shiver, moving her hips into his touch.

He straightened, meeting her drugged fawn-brown eyes with a blazing look of reckless male triumph. To her astonishment, Arlisa felt her red-hot blood fire into her perspiring face, and Brad gloated openly at the betraying crack in her facade of worldly sophistication. Arlisa Davenport, doyenne of her time, submitting to his will. His hands settled firmly back on her waist, holding her steady against the slippery floor of the shower cubicle as he ordered gruffly, "Come to me."

Arlisa obeyed, her legs brushing against his, trembling slightly in response to his sensual aura of blatant sexual excitement. She liked the way he gave the order and her meek show of obedience was all the incitement she needed to exert the boldness in Brad.

"I'm right here," she intoned, in a low, smoky growl, dropping kisses against Brad's glorious wet chest. Even the olive-brown complexion of his skin appealed to her, where the mixed racial identity of his roots were as much a part of Brad as all the facets of his character, giving her desire an added piquancy.

A slow wave of heat washed over Brad as he reached out and cupped one of Arlisa's breasts, lifting the soft mounds and smoothing his thumb over the nipples until he heard her cry of utter surrender. He felt her breasts ripen and become heavy in his cradling hand, and his gaze lowered, unable to stop himself from grasping her lips into his mouth. The sweet, clean flavor of her nipples incited him.

He was playing with her. This naked, gorgeous woman in his steaming shower cubicle was at his fingertips to do as he pleased. And he wanted to pleasure her. The mist on her body was like a glistening sheen, her braided hair was dripping wet, the face that stared up at him when he removed his mouth was as eager as his intention to take her. He bit into the tender flesh at the side of her neck, inflaming her senses as his lips delved lower to take her swollen breasts into his mouth.

Brad sucked fiercely on the engorged nipples, enjoying Arlisa's frantic writhing and gasps of helpless anticipation as her feet stepped slightly apart. It was the encouragement Brad needed to press one hand between her legs, his fingers probing for the moist center. He found it with little effort, exploring the area so leisurely and with expert control that Arlisa almost lost all balance on her legs.

The shudders that shook her body was the telling sign Brad needed. She couldn't wait for him any longer and he needed her. She was light, as he picked her up off her feet, holding the sides of her waistline as he leaned her back against the shower cubicle, his senses already aware that she'd wrapped her legs around him. The water flowing sensually around them was the edge that spurred them both as Arlisa arched her back and accepted Brad's manhood as it drove its way into her, a guttural shout of gratification escaping his throat.

Arlisa echoed the cry, clutching his slippery, straining back as he sheathed himself to the hilt in her wet warmth. She barely had time to adjust to the agonizing pleasure of being invaded and stretched to the brink of bursting, before Brad was drawing back with a harsh moan, heaving convulsively as he pulled himself out of her.

"What . . . what is it?" Arlisa gasped, her face contorting in a mask of disbelief.

"Condom," Brad gushed murderously, planting his head into her shoulder, laboring his breath. "Wait there."

He gently placed her down and Arlisa felt the break of cold air as Brad opened the shower cubicle and disappeared. She stood blinking over her lax shoulder and then at the paneled interior of the cubicle itself, stunned by the sheer despair of Brad leaving her so suddenly. But the shudder of violent spasms that had shaken her system was back in a flurry when Brad returned almost as quickly as he'd left, his throbbing manhood fully protected. "No glove, no love," he whispered, stroking Arlisa's shoulder.

She smiled, allowing Brad to reposition her again. "I know," she whispered in return, her body pulsing hotly as Brad entered with one massive powerful thrust. A shadow of a smile quivered at the corner of his mouth, and Arlisa couldn't resist planting a kiss against it as her arms locked possessively around Brad's shoulders. She felt a burst of joy when Brad instantly attuned himself to her movement, playfully biting into his neck as he kept careful pace with her, exercising a fierce self-control as she rode his iron-hard body.

"Scratch me," Brad whimpered, his thrust becoming much bolder, though he was withholding his own shattering release until he knew he had driven Arlisa over the edge into the ecstasy that every woman craved to experience.

Arlisa proved responsive in both curiosity and desire as she did Brad's bidding and used her fingernails to playfully mark his back and chest. He'd asked her to do this before—the last time they'd made love, and she hadn't forgotten that he liked it. With eager inventiveness, she dug her nails in and pulled gently at the skin, her senses rising to a pinnacle when the very action heightened Brad's sexual excitement to its natural, raw state.

His pace quickened, and the water slapping against their steamy, perspiring skin was as glorious as it was sedating. It was comforting, arousing, and sleepily seductive all at once. And when the time came for Arlisa to scream out, the tension that had built up within her escaped, too, lost in the heavy droplets that smothered her skin. When Brad joined her, crushing her against him as he released, she cradled the classic oval of his face, and leaned her contented head into the hollow between his shoulders and his neck.

In that brief moment of sensual satisfaction, Arlisa knew that she'd once again tasted that sweet nectar from God, and that Brad was the one she was looking for. His lovemaking still earned a resounding *ten*.

Nine

By the time Arlisa had dried her hair and changed into her clothes, she felt as though she'd been swept into the depth of love and sensitivity Brad had shown toward her. Never before had she experienced such intensity, and in the shower, too. It was excellent. Absolutely exquisite. And as she stared at the bacon, eggs, and fried potatoes Brad had prepared—her forbidden favorites if she were ever to keep her figure in check—Arlisa felt completely smitten.

Her dreamy fawn-brown gaze ensnared his as Brad left his bedroom to join her at the table in the lounge, dressed in an expensive azure-blue suit, with his white shirt perfectly pressed, tie neatly positioned in place and his manner relaxed and comfortably sedated. Arlisa's gaze followed him as he sat at the table, though she was somewhat bemused as to why he was wearing a suit. Surely something much more casual would be appropriate to follow her back home, and then to the offices of the *Nubian Chronicle,* where she was planning to call Joel in New York for an access number to his brother, Shay Brentwood.

But as Brad seated himself what became more pressing on her mind was what they'd just shared in the shower cubicle. "I didn't think we'd be doing that again," she assayed smoothly, decidedly cutting into a piece of bacon.

Brad winced in irritation. "I don't want to talk about

this now." He fixed his tie. "Before I can help you today, I have to go into the office—"

"The office?" Arlisa interrupted, placing her fork on her plate.

"I have an office at Shepherds Bush," Brad responded, "and I need to go there and see my partner first. He's putting a lot of money into Kudos Entertainment and I can't just pretend that I don't have a schedule."

Arlisa glared at him, feeling something sickly and snakelike churn within her gut. It was clear to her that Brad was regretting already the blissful time they'd spent in his bathroom. Wasn't this how men always behaved when they'd gotten what they wanted and were trying to find a way out? Cold. Reserved. Offhanded. And she could almost see the scenario in her head on when he would back out entirely on helping her to find her sister. It was just a matter of time, she thought, before he would insist to her that she should call the police and involve her father in the whole intrigue of the ransom note.

To Brad, more was on offer than the obvious thrill of having caught her a second time around. He had his work. He had his well-achieved lifestyle. And he had Bernadetta Crossland dangling in the wings. What did he really need with her? This was one sore lesson that knocked Arlisa right in the face, and not only on the tactics of being wooed by a player. For every lesson that had touched upon the complexities of her life, there were others, equally useful, on the intricacies of dealing with her self-esteem whenever she'd been thrown into confusion by a man.

The first was to play it cool. Brad was the kind of man who exercised discretion. That told her immediately that he was the type who also liked to end his brief interludes diplomatically. And as a *Hypermega,* she could handle that. She would not behave like the silly little fool who'd buckled beneath every knock Brad had ever given her. At twenty-six, she would take this drawback with a good measure of maturity. Lord knows she didn't want to appear possessive, grasping, even hysterical.

"You're busy," she clarified, with a lump in her throat. "Why don't I meet you at the *Nubian Chronicle?*"

She was surprised to find that Brad looked horrified. "Why am I meeting you there?"

Arlisa had a swift, unbidden recollection on how Brad had disappeared from her life the last time they'd made love. In some absurd fashion, she expected him to do the same again. "Well," she began, praying that her voice would remain steady. "I have to go home and change, and I have a few phone calls to make."

"Phone calls?"

"To Joel in New York," she explained. "And then to Shay in Cuba."

Brad's face sympathized slightly. "You can make your calls from my office."

"You have a schedule," Arlisa appended, repeating his earlier remark, the very words making her feel vaguely betrayed. For all Brad's protestations about love, when it came to the bottom line, he looked after Number One. Just like everybody else. "I can manage without you."

Brad shook his head irritably. "You asked for my help and—"

"You asked me what was in it for you," Arlisa finished, lowering her gaze, loathing herself for having gotten caught up in Brad's little hush-hush love nest. "Well, I'd say you've been duly rewarded for your efforts," she dared to suggest, schooling her tone in a businesslike, formal manner. "And if I find myself undercover again, it'd be because I've become an M15 agent working for the British secret service, okay?"

An awful quietness descended on the room. Two minds sharing a single thought. It was Brad who'd said that his prior affairs had been tastefully discreet. In Arlisa's mind, he knew this had to mean that she was thinking he was protecting Bernadetta Crossland from being hurt. But nothing could be further from the truth.

His sister and her husband needed his help, though he had long ago decided that he was not going to use his influence with another woman to protect what Erica had at stake. At the same time, he did not want to see Erica lose everything that was dear to her if Minister Tyrone J. Brown III, her husband of four years, were to be barred from practicing law. Though Judge Crossland had the sort of clout to pull strings and tie them into knots and bows, Brad was not interested in dating his daughter. He began to wonder when Arlisa was going to be in the state of mind to understand all of this.

"I'm not going to ask you to do anything you don't want to do," Brad found himself saying, annoyed that he had not the time nor the patience to deal with this now. "I offered my help and I'm still prepared to help, with no strings attached if you prefer."

"I see," Arlisa rebutted, finding Brad's attitude rather cold. "This is the way things are done, right? You try me out to see if I'm worth you upgrading from the woman you've already got. Your opinion of me hasn't changed at all."

Brad placed his fork against his plate and folded his arms in unabashed amazement. Arlisa could see that his picture of her had begun to reshape. How little he knew her after all this time. "You're making a mistake," Brad said quietly. "You've explained everything to me about—"

"The money," Arlisa spat out. "Yes, I did squander a lot of it, you might say, and I know you must still think that I'm the world's biggest sucker. To you, I don't know my own mind. Well, Brad Belleville, you're wrong. My father once told me that I was self-destructive, concerning money and men. But at gut level, I've always distrusted currency with the same equal distrust I have for men." She paused to catch her breath. "I've seen what money does to people, from as early as having met you and Erica. It makes people shallow, vicious and self-obsessed, and I still think that you and your sister are like that now."

"Arlisa!" Brad's tone sounded positively wounded.

"Don't," Arlisa rebounded. "I've met a lot of rich shits who use people. God knows, I've dated enough of them. And the bottom line, Brad, is that I confuse them, because I have something I learned from my mother called integrity. Don't ask me how I've managed to keep it. It's there. And it's precious to me. So . . ." She paused again. ". . . let's just forget that this morning ever happened."

Brad didn't know what to say. It hardly mattered whether Arlisa was telling him the truth or not. Only one thing was clear. Despite her talk of conforming to the standards set out in the world by men, where beauty and money went hand in hand, Arlisa Davenport wanted love. In his mind, she wanted marriage, too.

So why was she hell-bent on giving him a load of bullshit about how love sucks, and that marriage was good for women, but not for men. She'd led him to believe that her life revolved around money, just like it had his mother. Marilyn Scott-Belleville had married Sir Paul Worthington to add some prestige to her life. Love never entered into the equation. But now Brad had come to realize that Arlisa was fooling herself if she had ever thought she could deny herself the love that, deep down, she really wanted. In that brief moment, he also suddenly realized that Arlisa was more sentimental than he'd first surmised.

"If you can forget that this morning ever happened," he proclaimed, piercing Arlisa with a stolid glare. "I can't."

That's right, Arlisa thought. *Throw the guilt back on me.* "Look, Brad." She measured her words carefully in an attempt to assuage the ineffable sadness that had coiled its way through her body, even relishing the epithet of what she was about to say—a long-standing motto she'd grown to rehearse so well. "I've learned that a woman cannot be friends with a man without having slept with him first. Now that we've done that, let's be realistic. Your past with me is not going to be your future. I can see now where I stand, so let's just eat so I can go about finding my sister."

"Fine." Brad shrugged, deciding to refrain from any debate.

"Good."

They ate in comparative silence, leaving Brad's apartment some twenty-five minutes later. Arlisa knew her ego was sore to the touch as Brad's MG cruised the streets with her reclined in the passenger seat, dejected and nervous. But she'd be damned if she was going to let him see how expertly he'd managed to hack away at her emotions. And she'd known that getting involved with Brad would be destructive, emotionally and mentally, to her health. It was time to come down to earth from the soft, fluffy clouds he'd placed her in, where no room was allowed for silly romantic fantasies or fairy tales.

She was about to plan exactly how she would handle it all, pledging that she would go on as normal, when there was the sudden screeching of tires. "Damn," Brad yelled, having slammed on the brakes.

"What is it?" Arlisa was suddenly alarmed as her seatbelt held her from being thrown forward.

"That car came from nowhere!" Brad objected loudly of the black Mercedes-Benz that had veered itself in front.

"He could've gotten us both killed." He began to steer the car forward again.

Arlisa looked straight ahead and noted the registration number. Foreign plates met her inquiring gaze. London was full of overseas drivers transporting ambassadors, state leaders and government officials to their embassies. She quickly hazarded that this early morning crazy driver was obviously from a country that drove on the right-hand side of the road. It was often confusing to meet Britain's standard of using the left-hand side of the freeway. "You handled that well," she told Brad calmly.

"Yeah," he acknowledged, keeping his eyes cautiously ahead.

They arrived at Brad's office a little after nine o'clock. Arlisa watched as the car pulled into an underground parking lot of a modern building close to Pinewood Studios, where the old black and white films of the forties and fifties were made. Brad told her that he was located on the seventh floor, and that he'd only recently moved there.

Kudos Entertainment proved to be an elegant suite of rooms which afforded a stunning contrast to the decor at the *Nubian Chronicle*. As Arlisa walked behind Brad to his office along the well-furnished suite, Erica instantly came into view, well-dressed and professionally presented, her hands intimately dressing fresh flowers in a vase of water.

"Brad." She walked over and greeted her brother, bursting with news. "I need to talk to you." She was wearing a glacial-blue silk shirt and deep-blue suede skirt, the jacket draped over Brad's upholstered chair. Yves Saint Laurent; Arlisa recognized the look. It spoke of confidence and assertiveness, though she was also to realize that Erica appeared nervous.

"Hello Erica." She offered the older woman a smile, only to receive the curious raising of well-plucked eyebrows. "Nice flowers."

"Brad?" The piqued curiosity was mirrored in Erica's tone.

"I want to talk to you, too," Brad remonstrated, heading straight for his desk. Arlisa glared at Erica as Brad picked up his phone. "I'll be with you both in a minute." He gestured that they should both sit down on the sofa. And as Arlisa did so, Brad cradled the phone between his shoulder and chin and began to walk around his desk, making calls from a list while simultaneously thumbing through the papers placed there for his attention.

Erica, she noticed, decided to perch herself on the same sofa, not too close to her, looking like she was unsure of how to take her brother. And all the while, as they both sat there silently, a stream of underlings began to enter the office with questions they wanted answered, papers that needed signing, or simply to acknowledge that Brad had arrived.

Ten minutes passed before Erica felt strained waiting to receive her brother's attention. "You'd think it was Grand Central Station the way people keep barging in here," she taunted, casting a disapproving eye at Brad. "Second to God, they believe my brother controls this universe."

"He's worked hard for all this, you—" Arlisa objected smoothly, before being rudely interrupted.

"He knows how important it is that I see him now," Erica responded, agitated.

"I'm sure whatever it is, it can wait," Arlisa rebutted.

Erica felt obliged to protest. "What are you doing here?" she asked in a sarcastic manner.

"I'm here with Brad," Arlisa intoned.

"That doesn't quite answer my question."

"Erica," Arlisa sighed, her sign of irritation. "Why don't you—"

"I'm all done." Brad's timely intrusion aborted the insult Arlisa was about to levy. He walked clean across the room and towered above them both, his eyes straying toward his sister. "Right, Erica." Brad dug both hands into his trouser pockets. "What is it that couldn't wait? And thanks for the flowers, by the way."

"It's mum," Erica immediately ventured, the two words spilling forth as though they'd been bursting to get out. "She's flying to Venice today."

"I know," Brad nodded. "She left a message on my machine."

"To get married," Erica added with a scowl.

"Married?" Brad's face widened with amazement.

"You'd never guess to who?" Erica floundered weakly. She looked across at Arlisa. "I'd like to talk to my brother alone."

"Arlisa is fine where she is," Brad rebounded, wavering aside his sister's request.

"This is private," Erica insisted quietly.

The measure of discretion in her tone prompted Arlisa to her feet. "I'll wait for you in your reception area," she assayed politely, already making her way toward the door. On closing it, she stared at the plush surroundings around her, overawed that Brad could be making so much money to afford standards such as these. She'd seen a maestro at work in his office; she hardly recognized this newly discovered side of Brad Belleville.

Style. That was the key word that thrust its way to the forefront of her mind. The British MG sports car he drove had style. As did the clothes he wore. As had his Pimlico apartment. Brad had style to burn. Immediately, her calculation of his ability to earn money was notched up four points, from a *six* to a *ten*.

In the reception area, above the silent buzz of his staff at work, a popular soloist played perfumed music to her ears. She felt positively regal as her fawn-brown inquiring gaze zeroed in on the only form of chaos she could see, which was a stack of newly delivered boxes of freshly printed letterhead and other stationery items. *Seventy-nine,* Arlisa told herself, before a male voice suddenly intruded.

"Are you waiting for someone?"

She turned to find herself staring into the chicory-brown gaze that smiled back into hers. The man's broad shoulders and straining paunch were constrained beneath an elegant gray suit, his clean-shaven, round face and drooping smile suggesting that he was pleased to see her.

"I'm waiting for Brad," Arlisa explained, realizing that she was facing a large catch in the small pool of accomplished black men.

"You are . . . ?"

"Arlisa Davenport," she introduced. "And you?"

"Brad's partner. The name's Kal Campbell."

"Nice to meet you." Arlisa affected a handshake, throwing him a smile.

"Would you like something to drink?" Kal asked. "Fresh orange, espresso, cappuccino?"

"Nothing, thank you," Arlisa declined. "Brad shouldn't be long. He's just with Erica."

"Then I'm sure he'd like me to show you some hospitality," Kal offered politely.

Arlisa smiled, catching the glimmer of hope in his eyes. "Will tongues wag?" she teased.

"Definitely," Kal laughed. "That's all part of the fun, right?"

Kal Campbell loved the film industry. "Let others paint pictures or write music," he said. His creativity, like Brad's, existed in film. In the short span of ten minutes, before Arlisa caught Brad bursting out of his office with a tearful Erica in tow, Kal had explained to her the purpose of the company and why he and Brad had embarked on their exciting joint venture. He'd also founded NYEUSI, Liverpool's first black professional theater company, and in addition to the fact that he also wrote extensively for radio, the stage, and television, Kal Campbell loved the movies.

As he began to conclude their talk, Arlisa now scrutinized Brad with skeptical eyes, less shocked than concerned. "You've met my partner," he proclaimed, tight-lipped, on meeting her at the reception desk.

"Yes." Arlisa offered a weak smile before throwing her gaze at Erica Belleville-Brown, who stood forlornly next to her brother. The older woman looked thoroughly shaken, as much by her mood as in the shaking of her bracelet-clad hands.

"Fine woman," Kal spoke in his approval, appraising Arlisa again. "Easy on the eyes."

Brad smiled deeply, though Arlisa could see the tension in his face. "You can use my telephone now," he suggested, stepping to one side so that she could return to his office.

As Arlisa did so, Erica stared at her silently across a sea of childhood years. "I've left my jacket in your office," she told Brad eagerly. "I'll just go with Arlisa."

They were finally alone together, not even acquaintances, but two estranged women having met down the corridors of time. Erica kept her back rigid as she crossed the room and reached for her suede jacket, slipping into it mechanically, before twisting her wedding ring in distress. She still had not looked Arlisa in the eye, but instead walked around Brad's desk and glanced out through the window. "I suppose Brad told you that I woke up one day and wondered where my life went," she began.

Arlisa's gaze rested thoughtfully on Erica, though the older woman still kept her back to her. "He vaguely mentioned something about it," Arlisa replied truthfully, deciding that she would remain standing by the upholstered sofa.

Erica scoffed. "My husband has a brilliant career and commitments he can't afford to break. Today I told Brad I'd do anything to save my marriage, including talking him into getting engaged to Bernadetta Crossland. But I don't think I can persuade him to do that, now that you're in the picture."

Arlisa's heart lit up like a candle in full flame. "I see," was all she could gasp, though the glorious sensation she felt was so deeply disquieting, Arlisa could hardly remain standing.

Erica chuckled, though her tone was one full of despair. "Perhaps you don't," she relented rather crossly. "You see, like my husband, my brother has a bright future. He's achieved the goals he wanted in his life and . . . well . . . with a woman like you . . ."

"Like me?" Arlisa objected.

"I asked you once before to leave Brad alone; now I'm pleading with you," Erica said sternly. Turning from the window, she faced Arlisa head-on. "Don't try and slot your way into his life. He deserves someone more socially acceptable than you, with a good, stable, mental capacity to stand by his side. You—"

"I what?" Arlisa interrupted harshly. "Gambled away a fortune. Let's not forget how I came to be put on that destructive treadmill. There was a little matter of you attempting to buy me off with a handout of five thousand pounds. And like a fool, I took it."

"And you promised me then you would never walk back into Brad's life," Erica accused hotly, pressing both hands against the rear of Brad's chair.

"Well you know what they say," Arlisa chided angrily. "A promise is only comfort to a fool. So I think our scoring is about equal."

"Our scoring?" Erica picked up on the two words rather airily. "I see you still have a gambler's mind."

"The only thing I gambled away that really cost me dearly was my pride when I took that check from you," Arlisa relented furiously. "Because of it, I got myself into an awful lot of trouble, at a time when I was feeling extremely low because of losing my mother. Brad never understood—"

"Brad was building his future," Erica interrupted, raising her eyes in a deriding gesture as though she was amazed Arlisa hadn't realized this. "Even I could see he had goals that getting involved with a woman like you would've destroyed at a stroke. I saved my brother from you once before, and if you had a shred of decency now, you would do us both this small justice and leave him, before he becomes too attached."

"Erica." Arlisa could feel her blood move in full fury. "You intimidated me once before, when I was weak, vulnerable and quite shortsighted. It's not going to happen again. I can't leave your brother. Not this time."

"I suppose a reasonable explanation would be that it's because he's forged out his career and the money he's—"

"That's what you would like to think," Arlisa cut in, absolutely seething. "But the simple matter is, I love your brother."

A silence descended upon the room as though it were

the approach of a herd of buffalos. It came quick, shaking the ground beneath; at least that was how the carpeted floor beneath Arlisa's feet felt. Could she have just heard herself make such a remarkable admission? Did she really just declare that she was in love with Brad Belleville?

Certainly, by the way Erica was looking at her, every measure of alarm in her face exaggerated, telling Arlisa that even she was acutely surprised, divulged to every sense in Arlisa's mind that she had indeed betrayed herself. She'd always known it, of course. There could never have been any denying how she'd truly felt about Brad, but she also had to ask herself the tormenting question: was she forced into the admission to goad Erica, or was she truly revealing the truth to herself?

Erica was hardly convinced. "You love my brother?" She laughed, almost hysterically. "You don't even respect the institution of marriage. I can't imagine you even know what marriage means, after all those husbands you've been through," she reproved.

"I never married," Arlisa answered in confusion, endeavoring to close the distance between herself and Erica by taking small strides to the opposite side of the desk, while desperately trying to force down her anger.

"I meant other women's husbands," Erica snarled.

"I don't know where you've come by all these snippets of misinformation about me," Arlisa shot back mildly, "but they're wrong."

An uncomfortable silence ensued between them again before Erica spoke. "I've never liked you, Arlisa," she admitted, turning to look at the woman she despised with large, limpid brown eyes. "When I was a teenager, I had a crush on Cory Robinson, and watched you effortlessly take him away from me. I've often judged you since then as being a woman other women would love to hate." She paused, her hands quivering. "I kept telling myself that I could actually like you, but you attract men in ways that have other women worrying about where their husbands are."

Arlisa shook her head, disbelieving. If she were ever to describe the character of Erica Belleville-Brown, two words sprang to mind. *Fiery* and *insecure*. Apt to flare up at any given moment. For the most part, Erica's manner was commendable and gracious, even with people she disliked. She recalled having seen that shallow facade once before when she'd been invited to Erica's eighteenth birthday party. To Arlisa, it suggested that Erica had been putting on a false front to please others and not herself. But this accusation of taking other women's husbands. That was wholly beneath the belt.

"There are some things more painful than the truth," she told Erica, "but I'm sure that you can't think of them. One day, I think you'll wake up to yourself."

"What's that supposed to mean?" Erica demanded.

"It means you just can't face up to who you are," Arlisa declared bluntly. "You're insecure with the people around you. You always have been. So what if you thought I took Cory Robinson—that was over ten years ago, but you've never forgotten it. The truth is, I only dated Cory to try and make Brad jealous. I never admitted to anyone that he was my boyfriend, not even to my mother. My cousin Nellie took the rap for that one. As for your husband—"

"You don't know anything about my husband."

"I know that he's married to a conniving, malicious little bitch," Arlisa reproved, venting her frustration. "In your eyes, I'll never be good enough for your brother. If your husband ever found out what kind of woman you really are—"

"Minister Tyrone would never divorce me," Erica interrupted, as though it were a vital point needed to be made plain.

"I hope for your sake he doesn't," Arlisa rasped. "My sister used to go out with a minister," she amended, disbelieving that she was having such an unsufferable conversation with Erica when her thoughts were desperately trained elsewhere. "And like you, he believed people should behave in a certain fashion, too."

"Then perhaps he went to my church?" Erica queried, tight-lipped.

"He was a Minister of Parliament," Arlisa quirked. "His name was Selwyn Owens and—"

"Selwyn Owens," Erica echoed the name. "I've heard of him. Didn't he escape from the Grovelands Priory Psychiatric Hospital a month ago?"

"Excuse me," Arlisa gasped.

"Yeah," Erica pounced, as though the very subject was giving her leverage to score points. "He suffered a nervous breakdown. And you say he dated your sister?"

"Before she married the joint heir to the Brentwood Communications Group in New York," Arlisa gloated, her brain doing overtime. This was all news to her. She now began to wonder whether there was any connection between Selwyn Owens and Kendra's kidnapping. This was something she just had to tell Brad. "I'll be right back." Arlisa grew excited.

"Wait a minute," Erica's voice restrained. She cut a clear distance directly toward Arlisa. "Brad told me today that he knew about the letter I should've given you last year." Erica's voice was slightly remorseful. "Anyway, I don't want my brother to hate me because of you, so I think you should have it now." She reached to her handbag, next to the vase of flowers, and pulled out an old, worn envelope. "I've always carried it," Erica confessed without shame.

It was Arlisa's turn to be thoroughly shaken as she looked at the sealed, creased white envelope that Erica held out to her. Her right hand almost fell weak as she took the paper and felt the weight of it in her hand.

She simply stared at it. Surely, if there was one redeeming thing Erica had ever done, this had to be it, she thought, even though her mind told her that Erica must have had some crazy mood swings in her time to have deliberately kept it from her. Suddenly, it felt as though they'd reached a meeting point at the end of some terrible war.

"What am I supposed to do with this?" Arlisa gasped, the shock almost rendering her into instant vindictiveness.

"Well, I know what I wanted to do with it," Erica croaked.

"Why didn't you?"

"I love my brother, too."

"If you do," Arlisa wavered, "you'd respect what he wants."

"I do," Erica debated. "That is why I'm giving you his letter. I hope it helps you decide that he is best suited to a woman like Bernadetta."

Arlisa sighed, shaking her head, feeling sorry for Erica. "You don't even know the woman, not as I do. As for this," she held up the worn envelope. "I don't know whether to read it or burn it. Probably that's something your conscience should decide."

"It's up to you," came Erica's noncommittal reply.

An apology was not what Arlisa expected, nor did she receive one. As she left the room to find Brad in the reception area, still talking with Kal Campbell, she'd come to see Erica for what she was; a very mixed-up person full of the kind of weaknesses that a woman who had not yet found herself possessed.

She would not show Brad the letter he'd meant her to

have, she decided, quickly placing it in the haven of her handbag. One day she would read it, and put it into perspective along with the passing of time. But right now, she was back to the problem of finding her kidnapped sister. The matters of her heart had to remain for another day.

Ten

When Brad emerged from Kal Campbell's office into the public reception area, Arlisa was waiting impatiently for him as he advanced silently across the carpeted floor, his oval face forming only half of a smile, like a man whose head was filled with other problems.

"Did you get through to New York?" he asked, once he'd reached a close enough distance to her.

"I didn't ring them," Arlisa confessed, taking hold of Brad's arm and pulling him discreetly to one side. "Your sister just told me something that's beginning to make me see sense."

Brad pulled his shoulders back, his face stolid and slightly irritated. "If this is about Bernadetta Crossland," he shot back.

"Brad?" Arlisa was bemused.

"I don't need a lecture from you, too," he began. "Erica's given me all the talk I need."

"Now wait a minute." Arlisa immediately felt the mettle between her teeth. "I was going to tell you about something your sister said. A clue I was overlooking, but it appears that you're more interested in your present great cause of grand passion to listen to what I have to say." She stood motionless and outstared him. "You remind me of a wind-up mechanical robot. A woman only needs to turn the key at the back and she's got you going smack into a brick wall. Doesn't anything ever break on you, or are all your emotions some form of mechanical device?"

"Arlisa—"

"Just forget it," she rasped. "I'm not a mechanical creature so I can't play your game. I don't even know what the rules are."

"Arlisa, I'm sorry. I thought—"

"I know what you thought," she interrupted again. "So maybe I should put the record straight for you. We had another one of those brief encounters and now it's over. We established that this morning. You've decided that any involvement with me is a messy, disruptive business to the point that you're confused. You don't know what you want and that isn't good enough for me."

"Arlisa."

"Never mind," she rasped. "You wouldn't understand."

Arlisa's eyes widened in realization that Brad wasn't paying any attention to what she had to say. "Are you listening to me?" she protested, overawed.

"Look," Brad began, knowing his mind was elsewhere. "This isn't a good time for me to be doing this, but I have to leave with Erica to go and see my mother." His eyes were swimming with regret. "She's leaving for Venice to get married—to our father, would you believe?" He shook his head in blatant denial. "I need some answers. We're going to have to talk later."

Arlisa was stunned. This couldn't be happening now, not when she was thinking that Selwyn Owens was some mad psychopath on the loose and may have already caused some harm to her sister. Brad was still busy looking after Number One. And where was she going? Nowhere. Everything was still in zigzags, jangled, wrapped in circles. Right at that very moment, she felt like she wanted to scream. "Go!" she yelled, all her frustrations echoing in the one simple word, causing the members of Brad's staff to distract themselves from their work and face her direction. "I can handle things by myself."

Brad felt the discomfort and took hold of Arlisa by the wrist, but she tactfully pulled away, sensing his dislike in her doing so. "I won't be long," he said, leading the way back into his office. Erica was getting ready to leave, having put on her jacket, and was currently in the activity of retouching pink lipstick to her chapped lips. "Are you ready?" Erica asked, as she replaced the top back on her lipstick tube and stared head-on at Arlisa and her brother.

"Yes." Brad nodded, turning to hold Arlisa by both arms. "You're making this difficult for me," he began in a low whisper. "I'll only be gone a couple of hours. You can stay here and make all the phone calls you need, and then we can talk as much as you want when I get back."

"If I'm here," Arlisa retorted madly.

"You'll be here," Brad conceded with a half smile, working his hands up and down her arms in an attempt to appease her mood. "I've asked Kal to look after you, if you need anything."

Arlisa cast her head downward. "Go and do what you need to do," she chided, knowing it would serve no purpose to debate the issue.

"Two hours," Brad promised.

Arlisa refused to acknowledge the time constraint. All she knew was that within ten seconds, she was on her own. Her dim mood lasted all of three minutes before she sufficiently pulled herself together again. The thought of remaining in Brad's office was beginning to wear thin, but she recalled that she wanted to speak to Shay Brentwood, her brother-in-law, and so found herself finally reclining nervously in Brad's chair at his desk, reaching frantically for the telephone handset.

"Joel Brentwood, please," she bellowed politely, when eventually the connection static joined her to the offices of the Brentwood Communication Group in Manhattan. Though it was still early in the morning, and New York was five hours behind Great Britain, Arlisa knew that BCG Inc was open twenty-four seven, and Joel could often be found there, even at late hours at night.

"Who shall I say is calling?" the receptionist asked in a deep Bronx monotone.

"Arlisa Davenport from England," she announced.

Two seconds later, Arlisa heard the reconnection. This time she was put through to Joel's secretary. "Mr. Brentwood is unavailable," she exclaimed. "Can I take a message for you?"

"Tell that man that I need to speak to him now," Arlisa burst out in frustration.

"Excuse me?"

"I'm the sister of his brother's wife."

"Shay Brentwood's sister-in-law?"

"That's right," Arlisa shrieked. "So find some way to connect me to J B now."

"Please hold."

Insufferable man, Arlisa recalled of Shay's older brother, whom she'd last spoken to when Kendra married into his illustrious family. That had been last year, just before Christmas and then shortly afterward, Christmas day to be exact, his mountain of a father, Benjamin Brentwood had died. She'd heard that it had been a turkey bone that killed him at the stroke of midnight, too. That was the news Joel's wife Rhona had passed around at the funeral on New Year's Eve, which was when she'd seen him last.

That poor woman, Arlisa sighed of Rhona, while waiting in annoyance for Joel to pick up the phone. To be married to someone like Joel Brentwood was obviously not what the senator's daughter had wanted for herself. Even when Rhona had borne him a son in early May, it was amidst rumour and scandal that J B was parading around town like the tyrant Benjamin Brentwood had been.

Gossip had surmounted that Joel was behaving exactly as his father had done. People said he'd begun to talk with a giant American baritone, that he'd begun to smoke Cuban cigars and that he'd commissioned a top African-American artist to paint a gigantic life-size portrait of himself, which hung majestically in what had once been his father's office.

Arlisa was starting to think how exactly she should take the reformed Joel Brentwood when his voice filtered down the line. "Arlisa Davenport," he drawled in a husky tone. "It's been a long time."

Not long enough, Arlisa thought as she began to measure her words carefully. The last thing she wanted was to alarm J B, so she was not about to divulge her latest predicament. "How have you been?" she asked slowly, her mind in a spin.

"Busy," Joel sighed. "You know how it is. I'm just getting ready to go home."

"No rest for the wicked," Arlisa broached.

"So says the good book," Joel declared, his tone brash and loud. "I suppose you've called me to say Kendra's had her baby."

"Not yet," Arlisa sighed. "I was calling for Shay's number in Cuba."

"She's gone into labor?"

"No," Arlisa bellowed, feeling her patience now beginning to wear thin, too. "I need to talk to him."

"Then why didn't you get the number from Kendra?" J B asked, rather hurriedly.

What is this, twenty-questions? Arlisa's mind screamed, but remarkably she kept her manner, not to mention her voice, quite equably calm. "Shay gave me some work to chase up on at the *Chronicle* before he left for New York," she lied. "There's a few things I need to clear up with him and I can't locate Kendra. She's staying at my cousin Nellie's and maybe they've gone shopping or—"

"Okay," J B interrupted warily. "Hold the line a minute."

Arlisa did exactly that, until minutes later, J B's voice returned, giving her the telephone number she required. "Tell my bro' 'hi,' okay," J B chuckled after he double-checked the number.

"Okay," Arlisa acknowledged quietly. "How is Senator Morgan Layton and his daughter?"

Arlisa didn't imagine the gulp that echoed down the line. "They're both very doting on Benjamin Jr," he evaded.

"As I'm sure your brother will be when Kendra has her baby."

"Of course," J B agreed, before finalizing their conversation.

Arlisa stared blankly at the number for the Gran Caribe Hotel in Cuba, then picked up the telephone handset again, dialing out a new set of digits. After several seconds, she heard the distant pause and then a lengthy static before she was connected to the hotel.

"Hola."

Oh shit. Arlisa's thoughts spiraled. She didn't understand a word of Spanish. "Hello," she began, rather slowly. "Can I speak to Mr. Shay Brentwood."

"¿Es Americano?" the female voiced asked.

"American," Arlisa insisted, recognizing one word.

"Hay un problema."

"Excuse me."

"Hay un problema," the woman admonished. "Todos los Americanos ya no están aqui."

"Wait!" Arlisa grew alarmed. "What does that mean?"

"Americanos not in Cuba."

"Is Mr. Brentwood at your hotel?" Arlisa demanded, trying desperately to remain calm.

"Todos los Americanos se han ido." The phone on the other line clicked dead.

Arlisa glared at the telephone completely perplexed. *She hung up on me,* she raged to herself, almost in disbelief. The anxiety was back and building in the pit of her stomach, the mixing of Kendra being kidnapped, and Brad's untimely departure having a lot to do with her present unsettled state. Now worrying as to what had happened to Shay Brentwood was the last thing Arlisa needed to topple her nerves.

She pushed her weary back into Brad's chair, prayers and curses sharing equal time under her breath as she fought to keep some semblance of control. As she sat there, staring miserably at the plush surroundings of Brad's office, Arlisa felt as though she was approaching another trial of her life. In fact, the more she floundered on just how dangerous was the situation, the more surely she knew how helpless she was. This once, she should call the police, a tiny voice pressed. But Arlisa could not convince herself. Kendra's life was at stake, came the reminder. And somewhere, though she knew not where, she held the secret to what her sister's captives wanted.

She didn't dare confide in anyone else or ask advice. All her friends at the *Nubian Chronicle* were not close. They were in essence passing ships in the night, temporary acquaintances whom only circumstances made friends. And even the ones who knew Kendra very well—Lynton, Irvin, Tony—her father's old aides—would scarcely rise to her rescue, given the schedule they had in getting the newspaper to press.

Heart pounding, she sat for a moment in silence, feeling like a small trapped animal. She was aware that she was facing the problem of her sister's kidnapping alone, and that fact now assembled in her head gave Arlisa a whole string of others to worry about. The most noting, being her father.

She covered her stricken tawny-brown face with trembling hands, the thought of telling Ramsey Davenport providing the sickly churning of feelings in her stomach. She couldn't face the thought of regaling to him, yet again, another heartless tragedy. The last time she'd done that was when she'd confessed the terrible truth of having gambled away one hundred and fifty thousand dollars.

Lost in a despair made worse by the knowledge that Brad had left to her to her own devices, Arlisa closed her eyes, realizing that there was no way of softening the blow. And that morning of folly she'd shared with Brad simply added to her uneasiness in a measure she had no wish to calculate.

How could I have been so stupid? she told herself with such harshness, she choked back the sob of shame that was threatening to erupt from her throat. She didn't want to cry. She dared not cry. It was not becoming of a *Hypermega* to break down during times of strife. She was now a woman with backbone, just like her sister Kendra, wasn't she? At least, that was what Arlisa told herself as she removed her hands from her face, only to find herself staring dazedly into a pair of honey-brown eyes.

"Brad!" The gasp left a positive echo in the room. "What . . . what are you doing back here?"

Brad stepped over the threshold into his office and closed the door before he continued his progress toward his desk. To Arlisa, he seemed to move by instinct, as though by automatic pilot. When he was within a yard from her, his desk separating them, in the hush, she could even hear him breathe. His eyes touched her skin like a searing burn.

"I heard on my car radio just now that martial law has been declared in Cuba." Brad's voice came across to her quietly. "I decided to do a U-turn."

"But your mother," Arlisa gushed in a breath of disbelief, her heart suddenly racing, thudding like a hammer in her ribcage.

"Erica can deal with her," Brad jabbed with a flat absence of emotion which he knew had been bred throughout the years of his mother almost denying his and Erica's very existence. "If she wants to marry my father a second time 'round, then that's her misfortune." Arlisa glared at him as he paused and then added, "Did you make any phone calls?"

She had to shake herself into a response. "Yes. I didn't get Shay. I think the hotel he was staying at has evicted him and all the other Americans."

"That's not good," Brad said on a steely note.

Arlisa rose up slowly out of his chair. Dizziness was sweeping through her like a red-hot fever, but she used every atom of strength to pull herself together, shake herself into action. The last thing she wanted was to brood or to have Brad see that he had plummeted her into a tearful abyss of pining need. "We're going," she said, briskly making heavy strides toward the door.

"Where're we going?" Brad asked, taken aback.

"Home," Arlisa rasped. "I want to check something in Kendra's address book."

"You're thinking of paying someone a visit?" Brad queried, turning to catch up with Arlisa.

"Damn right I am," Arlisa rebutted in defiance. "And Brad." She paused as he joined her at the door, unable to shrug off entirely the physical attraction that flickered like electricity between them. "Thank you for coming back."

Brad did not let her go so easily. He touched her fingers and Arlisa felt the fiery spasm shoot up her arm. The sensation was all too revealing of what her feelings were for Brad, of the admission she'd made to herself in front of Erica. Arlisa hesitated when Brad took hold of her hand, his grip tightening as she tried to pull away. He turned the palm up, then raised his fingers midway, lowering his head to gently brush his lips across her soft skin. Arlisa bit hard on the inner flesh of her mouth, but could not suppress the gasp that came out.

She gazed up into Brad's dark eyes, the long black lashes casting a shadow to his cheekbones, and felt a spasm of exquisite delight shoot through her veins. Arlisa gasped again, quickly refocusing her attention. She had no wish to analyze herself now. "We really have to go," she protested weakly.

Brad reluctantly released her and she followed him to his car. Arlisa deliberately forced her mind to other matters, like taking the law into her own hands. Seating herself, and casting all thoughts of Brad to one side, she did not know if she had the sort of nerve it would take to do precisely that. And she knew that she had never had to face such shattering odds in her life before. She may have gambled once and lost far more than she had even realized, but now she did not know how she was going to cope with the consequences of her wild gamble this time around.

But while sitting next to Brad as he pumped up the engine, Arlisa felt certain that she was going to get across this dangerously high fence somehow or crash in the attempt. It was an all-out win or lose situation. And it scarcely occurred to her that Brad Belleville wasn't the only one in over his head.

It was just after noon when Arlisa turned a gold key in the Chelsea door lock and entered her father's house. She felt the absence of not having been there the night before wash over her as she walked into the lobby, inviting Brad in before she closed the door.

The house was silent. Only the tone of the motion detector blared, telling Arlisa that no one was home. She aptly punched at the relevant release buttons before venturing into the lounge. The wine cabinet instantly caught her attention and Arlisa felt more than willing to dampen her frazzled nerves. "Drink?" she asked Brad, heading straight for the bottle of Scotch, from which she poured herself a large measure into the glass she extracted from the same shelf.

"No, thanks," Brad said smiling, his gaze searching the room. He seemed to appreciate the coordinated pastel colors, the large fireplace that was the dominating feature of the room, and the split-level archway that led directly to what appeared to be a sun den from his vantage point.

Arlisa fabricated a smile as she took a sip from the glass, feeling her fingers tremble as she returned the bottle to the cabinet. "I'm a little on edge," she confessed, taking off her leather jacket and throwing it, along with her handbag, into one of the soft, floral chairs closest to the window. Taking refuge there herself, she added, "I feel so relieved my father isn't here."

Brad remained standing, though he slipped both hands into his trouser pockets and silently contemplated Arlisa with concern. "What was this clue you wanted to tell me about?"

Arlisa could no longer hide the tremors of anxiety and frustration that coursed their way through her body. It was now evident in her voice. "Selwyn Owens," she declared, quite panicked. "My sister dated him before she met and married Shay Brentwood. You could say they were a social item." She took another sip of Scotch and then continued. "He was the first black M.P. to be elected at the Brent-South constituency in Middlesex, North London. My sister was fascinated with him, don't ask me why. He always sounded like an old stick-in-the-mud to me." Arlisa sank her shoulders into the chair and sighed heavily. "Anyway," she began, dejected. "He asked Kendra to marry him, but she was caught up with trying to help me save Daddy's newspaper from Benjamin Brentwood. His son Shay had loaned me the money to pay off my debts. But he wanted the *Nubian Chronicle* in return."

"So that was why you called me to lend you the money?" Brad acknowledged sympathetically.

"Yes," Arlisa nodded. "Then, like I said, Kendra got into a united state with Shay Brentwood and ended up marrying him."

"Which did not go down well with the M.P.," Brad surmised.

"No." Arlisa shook her head. "Benjamin Brentwood died and Kendra came back to England. That was when she found out about the terrible things Selwyn had done. He was forced to resign from his office."

"Terrible things?" Brad's eyes widened.

"He was sending her poison pen letters and he tampered with the brakes of her car. He was also responsible for rigging the computers at the *Nubian Chronicle.*"

"So what happened to him?" Brad asked curiously.

Arlisa heaved a sickly breath. "He tried to kill Kendra." Her voice trembled.

"Unbelievable," Brad wavered uncomfortably.

"He was eventually hospitalized," Arlisa exclaimed, hardly believing herself the picture she'd painted of the traumatic experience her sister had gone through. "The newspapers reported that he'd had some kind of nervous breakdown and that it had been triggered by the death of his first wife. She died in some freak boating accident."

"But you think differently?" Brad queried suspiciously, his eyes narrowing at everything he'd heard. Again he felt as though he was bordering on the intrigue, that he was in unknown territory, and Arlisa's latest revelations were coming wholly as a shock.

"I don't know," Arlisa said truthfully. "All I know is that Kendra was never convinced. Then today your sister told me something that got me thinking. She said that Selwyn Owens had escaped from a psychiatric hospital a month ago."

"A month ago," Brad repeated, his mind running into overdrive. "That means . . ."

Arlisa looked at Brad nervously. "I think he's kidnapped Kendra."

"Wait a minute." Brad shook his head in denial, feeling truly out of his depth. He began to correlate the information quickly in his head, making twists and turns and taking strategic bends before formulating an answer to the bizarre story Arlisa had given him. "If this . . . Selwyn Owens has your sister," he began slowly, "where does this Cuban People's Power Party come in?"

"That's the bit that doesn't make sense," Arlisa responded, herself refusing to see the connection, her eyes bleak with worry and tension.

Brad immediately cut the distance between them and took a seat next to Arlisa. Holding her hand in a bond of support, he rubbed gently at her fingers. "Is there anything else you know about this man, like what he looks like?" he spoke seriously.

"Why?" Arlisa asked, fretful.

"I'm thinking maybe it's time we involved the police," Brad reasoned.

"No." Arlisa jumped to her feet, downing the last of the whiskey in her glass in one quick flurry. "We don't know what he's capable of." She paced the floor, only pausing once to deposit her empty glass on the cabinet. "I've no idea what he looks like. We were never introduced. All I know is that he was born in Guyana, that he spoke with a mild accent that was hardly noticeable and . . ."

Arlisa quickly dissolved into silence. A quick flash of memory invaded her like a stroke of lightning, almost taking her breath away. Her bar stool adversary at La Casa de la Salsa, with the receding hairline and alert hazel-brown eyes that looked riddled with guilt, had spoken with a Guyana accent. She felt certain he was the man she'd seen outside Brad's apartment last night and now that she knew Selwyn was missing, Arlisa began to feel like the pieces of some great puzzle were being put into place.

"What is it?" Brad's eyes widened in genuine worry.

"Mr. Burnt Out, the man at La Casa de la Salsa," Arlisa gasped, frightened. "I think he was Selwyn Owens."

Brad leaned forward in his seat and braced both arms on his knees. He stared at Arlisa as she stopped dead in her tracks, the enormity of what she was telling him weighing heavy with suspense. "Are you sure?"

He put it rather strangely, but Arlisa nodded reluctantly. "As sure as I'm ever going to be," she rasped, her lips trembling.

The troubled little silence between them did not go unnoticed. The room seemed filled with the awful truth. Brad was unsure what to make of the entire situation. He'd never heard such a story before. He scrutinized Arlisa with skeptical eyes, less intrigued than profoundly shocked. It wasn't that unusual for him to plot something on the dimensions he'd heard for a movie, and perhaps if he were to read a screenplay on the scale Arlisa had relayed, it wouldn't have bothered him. But to actually find himself partaking in some big, thrilling adventure with the one woman he'd never been able to forget was beginning to prove a hard pill to swallow.

Was this really happening to him? He began to fathom the question. Firstly, there had been the man at La Casa de la Salsa and then the break-in at the *Nubian Chronicle*. Then Arlisa had told him that she'd seen that same man outside his apartment. And what of the Internet page they'd read, which had given instructions about meeting a queen of pharaoh to return an item allegedly in Arlisa's possession? There had also been the lucky escape with the Mercedes-Benz carrying the foreign number plates, which had almost collided with his car. The whole matter heightened by the fact that Kendra Brentwood had been kidnapped made Brad realize more than ever that he was not part of some movie script.

All he'd wanted was to get to know Arlisa, to catch up where they'd left off. Though he had shut off his thoughts about her months ago, never expecting to see her again, he'd often found the memory of her returning whenever he relaxed his guard. He felt sure it had been more of a surprise to him than it had been for her, to come to her rescue at La Casa de la Salsa. There she was, back in his life, and he did not fail to recognize her.

Now it seemed ludicrous that instead of conducting an intimately wonderful affair, of indulging in some wild passion of mercy, he should be embroiled in something elementally deep that held hidden dangers and traps that were unseen. And now he was to learn that a former M.P. was the master culprit and the one person responsible for the absurd twist of pain he felt within. For until Arlisa had found her sister, there would be no chance for him to explore what he was really feeling.

He did not know why he felt the pain. A part of him was afraid that Arlisa might see it in his expression or in the betrayal of his actions. And of course he had to remind himself that he had no claims on her, apart from having jaywalked into her life like some knight in shining armour having come to her rescue.

And what was more tiresome was that there was no time to ponder his thoughts, either. Another more important factor had sprang to his mind that was imperative to Arlisa resolving her crisis. "The man at the nightclub gave you something, didn't he?"

Arlisa didn't answer or move for a second or two. Then the memory came flooding back. "A compact disc," she said suddenly. "It's in my white handbag in my room."

"Go and get it, quickly," Brad interjected, his heart pulsating faster. "Maybe that's what we're looking for."

Arlisa didn't waste any time. Within minutes, she was up in her bedroom, throwing clothes in all directions, rummaging under her bed, sieving through her wardrobe and pulling out all her drawers, shaking loose every item until she'd thoroughly exhausted all her energy. But to no avail could she find the CD Selwyn Owens had given her. *Where is it?* Her mind raged, recalling that she'd last seen the offending item on her bed, it having dropped from her white handbag along with the ransom note Leola had given her.

She'd thrown the CD to one side and placed the ransom note in her black bag. But as Arlisa looked at her bed, she saw that it was freshly made. Her heart sank into instant despair. Her father's regular housekeeper had obviously moved the CD when she'd cleaned the room. Dejected, Arlisa returned to the lounge, her face expressionless as she caught Brad sitting impatiently, waiting for her.

She saw a muscular spasm in his hard cheek move. "Well?" he inquired, his tone raised in anticipation.

"The damned hired help's done something with it," Arlisa bellowed, oddly at a loss.

"Well she must've put it somewhere," Brad barked anxiously.

"Don't shout at me," Arlisa screeched in return, hearing the flat edge in her voice.

Brad pulled himself up short, Arlisa's tale still unfolding in all its convolutions, making him feel his credulity was being strained. He hadn't meant to shout, but the circumstances were putting him on edge, too. "I'm sorry," he backed down. "Where did you see it last?"

"I threw it on my bed," Arlisa said.

"Your cleaner, she must have put it with the other CDs you have," Brad exclaimed, thinking fast as he rose to his feet.

Arlisa's brows rose marginally. "That's right," she bridled. "I have a CD player in my room, on my dressing table."

"Come on."

They took the stairs together. Before long, Brad was in Arlisa's room, but there was nothing except the stack of salsa CDs among the pile of branded cosmetics on her dressing table. "Let's check the bed," he suggested as a last resort.

He began helping her pull back all the bed coverings in search of the one item Mr. Burnt Out had given her. It was only when Brad removed one of the pillows did he see the small transparent casing lodged between the mattress and the headboard itself. Pulling it clear, he showed it to Arlisa. "This it?"

Arlisa stared at Brad from across the other side of the bed. "Goodness, you've found it," she breathed, sighing with mitigating relief. She drew in a breath as though he'd said something spectacular.

Brad watched the fawn-brown eyes widen, and then he knew. Arlisa desired him. It was incredible. He felt his mouth go dry as his body and loins reacted to the glittering sensual longing mirrored in her eyes. That same sparkle was in his own, too.

He hadn't planned this moment, hadn't even envisioned it. Yet to make love to Arlisa right there, right now, when they'd just stripped all the covers from her bed, down to the last one remaining, when their hearts were still pumping with panic and adrenaline, seemed right. There was an inevitability about it, as though their coming together was in celebration of having attained the one goal they'd sought.

But when Brad stepped forward, he tensed like a cat about to pounce. Their lovemaking that morning was now playing in his mind. Arlisa had accused him of it being another brief encounter; to him it was not. He was never one to take chances where his heart was concerned. Much of the childhood memories of his mother had hardened him that way, and he'd always wondered whether Arlisa was different. He wanted her to be. Deep down, he knew that she was.

As he held her gaze of relief, rich and potent with need, something of the pain he felt within begged that he clarified the content of what they meant to one another. "Arlisa . . ." He stopped. His breathing had become irregular.

Arlisa felt a hot confusion inside herself, too, at the silky mention of her name. Every fiber in her body was in answer to it. Instinctively, she inched forward. "Yes," she said automatically, her voice struggling to sound normal and not husky.

Brad dropped his knees onto the mattress and Arlisa's eyes flew to his face. His hand found her wrist and pulled her to join him. He bent forward, breathing unevenly, and she felt his lips brush the side of her neck, sliding coaxingly over her skin, while those dangerously seductive fingers she'd grown to know so well sent shock waves of intense feelings beating along the paths of her nerves.

Arlisa's breath stood still. The CD slipped from Brad's hand to the floor. She opened her lips to protest, though she knew not why, but it was her tongue that escaped her mouth and not words. Her reaction was too strong. Her eyelids closed and her head fell back, welcoming Brad's lips as he teased them down her neck to her throat. Her body was melting into total surrender and Arlisa knew it, but she felt helpless to resist.

When his mouth covered her own, she found herself clinging to Brad in reckless frenzy, kissing him back with all the pent-up, anxious frustration that was bursting for some form of release. Her hands against his neck, she felt herself being lowered onto the bed, sensing the rapid beat of Brad's pulse under her fingers, her body flexing and yielding in his hands as her heightened sexual awareness drowned every attempt at rational thought.

The heated, restless movements of their bodies became fevered the instant Brad began to remove items of her clothing. Suddenly, Arlisa felt oddly clearheaded in a crazy sort of way. She knew she was behaving against every logical reasoning she'd given herself about Brad, but she was enjoying this strange sense of dreamlike unreality, where there was no past and no future, no danger and no lives at stake. There was only the present, and the shot of magic that lingered in Brad's kiss. No hang-ups, no problems. Adrift from consequences, Arlisa felt able to do exactly as she pleased.

Brad pulled off his shirt and jacket and dropped them, along with Arlisa's clothing to the floor. His bare chest, with his tie still askew around his neck came into focus. His torso was firmly muscled, as she remembered it, his skin a perfect olive-brown where dark curling hairs growing up from the planes of his flat stomach tickled against her searching fingers. Through the languorous contentment that washed over Arlisa came another feeling, a piercing excitement which made her body ache with a deeper heat than the one she'd known before.

And to Brad, he felt as though he was riding a surf, where the current was unstoppable even to a man of his control. He was so engrossed in Arlisa, too eager to make further discoveries of her, that the driving power of his mounting excitement made hurried movements to remove the rest of her clothing entirely. His own were flung frantically about the room until he cried out in delight at the feel of Arlisa's naked skin.

His own naked body twisted restlessly, the roughness of his thigh on smooth female flesh teaching him new insights into the pleasure that only this woman seemed able to give him. That was the reality to Brad. Or maybe it wasn't reality, but fate. Kismet. Their becoming lovers had always been a certainty to him, even from when he'd first kissed Arlisa when she was fourteen years old.

Arlisa heard Brad's thick groan of pleasure with an answering cry of her own. Then he was kissing her once again with a swirling foray that was all but new to her. It ignited the gathering heat between her legs. "Brad, I like this so much," she gasped, as she unknotted his tie and whipped the patterned blue silk over his neck, tossing it over her shoulder.

"It feels good?" he whispered, tracing her lips with one thumb when she resettled down beside him and snuggled herself into the very heart of his chest.

Arlisa grazed his thumb with her teeth. "It feels like nectar from heaven," she gasped.

Looking up into each other's eyes, they both found and expected a growing passion that seemed untamed and uncontrollable. In eagerness, Arlisa hooked her leg over Brad's hips, caging him in with her thighs, holding herself steady as he just as eagerly centered himself on top. And in a frenzy, she felt him crush into her, gently, impatiently, both willing to fulfill the other.

They made love once—swiftly, desperately, with a kind of first-time flurry of shyness and urgency. Then once again, slowly, leisurely, as though they'd needed to catch up on what they'd missed or overlooked. The third time they made love, it was for fun. For knowing that they'd found what they were looking for, though Arlisa told herself it was not in commemoration for having found the CD. And sometime during the late afternoon, they made love for a last time, because Brad had run out of condoms. And as Arlisa fell back and lay content in his arms, she also realized that their final taking of each other had also been for good luck.

Eleven

"Brad." Arlisa propped herself up on one elbow and looked deeply into the eyes of the man she'd just made love to. They were still in her bed, leisurely calming the emotions that had taken them both into ecstasy. "Did you ever get into a serious relationship with anyone?" she asked.

The question took Brad by surprise. "Why do you want to know?" came his weak reply, his voice holding a touch of asperity.

"I was just wondering," Arlisa said. "Simple question."

Brad looked perplexed. Even uncomfortable. He shook his head marginally, as though fighting off an answer. An unbidden silence marked the discomfort Arlisa felt, too. She hadn't realized she'd hit a nerve. With her index finger, she drew an absent circle on Brad's chest, entrapped in the quietness that invaded the room, until Brad said finally, "She was an actress."

Arlisa's finger stopped, poised at Brad's right nipple. The message was clear. Brad had been hurt. She felt herself now to be in the real world, where prior ties and past affections, personal history and acrimonious partings were part and parcel of the social code. "How old was she?" she asked curiously, fighting the touch of jealousy she felt deep within that another woman had attempted to find a place in his life.

"Young. Younger than you."

Arlisa grew alarmed. She placed her hand under her chin, wondering absurdly whether she'd aged suddenly. "Mid-twenties?" she probed.

"Early twenties."

"What . . . like twenty-one, twenty-two?"

"Twenty."

"I see."

"Where did you meet her?"

Brad tossed her a skeptical eye. "At a hotel in New York."

Arlisa immediately discarded her curiosity and went in for the full kill. "This was before you met me again . . . that time when . . ."

"I know," Brad admitted. He pulled himself up on one elbow, too, and faced Arlisa with serious intent. "When I told you that our paths had crossed at a time when neither of us were ready to take things further, I believed it then. When I met you a year and a half ago, seeing you again felt like a dream. I felt like I'd been given a second chance with you."

"Are you telling me that you hadn't thought of me then as a one-night stand?" Arlisa asked tersely.

"You were never expendable," Brad confessed, "as you put it," he added.

"So you wanted to see me again?" Arlisa repeated slowly.

Brad took ahold of Arlisa's hand and worked her fingers between his. "What is this? The Spanish Inquisition?" he laughed.

Arlisa smiled, delving unashamedly into the fray. "So . . . how did this girl hurt you?"

Brad flinched and then cast his eyes sideways. "She was only interested in the novelty that she was dating an aspiring film director," he sighed. "We lasted nearly six months before I left New York and came back to England. Less than a week of having arrived back here, I saw you, by chance, outside the parish church."

"My mother was buried there," Arlisa interjected wistfully.

"You told me." Brad smiled compassionately.

"Like you said, we told each other many things that night."

Brad smiled deeply at the recollection. "I remember you told me you'd graduated at university the year before your mother died," Brad affirmed. "Why didn't you ever go into fashion design? It was what you told me you wanted to do."

"I can't compete with the Earl Vanis of this world," Arlisa cajoled warmly. "Ghetto culture has fascinated everything from sneakers to windbreakers."

"So, was that why you were waiting for Earl Vani at La Casa de la Salsa?" Brad returned with a cheeky tease. "Were you thinking of asking him for a job or was it more of a merger you were interested in?"

Arlisa did not miss the feisty innuendo. Funny enough, statistics did not play on her mind. "You thought I was trying to crack on to him, didn't you?"

"Well the last I heard, you were still collecting boyfriends, especially the gilt-edged, grade-one listed kind," Brad said.

It was Arlisa's turn to flinch. "There was a time when I thought like that," she admitted ruefully. "Sometimes I still view men in that way. Then I really saw how much money could change people, and how it made them want to imprint their standards of behavior on others. There was even a time when I felt confused about what exactly was middle ground."

"You said it was because of how Erica and I had treated you as a child, which . . ."

"It wasn't just that." Arlisa thought back, taking her memories to when she was a child. "I remember Daddy rearranging the house furniture to hide the threadbare carpet in the living room. And the mice that ran beneath the floorboards at night when Kendra and I were sleeping."

"That's how things were in the nineteen sixties for everybody," Brad intoned truthfully.

"That's how things were if you were black," Arlisa jabbed, almost cruelly. "I've always wanted to be different, and when Daddy made a success out of his newspaper, I felt I could be a success, too. Now I feel the disappointments of a twenty-six-year-old woman who hasn't really achieved anything. Your sister was the first to make me feel like that."

"Erica!"

"Yes, Erica," Arlisa underlined coldly. "My mother used to have me always believe that I was this absolutely wonderful person, just like my school report had said. Her Methodist influence has always given me some degree of . . . integrity. But when the blows came, I realized I was like everybody else."

"The blows?" Brad felt intrigued.

"Your sister making me feel like I was a woman without standards." Arlisa felt herself wince. "I've always been judged on the way I look. What's beneath the exterior has never been given consideration."

"Arlisa." Brad's voice was wounded and marred with guilt.

"It's all right," Arlisa felt her confidence rise up within. "Today, I spoke to Erica and realized that she is a woman with a very low self-image. Even though she rarely wears anything other than haute couture and her nightdresses are probably by Givenchy, she's a phony. She doesn't believe in herself."

"A little bit of our absent parenting rubbed off on both of us," Brad explained, ashamed. "That's why I changed my mind about seeing my mother today. Erica still went, though. She's probably at this very moment arguing with our mother about her decision—to remarry our father."

"You're against it?"

"Well, what is she trying to prove?" Brad implored, agitated and hurt. "When she was married to my father, it was unusual for a white woman to be seen with a black man, let alone them having children. When things got tough, they divorced, but that did not have to mean she should divorce her children. Erica and I have had to stick together through thick and thin. As the younger one, she grew to be very protective of me—even more so now that I'm successful and there are many gold diggers out on the hunt."

"Like me," Arlisa prompted.

Brad chuckled weakly. "I used to think that about you, from when you were a kid," he proclaimed. "Especially when I saw Cory Robinson give you that friendship ring at Erica's eighteenth birthday party. You were so pleased to take it, you reminded me of my mother." He leaned heavily on his elbow and something changed in the depth of Brad's eyes. "Did you know she was married to Sir Paul Worthington for nearly eighteen years and never introduced me or Erica to him once?"

Arlisa heard the pain in Brad's voice. "Why?"

"Our mixed heritage, I expect."

"Did your mother have more children?" Arlisa asked.

"No," Brad responded happily. "I think he was past his sell-by date in that department."

She giggled. "You've never liked him, have you?"

Brad smiled demurely. "No. I never did like the sound of him."

Arlisa turned on her back and stared up at the ceiling. "Do you think your mother is thinking that she is being given a second chance?"

"What?" The surprise echoed in Brad's tone.

"You told me just now that when you saw me again, you felt like you were being given a second chance," Arlisa remonstrated. "Do you think that is how your mother is feeling?"

"Arlisa . . ." Brad seemed amazed. "I don't know if . . ."

"Your past can be your future," Arlisa finished. "You told me that, too."

"What are you saying?"

"I'm saying that your mother is human, and maybe she's still in love with your father."

"In love." Brad scoffed out the two words contemptuously. "I don't think my mother knows what 'in love' is."

"Well, what is it?" Arlisa turned her face from the ceiling to study the wide-eyed amazement in Brad's face. She saw a flicker of something in his eyes, unable to decipher what it meant, for she'd never asked a man this question before.

Brad hesitated before he spoke. Only because he had put this question to himself once before, especially where Arlisa was concerned. There had been the time when he'd thought what he felt for her to be nothing more than the lustful embers of a teenage crush. Then there was the time he'd thought that the word "love" would mean to Arlisa the same as it had meant to his mother, something available to the highest bidder. And there had been women he'd met who viewed it that way. But now, Brad had formulated his own ideals about love.

"I think when you're in love with somebody," he began, "you would think about that person all the time. The world would suddenly feel like a wonderful, happier place. Your future would look rosy and bright. And people in love plan together. They would feel a part of each other."

Arlisa felt thoroughly touched. "I like the way you explained that," she said quite honestly. "I've often believed that if a man truly loved me, and wanted to prove it, he would give me something he hadn't thought he would ever part with."

"Like what?" Brad asked.

"I don't know," Arlisa chuckled, before adding, "When my sister and I started dating, we used to play a numbers game to discover how we felt about the guys we liked best."

"You scored your dates?" Brad crooned hysterically.

"We were young," Arlisa chided, realizing that this was a peculiarity that hadn't ended with her. "Kendra only graded kisses. I sort of . . . excelled myself."

Brad's honey-brown gaze honed in on her and widened. Suddenly, all his attention was diverted on her face. "In what way?"

"Criterions. Stuff I felt was important for a woman to look for in a man."

"But you're not going to tell me what these are, right?"

"Now that would be giving away a trade secret," Arlisa laughed.

"Well, I know my dancing got me an . . . eight," Brad cajoled cheekily. "How much did what we just did score?"

"Brad!" Arlisa felt thoroughly embarrassed.

Brad rolled over and pulled her into his arms. "Okay," he laughed. "How much did my kiss earn?"

"I will never tell," Arlisa chimed, though something in her brain yelled a new top score of *nine*.

"I'll ask your sister when I see her," Brad teased. "How many months pregnant is she anyway?"

Arlisa tensed, feeling an instant sickly feeling rise up in her gut. "Seven months. Where's the CD?" she countered quickly.

"On the floor," Brad broached. He paused for a moment, seeing the sudden seriousness in Arlisa's face. "Let's get dressed and take a look at it."

Arlisa had never been good at waiting. Her imagination was far too vivid and she had a tendency to think up all manners of catastrophe. Only in activity could she avoid dreaming up a scenario that something terrible had happened to her sister.

She was fully dressed, having changed her clothes to a pair of designer jeans and a Jasper Conran sweater. She was waiting for Brad to adjust his tie. He seemed to be taking an age about fixing the damned thing, though in reality, Arlisa knew he'd only been at her dressing table a mere thirty seconds. While tapping one foot impatiently, she'd trained her mind on the numbers game she often played in her head. Unusually enough, aside from realizing that Brad was now an *eighty-one,* she'd noticed that while she changed into a new set of clothes, she hadn't mentally calculated the value of every item.

That was the first surprising change her afternoon with Brad had revealed. Secondly, aside from her impatience, she felt much calmer and assured of herself. The only main surface anxiety at that point was making sure that she and Brad had checked out what was on the CD before her father arrived home.

She glanced at her Rolex, which read 5:45. Ramsey Davenport hadn't been in the house when she'd arrived at lunch time, so she wasn't sure where he was. "Brad!" She announced her urgency.

"You got the CD?" he asked, turning to face her as he fixed his jacket.

"Right here," Arlisa drawled, holding it up in her hand to show him.

"And what about this address you wanted?"

"Oh, that," Arlisa gasped. "I'd better search Kendra's old room."

Brad was in tow as Arlisa entered what was once her sister's bedroom. It had remained tidy ever since she'd moved to live with her husband at their new home at Wimbledon. Only a few items remained that showed that a young girl had matured from adolescence into adulthood there. Soft toys, schoolbooks, posters of favorite film stars and pop idols were stacked in a corner that was reserved for the part of Kendra she'd wanted to retain and which held no place in womanhood as the wife of a business executive.

Arlisa went among them and searched swiftly, finding nothing but childhood diaries and old Disney stationery sets, felt-tip and ink pens, most of which had dried up. She sighed heavily and faced Brad. "This is all old stuff," she appended weakly. "I'll have to go to Kendra's house at Wimbledon."

"Do you have a key?"

"Yes. It's the spare."

"Let's go now." Brad didn't want to wait. "We can listen to the CD in my car along the way."

They did precisely that. The MG branded, security coded, in-car entertainment system was at mid-volume when Brad inserted the CD and punched the detachable keypad to engage the play mode. Neither he nor Arlisa knew what to expect, other than perhaps a little soul music, hip hop perhaps. In Arlisa's case, the salsa. It came as a shock to them both when strange deep voices in Spanish accents, began to reiterate what sounded like a diverse international guest list.

To Arlisa, even without understanding many of the words, she felt as though theories, eccentricities and pretensions were being announced, along with the first names, nicknames and aliases of those who were obviously enemies to the Cuban republic. And the prevailing tone was obviously anti-establishment, too. Crimes, misdemeanors, and theft were flung out in broken English in a panache, impudent, daring sort of way.

"My god," Arlisa broached, suddenly panicked. "What the hell are we involved in?"

"Let's stay calm." Brad tried to reason against the running dialogue that was quick to damn all evils. "This is obviously what the men at the *Nubian Chronicle* were looking for."

"So this is what we have to deliver to get my sister back?"

"I guess so," Brad intoned.

"Brad . . . I'm scared." Arlisa began to feel weak. Something snakelike began to coil its way to her throat and at any moment, she felt herself about to choke.

"I'm sure everything's going to be all right," Brad urged, rubbing his left hand on Arlisa's knee. "We're on our way to your sister's house now. We'll find this . . . Selwyn Owens's address and go see him. And if he's there, I'll wring his neck first."

"I wonder where my father is." Arlisa began to worry unduly. "I'm now wondering whether I should have told him about all this."

Brad kept his eyes trained on the road, though he digested Arlisa's genuine concern. "Is he normally out at this hour?"

"Daddy goes all over the place," Arlisa wavered in agitation. "He could be anywhere." She sighed. "Perhaps it's just as well I didn't see him. I told him Kendra is at our cousin Nellie's. I'll try and call him later."

"You're getting stressed." Brad rebutted, flicking off the CD. "Until we get to your sister's house, try and relax for a while. I don't think either of us should get nervous at this stage."

"I can't relax," Arlisa protested, pulling back the long braids of hair away from her face. "I've already—"

"You didn't tell me what 'in love' means to you," Brad interrupted with more interest and energy than was necessary to keep Arlisa calm.

Arlisa half turned her head and looked at Brad. Her profile, plucked brows, rounded cheekbones, and endowed lips was clearly etched against the bright, late afternoon light that came through the car window. "I've . . . I've never thought about it," she stammered out in half truth, trying to forget what she'd told Erica, trying to forget her present ordeal.

She'd always thought herself to be infatuated with Brad. He'd always hovered at the back of her mind, ever since the very day she'd first kissed him. It was unhealthy for a man to remain in a woman's mind for so long, she'd tried to convince herself once. Maybe what she was feeling for Brad wasn't so much love, but an unnatural obsession. Arlisa paused and thought for a moment.

"Well?" Brad gently insisted.

"Oh, I don't know," Arlisa rapped. "I think true love continues to grow over time and the longest distance."

"Like when we were apart?" Brad probed.

Arlisa winced. "There are many ways of falling and staying in love."

Brad's brows rose with deeper interest. "Really."

"Yes." Arlisa's mind was suddenly refocused. "Regardless of how hot and steamy a relationship is at the beginning, when the passion fades, there has to be something else, something better to take its place. Whatever that something is, that's the 'in love' bit."

"I like the way you explained that," Brad agreed. "I remember when my sister got married, she and her husband both wrote poems to one another. I've never seen them argue or fight."

"Just because two people don't argue doesn't mean they love each other," Arlisa reasoned. "And just because two people do argue, doesn't mean they don't. Am I making any sense?"

"Are you trying to say that Erica doesn't love Tyrone?"

"I think your sister's life revolves around duty," Arlisa relented. "In her world, marital bliss equals natural male superiority."

Brad reflexively flew to Erica's defense. "A woman should have a loyal, selfless duty to her husband."

"That's small-island mentality," Arlisa contradicted.

"Don't bring Barbados into this," Brad objected smoothly. "Erica was born there, but I was born here. And regardless of that, I happen to share her views."

Arlisa's eyes welled. "Are you telling me that you have ground rules for a successful marriage?" Arlisa mocked arrogantly.

"I think every woman should know how to prepare a good home-cooked meal, and should have a mature, caring and intelligent attitude toward her man."

"Any other precepts?" Arlisa jibed.

"She should be athletic, love children, and have the ability to recognize life's experiences, both bad and good, and use them as opportunities to grow and moments to savor."

"Are you really talking about someone human?" Arlisa flinched, throwing him a wry grin.

Brad slowed the car as he approached a stoplight, taking the advantage to look across at Arlisa. "I think she should also take pride in herself. By knowing herself, she can be a true friend to her partner."

The grin dropped from Arlisa's face and she became thoroughly rattled. "Are you trying to insinuate that I don't love myself?" she broached, wounded by the conjecture.

"You told me once that marriage is good for women, but not for men," Brad remarked with ardor, taking the subject seriously. "It made me think, and I've come to realize that maybe you believe that having a man in your life will make you happy. You should not have to depend on a mate to make you happy."

"That was not why I said it," Arlisa railed. She turned her face away from Brad, taking her mind back to when she'd felt her first real pain of being jilted in favor of someone else. "Women have searched the globe to find ways of keeping their men engaged in a relationship," she began. "The truth is, men don't want to be held down because there are always going to be women out there to seduce. Women like Bernadetta Crossland."

"What is this?" Brad admonished, feeling as though he'd been ensnared into something he hadn't seen coming.

"Wait a minute," Arlisa interjected calmly. "Jerome Morrison," she began of the barrister she once knew, "was a man who made me believe that there was no such thing called love. To me, it was something women chased and men did not. I told myself that if I couldn't find love, I'd find a rich mate instead. But I couldn't do that either, because despite what you think, I couldn't convince myself that it was what I wanted. And since my sister's kidnapping, I've discovered that I like my integrity. I like the way I've matured."

"You have blossomed," Brad conceded. "I've told you that before."

And he knew that she had matured, too. Brad had discovered that Arlisa had found out that there was no such thing as free love, that finding love was not through a rich mate with money or position. At times, he had wondered how she had learned that lesson. Had she loved a man and lost him? Had she been hurt in some way as he had been? For the first time, he felt as though he was finally getting some answers. She had been right, too. They knew each other, but did not *know* each other. To him, this was the final testing on whether Arlisa could mean anything to him.

"I'm glad you can see my point of view," Arlisa said quietly. "It hasn't been easy for me, Brad. I'm not going to pretend that it has. Even now, I'm still trying to keep to some New Year's resolutions I made while I was in New York, when Shay Brentwood and his brother buried their father. One of them was acquiring wisdom. I still believe I'm on track for that one."

"You know," Brad said, while steering the car smoothly around a juncture in the road, "I didn't realize you'd become so sensible. I think I've misjudged you."

"You have," Arlisa said. "To you and Erica, there has always been the Belleville principles. No one else's count. I don't think either one of you had ever considered that I lived by rules, too. In fact, I refer to myself as a *Hypermega.*"

"A what."

Arlisa chuckled quietly to herself. "I made it up," she crooned. "Basically, it means that I have a sense of my own perfection." Arlisa was also truly honest with herself in knowing that such pride was for personal growth and not for wedding her way into a fortune. "I think it's made me a better person."

Brad chuckled, too. Arlisa never ceased to amaze him. "I take back everything I ever said against you," he declared with self-loathing. "From here on, I'm going to have to put my Belleville arrogance to one side and pay attention. With Erica," he added, pulling into a flotsam of traffic. "You're going to have to give her time. I still can't believe she didn't give you that letter I wrote you, but if we ever get out of this mess—"

The letter. Arlisa had forgotten all about that. "What did you write me?" she interrupted curiously, recalling that she still had the item in her bag.

Brad turned toward her, briefly, his eyes ablaze with such intensity, Arlisa felt her nerves quiver in response. "I just explained that I was going away for a while and that I'd hoped you could join me."

"You wanted me to go to the Bahamas with you?" Arlisa coiled in shock.

Brad shrugged his shoulders. "Would you have?"

"I don't know," Arlisa relented in truth. "Were you really serious at the time?"

"I told you before, I never enter into anything without good intentions," Brad said. "We had a good time, and yes, you being there with me would've been nice."

"That's what you wrote?"

"That's what I wrote."

Arlisa's heart seemed to lurch against her ribs. She knew only too well what Brad meant when he talked about the good time they'd shared. He meant the night they'd talked and made love together for the first time, when he had taken her down the path of sensual discovery, teaching her to arouse his passion while he had aroused in her a powerful, overwhelming desire to be a part of him so that she had surrendered willingly to everything he had to offer, and to his possession of her. And she had believed she'd possessed him completely. Had it not been for Erica, things could have worked out differently. She would not have thought that he'd let her down. She would not have taken those trips to Monte Carlo.

Arlisa turned and smiled at Brad in return, believing his every revelation. She had obviously misjudged him, as he had her. She had meant something to him after all. There was something refreshing in knowing that she had not been someone he'd used, as men do, to add to their sexual experience as she'd once thought. Perhaps this was their way of finally getting to know one another. Secretly, Arlisa hoped that it was. "I'm glad." Her smile deepened nervously. As the car took her closer to her sister's home, Arlisa suddenly felt as though everything was going to be all right.

Twelve

Kendra's home was empty. It took Arlisa a while to disable the security alarm before she could enter. In fact, the damn thing had gone off before she could rethink the four digits that were required to shut the system down entirely. It was becoming increasingly hard for her to think up numbers. This was a surprise to Arlisa. She'd always been a calculating sort of person: making additions, subtractions and divisions, multiplying statistics as though they were second nature to her. Perhaps it was being with Brad, she thought. He'd certainly opened her eyes to a lot of things recently, and she was beginning to see the startling change.

She closed the door and marched on into the sitting room, knowingly aware that the very man on her mind was taking his own short strides behind her. The room felt pleasantly warm and she recalled that the weather had been mild, the sky still pale with light, as it should be for late August. But the red roses in the vase stationed next to the chimney breast were dead, providing the blatant reminder Arlisa needed that Kendra and Shay had been absent from their home.

"I'll put these in the garbage," she told Brad quietly, immediately deciding that the roses no longer belonged where they were presently. "Would you like a cup of tea?"

"Sounds great," Brad accepted quickly, watching as Arlisa picked up the vase before he followed after her. "After that long ride, and getting lost twice, I think we could both do with a cup," he added.

"I'm sorry." Arlisa headed toward the kitchen, sensing Brad's footsteps not too far behind. "I rarely drive. In fact, I hate driving. Most times I come here, I travel by taxi."

Brad seated himself at the kitchen table and looked around the elaborately designed room. It held all the utensils of the modern age, the built-in appliances uniquely designed to provide a bright and airy environment. "Nice house," he acknowledged.

"Kendra's husband bought it a couple of years ago," Arlisa explained, as she switched on the electric kettle and began to place on the table two cups with saucers.

Brad's gaze searched the interior again, appreciating what he saw. "Your sister," he began inquiringly. "Did she and her husband take a honeymoon?"

The question, potent and personal, took Arlisa aback. She was already beginning to feel a little nervous being in Brad's company after the more revealing conversation they'd had in his car. But now his persistent probing was leaving her a little uneasy. Maybe everything wasn't going to be all right, as she'd first thought. Maybe she was having illusions again that had first taken root in her childhood with Brad.

"They went to Fisher Island, just off Miami's Biscayne Bay," she answered, wondering why Brad had asked such a question. "Kendra told me it was very romantic."

"And you're not romantic?" Brad returned.

Arlisa shrugged noncommittally. She shouldn't be giving in so soon, she told herself harshly. There were many facets of her emotions that were still undecided. "I've told you before," she said. "I don't read fairy tales."

"You should," Brad prompted, taking the sugar bowl Arlisa suddenly thrust at him.

There was a moment's silence, then Brad wavered, unsure. "Arlisa. Can I ask you something?"

Arlisa held her back toward Brad at the kitchen sink. She felt her shoulders tense as she dropped two tea bags into a tea pot. Whatever could he possibly want to know now? Her mind felt in turmoil at the inevitable tone of inquisition. "What is it?" She threw her own question out in agitation.

Brad was neither taunted nor intimidated by it. "Why have you never married?" He sounded more than curious.

Unusually, Arlisa felt reluctant to give him the same answer she'd given him before. It wasn't so much that she believed marriage was good for women and not for men. It was more the fact that she'd never thought it possible for herself. Not while the peculiarity of Brad's image lurked in those wistful moments of fantasy that she'd longed to shed, but which had never seemed to disappear. "I was disappointed with the quality of men out there," she rebutted swiftly.

"But what about this . . . this Morris Walker?"

Arlisa's gaze flew to heaven in wayward anticipation before they resettled on the tea bags nestled comfortably in the tea pot. She felt her eyes glaze over. Morris was intelligent and physically handsome, and by all accounts had all the credentials to tempt any woman. He was also the kissing and cuddling type, who liked to go out for dinner often and talk about current affairs, particularly when related to his work as the British Representative for the Jamaican High Commission. But he was not for her. How could he have been, when she still harbored such confused feelings for a man who had been nothing more than a blip in her life. "You know about him?" She could hardly believe her ears.

"Erica mentioned him, once."

"I see," Arlisa jabbed, knowing that Erica had probably tainted her gossip with a few unclear facts that would be untrue. "Well, the truth is, I think he was scared of me."

"Scared of you!" Brad was amazed.

Arlisa leaned against the kitchen sink and folded her arms under her heaving breasts. She tipped her chin arrogantly, preparing to make her point known. "Morris Walker was a rich man who expected me to have an affair with him as some kind of payment for what he'd spent on me. I told him I don't do one-night stands." She felt the sting at the back of her eyes as she recalled exactly why she'd made that decision. Even now, knowing that Brad had intended to see her again, the pain of what she'd felt when he left for the Bahamas still remained in that part of her that was cautious and careful. "I hate the thought of being used," she continued in earnest. "I scared Morris because it was not within his comprehension for a good-looking, single girl like me not to be having sex and actually to be happy about it."

Brad smiled in admiration. "You were like that with the others?"

"Most of them."

He shook his head, disbelieving. "How many have you—"

"I don't want to answer that," Arlisa interjected coolly. "Even though I know that in this day and age it's important, you will begin to judge me again. And I don't want that."

Brad nodded, accepting Arlisa's remark. He was not going to pressure her any further. He knew enough already. Enough to realize that Arlisa was appealing to him more than ever. She had morals he'd never expected. She'd once had a Methodist mother and that meant something, too.

Not that he was overly religious, but a woman who was raised with some pride in the church meant something to him. It stroked at his old-fashioned values. It made him feel that there was something innately there that made a woman more worthy of attention.

Brad found himself smiling ever more affectionately. Arlisa noticed it, too. It touched at her heartstrings in a way she'd never known was possible. Her fingers sensed it; her toes felt it. Her very lips trembled at the strength of it. That thing which was successful in melting her at a stroke. Suddenly, she was reminded of the kiss they'd first shared beneath the stairs at his grandfather's home. It was incredible that that first flurry of excitement should still be present after all these years. Only now it was more pronounced. More intense. "How do you take your tea?" Her voice was muffled.

"White. One sugar." Brad's smile deepened. "Actually, I'm hungry. Do you mind if we eat here before you look for that M.P.'s address?"

Arlisa stared at Brad, seated with his hands on his knees, staring at her across the space between them. "I should cook something," she frowned, feeling the emptiness in her own stomach, and the sickly nausea of knowing that the intrigue surrounding her sister was not yet over. "There should be some food around here."

"Need any help?" Brad offered persuasively.

"You can see if there's some wine in the pantry over there," Arlisa prompted, a smile trembling around the corners of her mouth.

They ate pineapple and smoked ham, followed by pasta and stewed lamb fried in onion, tomato and barbecue sauce. Then they talked and smiled at each other across the kitchen table and slowly, Arlisa found herself relaxing a little more. Their conversation wandered from books to music to the theater, and if their opinions were disagreeable in any way, it was without heat or argument, serving as a lively understanding that grew between them as they stretched each other's tastes even further.

"Your grandfather," Arlisa asked, as she handed Brad another glass of red wine. "Do you think he would approve of your father marrying his first wife again?"

Brad hesitated for a beat of time and his honey-brown gaze skewered Arlisa with pinpointed ambivalence. "If he's as suspicious as me, maybe not," Brad affirmed, his lips drooping in disappointment. "I think my mother is marrying my father again because of his inheritance. It's a status thing."

"Him inheriting the Belleville Lagoons?" Arlisa surmised slowly.

"Exactly."

"When was the last time you saw your father?" Arlisa began, curious.

"Reuben?" Brad shrugged, uncaring. "Two years ago. Maybe two and a half."

"That long?"

"I'm grown now," Brad explained. "It's not as though I'm a kid anymore."

"When was the last time you saw your mother?"

"Last month," Brad breathed easily, taking a swallow of red wine. "She lives not far from here, in this rambling big house in Kent."

"I see," Arlisa nodded.

"It's far too big for her, but she won't be told," Brad added disapprovingly. "Seven bedrooms, three bathrooms. And a gym."

"She works out?" Arlisa was surprised.

"Twice a day, would you believe," Brad chided warily.

"She's forty-eight years old and she behaves like she's twenty."

"But if she looks well for her age, why shouldn't she?" Arlisa temporized in silent admiration. She'd often wondered what Brad's mother looked like and she was finding herself beginning to like the picture he was painting, however disagreeable his mother's behavior was to him.

"Whose side are you on?" Brad asked with an inquiring expression.

"No one's." Arlisa smiled. "I just happen to admire older women who look after themselves."

"I don't remember you saying that about Bernadetta Crossland," Brad responded coolly.

Arlisa winced, staring into Brad's face, her nerves flickering with fire. Why did he have to mention her, especially when they'd been having such a good time? "Bernadetta and I . . ." Her voice tapered off. "You really like her, don't you?"

"She's a friend, and that is all," Brad stressed, staring right back at her. "I've told you that before." His eyes narrowed determined.

"Let's just forget it." Arlisa shrugged off the subject. "I'm tired. What time is it?" She glared at her Rolex. "It's a quarter to ten. Oh god, I haven't done anything all day except—"

"Arlisa." Brad's tone was firm. "Calm down. We found the CD, remember?"

Arlisa rose up out of her chair, panicked and nervous, taking the dinner plates and cutlery with her to the kitchen sink. "I'd better go and see if I can find Kendra's address book." She placed the items down, turning to face Brad. "How do you feel about staying here tonight? It's just that, I want to avoid my father and—"

"That's fine with me," Brad nodded. "In fact, while I

wash up the dishes, you go and find Kendra's address book."

Arlisa's smile was half-hearted. "Thank you."

It did not go unnoticed by Brad. He unerringly caught hold of her wrist as she passed by the kitchen table, his compelling honey-brown eyes searching her face endlessly. The heart-wrenching gaze tripled Arlisa's pulse rate immediately, but she stoically repressed the feeling, fighting back the fluid heat of burning need that coursed through her body. "Don't feel guilty because I distracted you," Brad drawled smoothly. "We had a lot to catch up on."

"I know," Arlisa nodded, smiling evasively.

But she couldn't fight the guilt by the time she'd reached the master bedroom and was working her way through the closets and drawers. Arlisa felt bitterly ashamed. While her sister was probably shackled, handcuffed, or even lay dying, she'd been making love to Brad Belleville.

She shook herself vigorously, trying to shake off the gloom which hung over her like a dark cloud in winter. Her face stiffened in an effort to remove the misery that suddenly seemed to claim her. *Where is Kendra's damned address book?* her mind screamed, as a strange kind of trepidation she recognized to be fear took hold and gripped her senses rigid.

The closet and drawer space revealed nothing, except an extensive wardrobe that could only rival her own. Equally, Kendra's dressing table displayed nothing but the finest in branded cosmetics and perfumery. She was twisting her hands in anguish by the time she returned to the kitchen, facing Brad, unsettled.

"I've washed up," he declared. "Did you find the address book?"

Arlisa's face grew alarmed. "No. I don't know where else to look."

"Would she have it at the office?" Brad asked sympathetically, wiping his hands dry with the kitchen cloth before folding it and placing it by the kitchen sink.

"Kendra never keeps personal things at the *Nubian Chronicle*," she said flatly.

"Look." Brad took the few paces required to cross the kitchen space toward Arlisa. On reaching her, he pulled her gently into his arms. Arlisa could not help leaning her head against his shoulder, finding restitution there as he spoke. "We've found the CD," he began gently, his own tone tinged with a note of apprehension. "The only thing we can do now is sit tight until Bank Holiday Monday, when we go to the Notting Hill Carnival and see the queen of pharaoh."

Arlisa reared back in Brad's arms, suddenly panicked. "What time did we have to meet her? Do you remember?"

"Westbourne Grove Church Center. Seventeen hundred hours."

"What about the days until then?" Arlisa gasped tearful. "I can't just sit back and do nothing. Tomorrow's Friday, then there's the weekend."

"I don't know what else to suggest," Brad shrugged, helpless. "There was no e-mail address for this People's Power Party, so we have no way of contacting them prior to Monday. We've no idea how to contact this Selwyn Owens either, and there's no knowing whether he's even involved. And as for Shay Brentwood, your sister's husband, you couldn't reach him in Cuba."

"Maybe he's been detained." Arlisa's mind was reeling.

"I'd rather worry about it all in the morning," Brad insisted, feeling himself suddenly pressured by the enormity of their ordeal. "If we don't get some sleep, and I mean sleep, we won't be able to function very well come tomorrow. And right now, I think that we both need our faculties in place."

Arlisa conceded to his common sense. "You're right," she nodded, sighing heavily. "There's a guest room upstairs. We can use that. We'll sit tight until the morning."

Arlisa awoke with a start. She heard a noise, or thought she'd heard a noise. She looked around the dark bedroom, the only light coming in from a break between the curtains on the window, where the moon was peeking in. Resting on one elbow, she listened attentively. There it was again. It sounded like footsteps, as though someone was walking around the house.

Panicked, she nudged Brad. Sleeping silently next to her, the quiet ebb of his snoring having successfully worked a most curious sedating effect on her, Brad was alien to the world. He was obviously tired, that much Arlisa knew for sure. When Brad had entered the bedroom and finally gotten into bed, he'd fallen asleep almost instantly. Arlisa felt unsure whether to awaken him, but when she heard a most definite thud, as though something heavy had fallen to the ground, she was practically pulling at Brad's hair to rouse him.

"Ouch!" His first word was harsh with agitation. "What's the matter?"

"Someone's downstairs," Arlisa broached, tense and frightened.

Brad's eyes opened and Arlisa could almost sense the smirk that crossed his lips. "Come on, Arlisa. I need some sleep."

"Brad, I'm serious," she whispered, fretful. "I heard them walking around."

"Them?"

Arlisa cast her eyes heavenward. "Well, I don't know."

"Arlisa . . ."

"Sssh. Listen." She held Brad's hand and twisted it tightly, stricken with fear.

After a moment of hush, Brad grew annoyed. "I can't hear anything," he objected quietly. "Maybe you're hearing the wind outside."

"This is August, Brad."

"I know," he jeered.

Arlisa stared at his shadowy exterior. Brad was obviously not taking her seriously. *Isn't that just like a man,* she thought wildly. There was someone downstairs, and at any given moment they could be murdered in their bed. Yet all Brad cared about was getting a little more sleep. Arlisa felt enraged. *I'll deal with this myself.* Sensing that Brad had comfortably repositioned himself on his side, snuggling back into the softness of his pillow, she raised herself from beneath the sheets, dressed in Kendra's nightwear, and plodded her bare feet toward the door.

"Now where are you going?" She heard Brad sigh as she braced her shaking fingers against the doorknob.

"Someone's got to check it out," Arlisa countered lightly, keeping her voice low as she edged the door open. The first thing that caught her attention was the stairway lights. They had been switched on, and Arlisa knew for a fact that she'd admired the lucid diamonds in the chandeliers downstairs before having gone to bed that night, switching the lights off. But now they were on and her body stirred in fear that her suspicions had not been wrong. Someone was definitely in the house. "The lights are on," she informed Brad in a loud whisper that carried enough anxiousness and anxiety to alert him instantly.

"What?" He bolted upright and immediately looked at

his watch. He made out 6:35 AM against the dull glare of the room. Jumping from the bed, he reached to the floor to pull on his pants. "You stay here," he ordered, pulling on his socks and then slipping into his shoes. "This could get nasty."

"What?" Arlisa blared.

"I don't want you to get hurt," Brad rephrased carefully.

"I better come, too," Arlisa decided.

"No," Brad debated, throwing on his shirt. "It could be our same friends who visited the *Nubian Chronicle,* and—"

The sudden sound of shuffling footsteps caused him to catch his breath. Arlisa's shaking fingers flew to her lips. She was aware that whoever was outside their bedroom door knew that they were up there. From the light of the stairway, she saw the long shadow cast against the wall, coming closer toward them. There was a sense of doom as the shuffling, enhanced by the muffling drag it made against the carpet, came nearer until Arlisa found herself attempting to force down the scream that was bridging itself to erupt from her throat.

"They know we're here," she breathed on a pinnacle note.

Brad looked around quickly for a suitable instrument to fight with, though he could not see anything appropriate to use. The room was too dark to even glimpse at an item, let alone select one. "You hide behind the door," he informed Arlisa, his own tone troubled, as he reached for the first thing he could feel with his hands. "I'll try and rush them and then you can hurry downstairs and call the police."

"Is that a plan?" Arlisa chimed in frustration.

"You have a better one?" Brad returned.

She did not, though she wished she had. For a woman

who'd decidedly taken control of much of her life, she felt very much out of control presently. But she did as Brad instructed and began to inch her way behind the door. As she did so, she could see through the crack in the door hinges that the dark shadow outside had loomed up, imposing and arrogant.

It stood at the door's threshold and Arlisa held her breath. From across the other side of the door, she could see Brad. His profile was but a glimmer in the light, but unusually, it made her feel safe just knowing that he was there. Then suddenly, the door shot open. Arlisa's stomach turned into knots as the involuntary scream left her throat.

"Arlisa?" The American accent was most definitely bemused.

"Shay?" Arlisa gushed in disbelief.

The light came on overhead. Both Arlisa and Shay glared at each other and then at Brad, who'd switched on the lights. "Hello," Brad swallowed convulsively, casting his gaze heavenward to the wicker chair held high above his head.

Arlisa smirked, almost comically, as she also caught the baseball bat Shay Brentwood held in his hand.

"So, it's my fireball sister-in-law," Shay announced, watching arrogantly as Brad replaced the wicker chair to the floor. "If you're one of her wild friends—" he directed toward Brad.

"I'm one of her tame friends," Brad remarked equally as arrogant, though his tone was somewhat apologetic. "And before you start," he added with a frown, "we need to tell you something."

Thirteen

"What do you mean Kendra is missing?" Shay's bark shook the room. Arlisa stood in fear, but decided she was going to face Shay head-on.

"I think you'd better sit down," she advised quickly, taking refuge immediately in the nearest chair situated at the kitchen table. She looked at Brad and gestured with her head that he should join her there, too. As he did so, Shay stood bewildered, then reluctantly took the advice. Seating himself across from Arlisa, his dusky brown eyes raked hers in challenge, as he clasped his fingers together and looked head-on with discontent.

Arlisa felt pathetically weak as she tried to gauge Shay's mood, aware that she hadn't seen him in nearly a month. The exhaustion of flying back to England had obviously taken its toll. Shay appeared worn out; his square-shaped face, where there were no softening features, displaying that he was evidently in need of some rest. Aside from his tiredness, his good looks were still intact: a broad nose which looked straight as a blade, the raven-black hair that was formed into tiny black curls, and his full pink lips set perfectly against a caramel complexion that had grown a little more burnished by the Cuban sun. She was reminded that Shay was not a man to be reckoned with.

"This had better be good," he bridled, his gaze guarded,

the very caution in his glare giving Arlisa a shiver that seemed to reach every nerve ending in her body.

The story unfolded as she recounted everything with speed and precision, hardly daring to look at Shay as every measure of disbelief and alarm flashed across his granite face. Shay drank it all in by the mugful. And Arlisa did not spare any detail either, adding the correct amount of sugar and cream that were all too enriching of the danger they were all in. Her only failing had been not to add a good dose of the law. And its absence did not go unnoticed by Shay.

"Are you telling me you haven't called the police?" he taunted with such rage, Arlisa felt the air vibrate with it. "That's my wife and unborn kid out there."

"And Kendra's my sister," Arlisa cried out, her voice trembling weakly.

"What's the news now. Have you heard?" he yelled.

"No, but we've found the CD," she clarified, chewing at her lower lip.

"You're not my idea of a detective," Shay shot back, his voice so full of contempt that it forced an iron grimness to the set of his jaw. He couldn't believe that after all the hassles he'd suffered in Cuba—his luggage having gone astray, delays at the airport, the emergence of martial law that produced chaos and anxiety, that he would be coming back to this.

Brad had sat silently listening to Arlisa replay the bizarre reel of circumstances that had plagued them since she received the ransom note. On one occasion, he'd even felt tempted to add to the version, only deciding against it because he'd felt it was within Shay's right to understand everything from one voice. It was only when he saw the reckless glitter in Shay's dusky brown eyes that his mind screamed a poignant warning. It was clear to him that Shay was blaming Arlisa, and he felt that she'd taken enough without having to deal with his arrogant nature.

"Listen, you two," Brad began in an arbitrary tone. "We don't—"

But Arlisa interrupted, fully in defense mode. "I don't recall you figuring out what Selwyn Owens was up to the first time he went off the rails," she launched in a full counterattack at Shay.

"I at least had some idea," Shay fired back.

"Then why was Kendra nearly killed?" Arlisa roared, laying down the ammunition among all her artillery. "I'll tell you why. Because you always like to get what you want."

"Okay," Shay seethed angrily. "That's one of my faults."

"What about the other ninety-nine?" Arlisa pounced harshly.

"I'm not proud of what I did," Shay conceded, taking the full force heavy and hard.

"That's a shame," Arlisa taunted, failing to rear back. "Your father would have been."

Shay leaned all his weight into his chair, taking the offensive head-on. "My father may have wronged a lot of people, but deep down he had a good heart."

"Really," Arlisa jibed, unforgiving. "There are many people who used to say he didn't have one."

"Arlisa!" Brad desperately tried to wedge his way in.

"I'd be careful what you say next, girl," Shay warned.

Arlisa made a grimace to disguise the flurry of tears she could feel rushing to her eyes. She turned and faced Brad, then rose up out of her seat, pacing the floor in an attempt to steady her nerves. She felt unsettled and fickle, and physically her heart was pounding in anxiety. Shay could never have any understanding of what she'd been through, of how she'd tormented herself on what was the wrong or right thing to do. Where Kendra and her unborn baby were concerned, she still felt certain that she'd made the right decision. The only ultimatum that was important to her now was getting her sister back, alive. "We shouldn't be fighting like this," she intoned, catching Shay's look of resignation.

"You do know I'm going to have to call New Scotland Yard," he announced firmly. "Detective Inspector Chandy Sullivan will be more than interested in this one."

"I take it he worked on the last case regarding this Owens fellow," Brad inquired curiously.

Shay fixed Brad a challenging stare. "He picked up Owens the last time he flipped," his menacing voice explained before his own curiosity piqued. "What's your part in all this?"

"I'm an old friend of Arlisa's," Brad announced. "She needed my help."

"What's your name?"

"Brad Belleville."

"Belleville . . . Belleville. Sounds familiar," Shay remonstrated, inhaling a slow, ragged breath. "I know of an Erica Belleville-Brown. Any relation to you?"

"My sister."

"Sister." Shay nodded his quiet approval. "I'd ask you how she's doing, but as you can imagine, my mind is elsewhere."

Brad saw the urgency to deal with the tension that enveloped the room. Being the only one who was detached from Kendra in an emotional way, he felt it appropriate that he did the thinking at that precise moment. "We have the CD," he reminded Shay wisely. "Whoever has Kendra, that's what they want in return. If this D.I. Sullivan does become involved, then I suggest we tell him everything first."

"Yeah," Shay agreed, studying the seriousness in Brad's face. "If there's one thing I'd like to see strapped up right now, it's Selwyn Owens." His eyes narrowed with fiery contempt. "And I intend to get him, too."

Arlisa stared at both men, feeling as though she'd just come out of a dream. Somehow, without her seeing how, Brad and Shay had struck a resolution. What it meant, she didn't dare guess. All she knew was that they'd found a way to move forward.

There was a hive of activity in the days which led up to the Notting Hill Carnival. All the intense activity had stretched Arlisa, but the excitement, the atmosphere, the steady rise of tension which was mounting to explosion point was worth it, she decided. Kendra's life was on the line.

New Scotland Yard was keenly interested the moment they heard what was on the CD. The government's Home Office of Foreign Affairs had been contacted immediately, but she was more than amazed at how swiftly every facet of information had been correlated. Aside from the other ministers of parliament, who would be hand-selected to partake of the news, she was made to understand by D.I. Chandy Sullivan that the Prime Minister had been informed, too.

"This is deadly serious," he'd shrieked from across the desk in his office at the recently established criminal investigation department. "Have you any idea how Selwyn Owens got hold of this information about officials in the Cuban government?"

"No," Arlisa answered truthfully. "But he's an M.P."

"He's a former M.P.," Sullivan reminded. "Maybe he had links to other government departments."

"What happens now?" Shay asked insistently.

To him, everything was hanging in the balance. His future, the life of his wife and child, and from all accounts, the very security of the country. Negligence was obviously at an all-time high. A former minister of parliament had been able to sneak into a government department and remove damaging information. But that wasn't on his mind right now.

"We'll have our men tail Arlisa and Brad to the Westbourne Grove Church Center," Sullivan clarified, reaching to the table for a packet of Marlboro cigarettes.

Arlisa anxiously scanned the room, which appeared regimentally designed in shades of blue, then schooled her features to one of complete blankness as Sullivan lit up his cigarette. The numbers game had started again. It was Sunday. The Carnival was tomorrow. She'd spent Friday and Saturday at her sister's Wimbledon home in an unhappy daze, while Brad and Shay departed and returned on numerous occasions. They'd visited D.I. Sullivan together, twice. Brad had stopped by his office, and Shay likewise at the *Nubian Chronicle*. Both had seemed able to cope with the inevitability of the big showdown on Monday, even to the point of deluding her father when he'd called the house and spoken with Shay.

She'd already popped four pain killers. And then there was the reminder that it was day *five*. Day *six* was tomorrow and by Tuesday, day *seven,* Kendra should be home. She paused heavily and stared at D.I. Sullivan. He looked capable, she decided astutely. He'd obviously solved his fair share of mysteries. But what mettle was he made of among people? There would be TV crews from all over the world, the press would be there in force, and security would be tight as always to control the throng of two million people, one-third the size of London's population.

Two million. There goes another number. She wondered whether Sullivan was hiding some cataclysmic surprise up his sleeve, but in reality, Arlisa knew differently. Ultimately, it was going to be down to her in the end. She was the one who was going to have to keep a level head while a platoon of armed plain-clothed officers would be tracking her every move.

"There's no chance of any of your men losing us, is there?" she breathed, her gaze trained on the inspector as he puffed out a breath of smoke before slipping the cigarette back between his lips. She felt the comfort of Brad's hand as he pressed it against her own in solidarity.

"They'll be seven thousand, eight hundred police officers on patrol tomorrow. Our men will be alongside them," Sullivan assured. "If you just do as we tell you, you'll be fine."

If only Arlisa could feel just as convinced. As she lay against Brad's chest later that night in the same room they'd shared at Kendra's and Shay's home, swallowing down the fear that was leapfrogging through her, she could only reflect on the past few days in silent trepidation. She was not aware that Brad knew she was awake until he said, "Are you afraid?"

"Yes," she sighed heavily.

He exhaled a breath and stroked at her shoulders. "For you?"

"No. For my sister."

"Arlisa."

Brad snuggled her into him, and Arlisa felt as though she was suddenly tangled in a web of emotions. There was the guilt as a swirling morass of desire suddenly took hold, caused by the gentle movement of Brad's fingers against her bare skin. Then there was the fear of reverting back to that foolhardy, mischievous woman she'd once been, who seemed to have an innate gift to cause mayhem and leave trouble wherever she went. For once in her life, she had to get this right. To Arlisa, it felt like the testing of a true *Hypermega*.

"I don't want to mess up," she sniveled, as those same heated fingers she'd grown to know so well traveled down the spinal cord at the back of her neck.

"You won't," Brad encouraged, planting a kiss against Arlisa's forehead. "I won't be far behind, remember."

"I know." She snuggled in deeper, feeling as though her very life depended on gaining strength from Brad. Then a question suddenly fell from her lips. "Am I?" she asked a little anxiously.

"Are you what?"

"Your love?"

Arlisa felt Brad tense, knowing not what senseless self-ishness had dared her to ask such a question, even to re-ceiving a response. She hardly expected Brad to give her an answer, given the circumstances presently plaguing them. Of their meeting, there had hardly been what could be termed a reckless passionate romance. Whatever ex-isted had been kindled with a certain spark of danger, in-trigue and general suspense. She was clutching at straws, but absurdly, she did not care. She needed something right then. Right now. Not sexual fulfillment, fantasy or hope. Just . . . words. That was it. Even if they were meaningless. Just to hear Brad say the words she desperately wanted to hear was all she needed.

Brad's voice seemed caught on a breath. "You were al-ways that." He hugged Arlisa close and gazed into her angelic face. She looked so adorable, vulnerable, innocent and sexy all at the same time. Brad felt his heartstrings stretch to their limit at the intensity of such a combination. The tenderness of her being in his arms was all too consuming, searing at his emotions. And when their eyes locked, he felt the fascination of her being with him touch his soul. "My one and only." The words were heartfelt.

Arlisa trembled, gazing deeply into Brad's honey-brown eyes. The kiss came impulsively, unexpectedly. She couldn't help but melt right into it, sensing the devotion that dripped from Brad's lips. He smothered and enraptured her all over again, and she could do nothing, except surrender . . .

It took one million man hours, thirty million sequins, fifteen thousand feather plumes and thirty liters of body paint to make the decorative costumes for the Notting Hill Carnival. Those were the statistics that came over the radio as Arlisa dressed that morning. *More numbers,* she sighed as slipped into the Calvin Klein jeans and pale blue T-shirt she'd hastily plucked from the wardrobe at her father's house the night before, en route to Wimbledon. She was amazed that she'd never calculated their value, and was even now more interested in digesting the running commentary about the biggest street procession in Europe. *Thirty-nine sound systems with a combination worth of three point five million sterling, playing over eighteen thousand records in twenty-six different types of music from across the Caribbean.* These were the new set of figures that ran through her head.

"Are you ready?" Brad emerged from the ensuite bathroom, clothed similarly in jeans and a white T-shirt, looking fresh to take on their task that day.

Arlisa sucked in her breath, aware that his very presence was tugging more at her amorous feelings than her fearful ones. She realized now that Brad would always affect her in this way. Everything about him seemed to be in answer to the yearning she'd always felt within, especially in the way Brad gazed at her. Though the look was one filled with concern, to Arlisa it spoke volumes in every sense. She was his love. He'd told her so last night. Her heart leapt with the prospect that after their present danger was over, he would want to continue seeing her.

Hadn't he told her that whatever he entered into, it was always with the best intentions? That he preferred something where the capacity for love could be explored? And he'd wanted her to go to the Bahamas with him. Hadn't he also told her so in the letter Erica had returned? *The letter.* The white envelope suddenly flashed through Arlisa's mind. She'd forgotten all about it. *I should read it later.* She made a mental note. Seeing those very words immortalized on paper would be the true testament of Brad's feelings toward her.

"I'm ready."

He helped her remake the bed and then together they both disembarked downstairs to find Shay drinking coffee and pacing the kitchen floor anxiously. He was dressed in stonewashed jeans, a sweater and Timberland boots. The hair was, as always, groomed, and he'd already thrown on a lightweight jacket.

"The radio said the weather would be hot today," Brad informed Shay as he began to help himself to coffee. "I don't think you're going to need that jacket."

Shay paused in his pace and thought for a minute. Then placing his coffee mug on the table, he began to remove his jacket. "I'm not thinking," he breathed. "I swear, when I see Selwyn Owens . . ." He ran nervous fingers through his hair. "Arlisa. I'm counting on you," he warned.

"You and seven thousand, eight hundred police officers," she broached, recalling what D.I. Sullivan had told her.

Shay shook his head. "What?"

"It's going to cost four million pounds to police this Carnival today," she wavered. "And the radio DJ this morning said that it would take ten hours for the procession of one hundred and twenty floats and fifteen thousand costumes to complete the full circuit route. I think you can safely count on me making my way through that lot."

Shay saw the perilous enormity of it all. "This isn't going to work," he rasped, annoyed and disbelieving. "You're right. There're going to be so many people. If this were America, the police would be more equipped to—"

"We may be from two countries divided by a common language," Arlisa interrupted, her tone defensive, "but over here, in England, the police know how to handle things, too."

Brad sought to bridge the gap of tension with a dose of humor. "Remember Sherlock Holmes?" he added with raised eyebrows.

Shay's lips formed a weak, conceding smile. "And New Scotland Yard."

That's precisely where they were two hours later, being briefed by Detective Inspector Chandy Sullivan.

"Sure you can handle this," he buzzed, handing Arlisa a vanilla-colored carry-all.

"I think so," she muttered, taking the bag.

"In here," D.I. Sullivan began with a growing sense of excitement, "is our latest state-of-the-art tracking device. It looks like a pen, so don't lose it," he added. "There's also a wiretap in the lining and a flask of orange juice inside. It's going to be a scorching hot day out there, so we don't want you thirsty by five o'clock. There're also some sandwiches and a mobile phone. Any problems, just press zero and it'll connect you to us direct. Questions?"

"Where's the CD?" Arlisa panicked.

"It's in the bag—in the lower compartment," D.I. Sullivan explained. "It's the original, but we've taken a copy. If these people are part of a Cuban exile group, then they can't be fooled. We have to remind ourselves that they may've duped this Owens fellow to help them. What's important is getting your sister back alive."

"I know," Arlisa agreed.

"And you both must behave quite naturally," the detective inspector insisted. "That means a lot of holding hands, kissing—you know—the usual stuff. Just appear as though you're enjoying yourselves."

Arlisa dipped her head, a little embarrassed. She knew she wouldn't have any problems where Brad was concerned.

"It's nearly noon now," Sullivan said. "So you have nearly five hours to circulate. We'll be watching to see if anyone makes contact."

Arlisa stared at Brad. It was time to go. She was now immersed in the biggest adventure of her life, and she was about to share it with the one man she loved.

The gray English streets were alight with extraordinary creations of wire, fiberglass, silk, foam and sequins, proving itself to be the United Kingdom's greatest annual spectacle as Arlisa and Brad walked among the mass of people. The capital city had taken the celebration to its heart, having started from meager beginnings thirty-five years ago, when a small group of steel pan men from the Caribbean came to a place called Notting Hill.

With the sun burning above their heads and the sky a clear picture of blue, where no clouds were present, Arlisa almost felt as though she was in the Caribbean itself, enjoying the calypso, soca and salsa rhythms she could hear the moment they'd emerged from the Notting Hill Gate underground station and began to make their way down Kensington Park Road.

The merrymakers and masqueraders were in full carnival spirit, high-energy and feel-good vibes, attracting and rocking the ever-increasing crowd of revelers as they began to flood the streets. Overawed, Arlisa and Brad hardly spoke, instead building up a silent communion that was bonded in their holding hands while they merged through the throng of human traffic. Even as all the excitement and noise swirled around them, the atmosphere becoming more bawdy and jovial, by tacit consent they maintained their quiet sense of comfort in one another. It was as though if one or the other spoke, something terrible would happen or go wrong.

And so the suspicion held until Arlisa's Rolex read a quarter past three. A steel band float, depicting fantastic allegorical themes, passed on by, filling the air with Caribbean music. Arlisa and Brad suddenly found themselves thrown among the revelers who'd snaked a colorful, staggering conga line which trailed the float along the designated procession route.

There were costumed people, all dancing in the tight space between the float ahead and the float behind, some swigging wine, others puffing *ganja,* other carnival-goers with garishly painted faces simply piping on whistles, clearly having a good time. It was clear they were not all part of the procession. These were members of the crowd who'd hopped on board to join in.

There were others, too, wearing grotesque masks that

represented the mystique parts of Africa, their papier-mâché camouflages used to preserve the secret of identities. Managing to break free from the human flow, Arlisa and Brad were able to return to the sidewalk, though it proved difficult because of the number of strangers coaxing and propelling them to come along. It was an intoxicating scene, being trapped among the bizarre atmosphere, where complex feathered masks, headdresses and animal disguises went hand in hand with men juggling flaming torches, women performing magic tricks and people tossing aside their clothes in abandon to do the limbo.

As the heat sweltered above them, an artfully dressed woman with legs like an ostrich leapt madly into the air and squatted at Brad's feet, entreating him to join her. Pulling him through the barricades that were erected to protect the dancers from the crowd, they whirled away together in a mad dance, laughing, while a gruesome devil-dancer leapt in front of Arlisa and did a few odd contortions before capering away gleefully to scare others.

Only when the steel band shifted tempo, and the trailing posse broke out into another rhythm, did Brad release himself from the strange woman and manage to make his way back toward where Arlisa remained, swaying her hips to be at one with the Bacchanal crowd. Impulsively, Brad took hold of her wrist, spinning her into an island dance that was a sweet cocktail of salsa grooves. Arlisa smiled, almost seductively, her fawn-brown gaze grateful that he'd returned.

He could feel the strong pull emanating from her, causing that odd feeling to creep up inside him again, a lingering, throbbing experience holding a semblance of pain. It made Brad's heart beat faster, caused his gaze to melt deep into Arlisa, and there was something else that made Brad tell himself that what he was feeling was simply the reaction of facing a beautiful woman.

Yet among the tidal wave of juggernauting chaos, the sensual kaleidoscopic frenzy of light, and the maelstrom of merciless satire where profane parody prevailed, no barricades could protect his heart from reacting to Arlisa the way it was presently. Everything he'd ever felt toward her suddenly seemed intensified, and he blamed it on the unusual paradox of the carnival that was making him feel so confused. Opposites were united, order was disorder, harmony dissonance and no laws and taboos sacred. One and all were changed, everything was reversed, inside out, inverted backward, as was his mind right now in attempting to merge their past with a future.

And then he reminded himself that the dancing, music, rhythm, mentality and aesthetics of black Africa was also at that moment in excess and infectious to all strands of sensitivity. The air was filled with unrestrained folly, joy and anger, kindness and cruelty—a mad fleeting moment where life phrenetically embraced death in a whirl of primal exclamation.

Carnival always tugged at the deepest, rawest, most sentimental consciousness, finding the heart of the African soul in spectators and bystanders alike. Its very roots were buried in the primordial mists of ancestral memories, far beyond history, when man lived by nature. It was knowing that he was being touched with the ancient spirit of primitive abandon that made Brad shrug aside the intensity of burning earnest which thrilled and rocked him as he looked into Arlisa's face.

"We should eat," he said coarsely, indicating at his watch, purposefully deciding that he should distract himself particularly when his mind thought of what he'd told Arlisa the night before. It was premature to confess to her that she was his one and only. He could not ignore the sense of unease in knowing that he wanted this woman when his past actions and words had not been in admission to it.

"Yes, let's eat. I'm hungry," Arlisa agreed, realizing that time had elapsed and it was now four-thirty in the afternoon.

Together, they were thrust, once again, into the canyon banked with shouting and singing people. The massive percussion section of sound systems roared down the street in a riptide wave of steel drums, whistles, tambourines, shakers, cowbells and triangles. The force of their sound was irresistible as Arlisa and Brad tried to make their way through the thickening crowd to a safe spot designed for taking a breather and would perhaps allow them to eat and drink something.

The huge sound systems of four floats, with their slogans and advertising painted across them, positioned themselves on the road to allow the main body of dancers to pass. The *sambistas* were the most dazzling highlight of Carnival because of their incredible double-time change-ups, dipping and cross-legged whirling routines; the *ragga girls,* who sensually arched their "bundas" or rear ends, pumping their torsos in a choreographed display of erotic exhibitionism, and the *fillers* did variations of samba, salsa and calypso. Arlisa paused for a brief moment to catch her breath while viewing the carnivalesque spirit around her.

African warriors, Indians, gladiators and girls wearing tangas and headdresses paraded by in a frenzy. They were followed almost anticlimatically by the *wings,* the often older, portly women traditionally dressed in costumes from old, colonial capitals. It was a paroxysm of cultures, and there had been times when the London police were unable to control the furor and keep it spilling into the avenue, inundating the passing dancers writhing and gyrating in a riot of color. Robberies, accidents and fights were sometimes unleashed among the fury and chaos of Carnival.

Moving again on her feet, she decidedly caught Brad's left hand so they would not lose each other in the chaos. The sheer contact made Arlisa start back as if her body had been seared by contact with white-hot metal, such was the affect Brad would always have on her. Carefully, they worked their way through the crowd, finally finding a suitable spot to rest in a corner, just off Wesbourne Grove. Arlisa sat down on top of a public dustbin, exhausted and intent on quenching her thirst. Brad chose to remain standing, though he leaned his weight against one of the metal barricades looking around him, as the noise thudded on.

"I'm so hot," Arlisa murmured, reaching to the carry-all Detective Inspector Sullivan had given her, from where she extracted a flask of orange juice. Screwing off the lid, she gulped down several mouthfuls of the stuff before handing the flask across to Brad. "I think the Westbourne Grove Church Center is just around the corner."

"We're early," Brad chided, looking around him as a procession of carnival participants dressed in sparrows, peacock and eagle-styled costumes danced their way down the road to the infectious rhythm of chutney-soca.

The intrusion of cultures was so amazing that it was impossible to dismiss the ultimate creation that sprang from the Portuguese and Spanish navigators. Arlisa's fawn-brown gaze took in the distinctive individuality of each participant as they passed along. So far, no Egyptian-styled costumes had caught their attention and she was reminded that there were at least eight hours of Carnival left to go. "There's no hurry for us to go inside the church now," she said, plunging her hand into the carry-all to retrieve the sandwiches. "We're not expected there until five o'clock."

"I know," Brad acknowledged. "But this waiting around is killing me."

"Me, too," Arlisa appended. "I always seem to get myself into a spot."

Brad laughed. "You mean walking on the wild side," Brad agreed. "You didn't so much paint a colorful lifestyle. You lived it."

"At least I can say I've lived," she broached.

She handed him a sandwich and he took it, shedding the wrapping diligently. For a while they ate in silence, simply watching as a further procession of twelve-, fourteen- and sixteen-foot costumes, all proportionately large sizes to the others, began to parade down the street. The expense and depth of work that had gone into creating them made Arlisa curious as to what led Brad to create his movie. "Tell me about 'The Price of Glory'," she prompted smoothly. "Are you proud of it?"

She saw the smile tug at Brad's lips, but Arlisa was also aware of the evasive expression in his face, too. "Very," he affirmed, nodding his head. "It was one of those climbing a mountain things. I was determined to reach the summit so I could say I'm on top of the world."

"You were proving something to yourself?" Arlisa asked, deeply interested.

"A sense of achievement I think," Brad answered in truth.

"What's the film about?" Arlisa ventured further, having opened her own sandwich, holding it poised ready for her to take a bite.

Brad chuckled, not expecting the question. "It's a story

about the African-American soldiers who fought in the Spanish-American War of 1898," he explained. "I've always been quite fascinated with war, regiments and soldiers."

"I remember," Arlisa drawled, her mouth full. "I picked up one of your toy soldiers when I was nine at your grandfather's house and—"

"I snatched it out of your hands and told you not to touch my things," Brad interjected.

"You remember, too," Arlisa smiled.

"Like I said, sometimes your past can be your future."

Arlisa's heart warmed to the suggestion Brad was making. "You believe that, don't you?" she probed, her heart suddenly beating more rapidly than usual.

"I believe that destiny is something you create," Brad returned. "When I first started out making films, I didn't know the difference between a 16mm and 35mm film. Now look where I am now. Every part of a person's life can be controlled and nourished to grow if they believe that they can achieve what they want."

"Even to make someone fall in love with them?" Arlisa chimed.

"That's tricky," Brad croaked. "Sometimes a person can get feelings that they don't understand because they're being introduced to them first time round. What I'm saying is, it's hard to know if you've fallen in love. It could simply be desire."

"Or lust," Arlisa chuckled weakly, attempting to quickly analyze what her feelings for Brad truly meant. She felt certain it was the real thing. *It's love,* her mind divulged. And in her heart, she wanted Brad to feel the same way, too. "Who can ever be sure?"

His honey-brown eyes suddenly penetrated hers, and Arlisa felt her fingers dig into her sandwich. "Personally,

I've realized that I have to be the right man in order to find the right woman," he told her astutely. "And I'll find perfection when I find the right woman, but until then, I work on building myself. After that, everything else falls into place, whether it's from your past or your future."

"I see." Arlisa's mind felt jarred by Brad's revelations. He was such a deep thinker, and in many ways quite complex. She now came to understand what he meant when he'd told her he was a difficult person to live with. Yet his clarity on the subject of *love* was so clear and precise that without intention, she'd notched up a mark. *Ten out of ten.* Her mind worked its magical arithmetic. *Brad was a ninety-one.*

"I'm glad you agree," Brad continued warmly. "Because it's not something a man goes into lightly."

"Tell me about it," Arlisa scoffed like a cynic. "I think most men don't want a woman to care about them because it makes it easier for them to feel free."

"There's two schools on that subject," Brad relented. "Most grow up in the end."

"Do they?" Arlisa rebuffed. "If there's one thing I can't abide in a man, it's immaturity, and I've seen much of that these last few years."

"It's just a sign of the times," Brad rationalized, swallowing hard on his sandwich. "People being confused. Many not seeing where they are going. We're in a new millennium; things are bound to change."

"Things are changing right now," Arlisa announced warily, her gaze alert as she looked at the street. "There's a group dressed in Egyptian masquerades heading this way."

"Where?"

"Over there." Arlisa pointed westward.

"Come on."

Brad returned the flask to her and binned the rest of his sandwich. Quickly Arlisa replaced it in her carry-all, pulling the bag over her shoulder in one fell swoop. In a short flurry of steps, she rushed after Brad, who had already begun to break his way through the thick crowd, who were either milling around the numerous craft stalls that were selling all manner of wares from the Caribbean, or dancing among themselves in intricate patterns that were traditionally attached to the music being played.

The Egyptian-style dancing group came into full sight the moment Brad and Arlisa turned the corner onto Westbourne Grove. From where they stood, the Westbourne Grove Church Center also came into view. Several steps led up to the main doors, but each was presently cluttered with people—mostly mothers with prams taking time out to feed their children, or the elderly who were too pooped with exhaustion from having walked a good while under the intense glare of the afternoon sun.

Arlisa realized that she and Brad would have to step over the entourage just to make it inside the church. If that was the only entrance and exit into the place, then how were they going to facilitate an escape, should they need one? They stood and watched for the fifteen minutes it took for the Egyptian dancers to parade down the street, before Arlisa and Brad watched two of its members depart and make their way toward the church.

"They're going in," Brad proclaimed, taking a firm hold of Arlisa's left hand and practically pulling her across Westbourne Grove through the procession, passing the many TV crews with their cameras, and then through yet another set of carnival lovers on the other side of the street. The sidewalk was crammed with revelers who were like ants on the run, but before long, they stood at the foot of

the imposing sandy-colored church building, wondering
whether to venture further.

"Did you see them go in?" Arlisa bellowed loudly,
above the new wave of troopers making their way down
Westbourne Grove.

"I'm not sure," Brad roared above the torrent of music.
"Let's go in anyway."

"Okay," Arlisa agreed.

There was no turning back for her now as she took the
steps one at a time behind Brad, carefully picking her way
through the people sitting around. She glanced backward,
expecting to see Detective Inspector Sullivan or a member
from his squadron, absurdly realizing that there was no
way of knowing or recognizing any one of them.

Finally, she was swallowed into the church and the first
sight that met Arlisa was one of chaos. Children were running around in all directions, the few craft stalls situated
at the entrance were swamped with buyers, and a long line
led to a coffee shop and another to the male and female
toilets. There was no question at all that the church was
being used more as a recreational center rather than a place
for worship. There was no aisle. No seats. No center stage
and no podium for a minister to talk over his congregation.
Arlisa was surprised. She'd expected something traditional
inside.

"Not like your usual place of worship," Brad objected
in irritation, noting a plaque on the wall which charac-
terized the building as having been founded as a Baptist
chapel in the middle of the last century.

"No," Arlisa drawled. "Where did they go?"

"They're over there." Brad discreetly pointed out the
two people they'd seen earlier.

Arlisa looked across at them. They'd joined a group
of six other members who remained huddled together

and in close contact to each other. They were all clearly dressed in Egyptian-style costumes, but there was no distinguishing a queen. There was a tall man among them who appeared to be a pharaoh, and the other participants were either eunichs, priestesses or mummies. Arlisa stared on, bemused, unsure how she and Brad should proceed.

Then suddenly, the pharaoh departed from the group and made his way toward an old, carved wooden oak door, situated in an obscure corner of the large room. No one paid attention to him as he rapped out three knocks on the door, such was the activity that was going on. But Arlisa and Brad paid close attention as they watched the door slowly open, seeing the distinct impression of a woman dressed to appear like an Egyptian queen inviting the young man in.

Arlisa looked at her watch. It was a shade off five o'clock. "That's where we go," she declared, fretful and full of nerves. "That must be where we make the hand-over."

Brad looked equally worried, but Arlisa was aware that he was putting up a remarkable bold front for her benefit. "Let's get this over with," he urged quite tersely.

They followed the same tracks the pharaoh had made, making their way to the same door. With three knocks, Arlisa stood back, immediately reaching for Brad's huge, sturdy hand, where she clasped her fingers around his and rubbed against the diamond-studded ring his father had given him, as they both waited for the door to open. It took five long seconds before it was pulled ajar and the head of a woman donned in a Nefertiti hat poked her head out. "Yes?" came the harsh tone.

Arlisa gulped. "We're here to see the queen of pharaoh," she swallowed. "We have what you want in exchange for my sister."

They were gazed at in deep suspicion and for a moment Arlisa thought she and Brad had come to the wrong church. After all, the sentence she'd verbalized sounded so bizarre, it was little wonder anyone would've thought her capable to be in full possession of her mind. But when a flicker of recognition flew across the woman's round, brown face and she pulled the door wider ajar to admit them in, Arlisa knew that she was one step closer to finding her sister.

The room was small, holding only four people, three seated at a table and the woman who'd admitted them, standing at the door. The only light came through a small latticed glass window, and there was another door behind the table which was steadfast closed and for all pretense and purposes, was probably locked.

Arlisa's gaze honed in on the people seated at the table, the first one she recognized to be the tall man dressed as a pharaoh whom they'd followed there. The other two were women. Though they were seated with their backs toward her and hadn't yet turned their heads to observe her presence, she could tell by the shapely outline of their bodies beneath the elaborate design of their costumes that they were of the female gender. Arlisa also knew they had not been part of the entourage she and Brad had seen inside the church. As the queen eyed Arlisa carefully and she threw her a cautious smile, Arlisa found her gaze returning to the table.

"Where's my sister?" she demanded murderously, feeling the hot sting of pain greet her eyes as the two women at the table turned their heads.

Suddenly the tears welled inside Arlisa. She recognized her sister instantly. "Kendra?"

"Arlisa!"

A flash of arrogance rose up in the pharaoh's eyes. As

Arlisa flew across to the table and hugged her sister, Brad was more than aware that they were certainly among people who were potentially dangerous, with deep-seated motives that were often unseen, even to the most discerning and street-wise. Returning an equally combative flash of arrogance, he exerted himself and pronounced quite clearly, "We have what you want. Let the girls go."

He was, however, unprepared for what happened next.

Fourteen

There was no mistaking the shock on Brad's face when the other woman at the table stood up and faced him. He felt hoodwinked. Duped. Ensnared in a harlot's nest when the familiar squirrel-brown eyes faced him head-on. She looked as bemused as he, though she could not have possibly understood the instant feelings that tormented Brad as his honey-brown eyes widened with incredulity. This had to be some kind of a hoax, he told himself. A pitfall devised for fools only. But harsh reality told him differently.

"Erica?" Even Brad's voice sounded bemused, the apparent noose he found himself flung into etched in the one word.

"Brad. What are you doing here?" Erica's tone was cool and collected.

"I think that's my question," he blared.

"I can't explain, not here," she exclaimed, glancing briefly at her friends.

"Erica!" Brad ate up the distance between them and took an immediate hold of his sister's wrist, alarm marked in every line of his profile. "Just what kind of trouble are you in?"

Arlisa wasn't oblivious to what was going on. From the moment she heard Brad's voice echo across the room, her senses were alert to whom he was directing his attention.

The last person she expected to see was Erica Belleville-Brown. It could hardly be true that such a snake in the grass had existed among them at a time when both she and Brad had desperately been in a struggle to find her sister.

Kendra seemed to be all right by all appearances. She looked well, had been fed well, and had presented no trouble at all to her captors. Her unborn baby was safe, too. Aside from having been forced to wear an Egyptian-styled costume to merge with the others, her face showing slight signs of exhaustion from lack of sleep, worry and the perilous danger she was in, her spirits were remarkably sedated. But Kendra had always been a rock. The anchor that had kept their family together since their mother had died.

Still, it had been an ordeal. Arlisa wouldn't have wished it on anyone, even her worst enemy. Now to find that the one adversary who had always been against her from child-hood was right there in that very room, obviously party to the entire kidnapping, heated Arlisa's blood to boil with such intensity, she hardly knew how to cope with it. "What in the devil are you doing here?" she boomed, her tone full of malice.

Kendra turned and faced the woman who'd kept her company throughout that morning. "Do you know her?" she intersected, facing Arlisa.

"Know her?" Arlisa scoffed, thinking perhaps she should spit. The fire was certainly mounting in her gut, looking for an avenue to escape. Adopting a deadly tone, she informed her sister, "This is Erica Belleville-Brown."

"You mean. . . ." Kendra wavered incredulously.

"Otis Belleville's granddaughter," Arlisa concluded, attempting a supreme effort to calm herself. "I hope you have a damned good explanation for being here," she threatened, taking two menacing steps toward the woman.

"Brad . . ." Erica pleaded sheepishly. "I did it for Tyrone."

Brad swallowed hard on the tightness of his throat, facing Erica's stricken expression. She'd gone pale suddenly and the contrite look of remorse in her eyes made his brows furrow with anger. "Did what for Tyrone?" he raged at full volume.

The man attired in the pharaoh costume took Brad's raised voice personally. Aiming accurately, he took ahold of Brad's arm and twisted it arrogantly behind his back, attempting to arrest Brad's rising temper. "Let go of me," Brad challenged, shrugging with enough brute force to release himself from the hand-held lock, pushing the heavyset man to the floor. "Touch me again and you'll get more than you bargained for," he warned off the man offensively. "What's my sister doing here?"

"Your sister?" the man screeched in a deeply Spanish accent, slowly picking himself up from the ground.

"My sister," Brad underlined murderously, baiting his gaze in challenge.

"Look," the man said, holding up both hands in surrender. "We just want the CD."

"Why?" Brad growled. "What is this all about?"

"Brad," Erica sighed heavily, nodding her head toward the pharaoh and the woman styled as queen Nefertiti. "This is Nico and his wife Claudia. They're members of the People's Power Party, an exiled group fighting for the emancipation of Cuba."

"So?" Brad chided in an unreasonable manner.

"Tyrone—"

"Tyrone!" Brad blazed in interruption.

Erica swallowed. "Tyrone has been fighting their case to get political asylum in this country."

"And?" he insisted.

"Three months ago, it was rumored that Fidel Castro was suffering from a mysterious illness and the Home Office turned down their application."

Brad shrugged his shoulders uneasily. "I fail to see the point," he grasped.

"In Cuba, they were accused of leaking information to the CIA. If they were to go back there, they would be arrested, imprisoned and probably murdered. One of their members was able to get hold of a CD which contain the master files of all the top secret officials in Cuba who are really working for the USA. He gave it to a minister of parliament who represented ethnic minority issues at the Brent-South constituency. It was hoped that the CD could be used as a plea bargain to get them political asylum."

"What happened?" Arlisa demanded hotly.

"The House of Commons public information office announced that the M.P. had resigned because of personal problems. These people thought the government was playing a game with them, because they located their M.P. at a psychiatric hospital and—"

"Selwyn Owens," Kendra wavered in alarm. "You're talking about Selwyn Owens."

"I swear I didn't know," Erica pleaded tearfully. "Tyrone only filled me in on everything yesterday and told me that he needed my help. I did not know these people had taken a hostage to try and get their CD back."

Brad shook his head, disbelieving. "What's this all got to do with Tyrone?"

"Someone is trying to frame him," Erica explained. "Cases were going missing, his telephone had been tapped and now he thinks he's going to be barred for malpractice. Someone's been—"

"That was why you wanted me to get involved with Bernadetta Crossland, so I could get information from Judge Crossland," Brad interrupted.

"Yes," Erica nodded. She looked at Arlisa in earnest. "I didn't know about your sister," she intoned with blatant sincerity. "When Tyrone told me that the PPP had taken a female hostage and that she was pregnant, I swear, I didn't know what to do. These people just want their CD. I told them—"

The slap came unexpectedly. To Arlisa it represented the release of all the pent-up anguished pain and frustration she'd ever suffered at the hands of Erica Belleville-Brown. "Because of you and your husband, my sister's life had been put in danger," she blazed. "How dare you try and explain things to me now? How did these people even know I had the CD, to think that they could have the arrogance to take my sister so I would return it?"

Erica rose a shaky hand to her face and rubbed slowly at the clean mark Arlisa's slap had left there. "One of the members of the People's Power Party followed Selwyn Owens to La Casa de la Salsa. The night I saw you there," she added. "He saw Selwyn give you the CD. He started following you and apparently caught you with Kendra one day at the Yaa Asantewaa Art Gallery."

"Funny, you were around both times," Arlisa proclaimed suspiciously.

"I tell you, I did not know all this was going on," Erica implored weakly.

Arlisa turned murderously toward Nico and Claudia. "You both put us through all this just because you want political asylum? I'll give you political . . ." She marched arrogantly toward the two in exile, but was instantly pulled back by Brad.

"Don't," he intoned sharply. "They're not worth it."

"Do you have any idea what we went through?" she admonished madly. "Having to pick up information on the Internet like we were part of some secret conspiracy. The *Nubian Chronicle* being searched. Even now, while we're trying to get our heads round all this," she waved her hands helplessly in the air, "police officers from New Scotland Yard are tracking our every move."

"We said no police," Nico's accent deepened to a threatening note. "Give me the CD," he demanded of Arlisa.

"No," she objected, standing her ground.

"I said give it to me," Nico repeated again more harshly.

"I said no," Arlisa rebutted.

Nico instantly caught everyone unaware when he pulled out a gun from beneath his costume and aimed it unerringly. If there was anything that was going to make Arlisa realize that he seriously intended to get what he wanted, seeing a Walter PPK .32 caliber had to be it. "The CD," he ordered, carefully pointing the gun at Kendra.

"Now, take it easy," Brad prevaricated slowly, inching one step forward, his gaze fixed.

"Stay where you are," Nico warned. He held out his hand toward Arlisa. "Give the CD to me, now."

He didn't have to tell her twice. Arlisa pulled the carry-all from across her shoulder, throwing a cautionary gaze at Kendra and another at Brad, before extracting from its interior what Nico required. Taking timorous steps forward, she handed it to him. "There." She planted the CD steadfast into his palm. "I hope it's your passport to hell."

Nico offered an arrogant, winning smile. "Let's just say it'll keep me and my wife safe." He turned briefly toward

Claudia. "Go get the others." He spoke in Spanish. "If the police are out there, we need to leave now."

As Claudia rushed to the door and pulled it open, the heavy noise of the Notting Hill Carnival filtered into the room. Arlisa felt the panic she'd stifled within begin to surface once again. There was no doubt the police had heard everything that was going on from the wiretap in the lining of her carry-all. But would they arrive in time?

"Arlisa." Kendra's voice was a mere whisper. "Where's Shay? Is he still in Cuba?"

"No." Arlisa looked at Nico. "Is it all right for me to go and sit with my sister?"

Nico glared at her arrogantly before nodding his head. "Don't try anything."

As if I would, Arlisa thought as she walked over to the table where Kendra was still seated. "Shay's here, outside somewhere, with Detective Inspector Sullivan," she whispered. "They know what's going on."

"Have they found Selwyn Owens?"

"No."

"Oh, god," Kendra muffled, taking a deep steadying breath. "I think . . . I'm not sure . . . but I think Selwyn Owens gave you that CD on purpose to get these people to react the way they have," she breathed. "It's his only way of getting to me. Remember, Shay took out a court injunction to ban him from coming anywhere within a foot of our house."

"But, he's never met me," Arlisa protested.

"He may've sought you out," Kendra sighed, the words struggling to get out.

"Kendra? Are you all right?"

"I don't . . ." She took a heavy breath. "All the excitement . . . seeing you again." She paused to take another heavy breath. "I think I'm going into labor."

"Labor!" Arlisa shrieked. She turned quickly and stared at Brad, completely panicked. "Kendra's in labor." Her voice echoed like a banshee.

"What?" he gasped, his malevolent glare still trained on Nico. He'd kept his eyes on the man the entire time, from the moment he'd pulled the gun—even when Claudia had left the room and the noise of music and laughter had invaded. Nico was still holding the damned thing unwaveringly, though he'd now redirected it at Brad's solar plexus.

"Don't try anything," he warned Brad. He looked across at Arlisa as though she'd just cracked a joke. "You're bluffing." He seemed slightly panicked.

While Kendra heaved heavily, Arlisa grew even more concerned. "I'll be the first to have your jugular if you let my sister have this baby squatting on the floor," she blazed. "Women may do that in Cuba or in Africa, but here in London—"

"Shut up," Nico snarled. "Move over there," he ordered Brad, directing with his eyes that he join Erica, Arlisa and Kendra by the small table. "All of you, sit down." As they did so, Nico inched his way toward the door. With his free hand, he was about to turn the brass knob when the door flew toward him violently, smacking his face and causing him to roll sideways, taking four stumbling backward steps. Nico's gun hand reflexively darted into the air, while the pistol fell to the floor with a thud.

Kendra's eyes widened with alarm when her vision focused on the person who'd barged into the room, and who she'd never expected to see again. "Selwyn!" she cursed on a crescendo note.

"Remember me?" he chided like a maniac, as the room door thumped shut. He was casually dressed in torn dungarees and a sweatshirt, which was so unlike him, having once been a man always in a pressed suit. And his hazel eyes were laughing dangerously as every unmuscled and tapered part of his body stood menacingly like a black cat ready to pounce.

Arlisa recognized the receding hairline instantly, the chicory profile and Guyana accent. Mr. Burnt Out had obviously gone to a lot of trouble, as Kendra had said, to bring their little situation about. From the moment he'd planted her with the CD at La Casa de la Salsa, he'd begun his game to reach Kendra.

Arlisa had to admit, he'd plotted it precisely. Using all his connections, liaisons and acquaintances, and motivated by his own selfish notions, he'd been able to involve a paramilitary group, two revolutionaries seeking political asylum and a sympathetic lawyer, whose wife had also inadvertently gotten embroiled, to get his hands on her sister. Arlisa's blood boiled.

"Still looking for your soul mate?" she temporized with a trace of bored sarcasm in her voice. Nico was attempting to steady himself on his feet when she rose quickly to her own, and walked steadily toward Selwyn Owens. "I don't think you'll find Khadija here."

"Keisha," Selwyn insisted nastily, shaking his head.

"Her name was Katherine," Kendra breathed weakly. "You killed her."

"No witnesses," Selwyn raged rather nastily.

"Señor Owens?" Nico rubbed the bridge of his nose where the door had caught him. "Remember me and my wife Claudia?"

"Get out," Selwyn blazed without even looking at the man, his eyes hot and fierce, trained only on Kendra. He was oblivious to her panting and the look of fear dashed across her face. He sensed only that Nico had paused before he left the room, throwing a backward sneering glance filled with disgust. "I've waited a long time for this," he told Kendra. "Now you belong to me."

When Brad saw that Selwyn made no attempt to reach to the floor for the pistol, which was in close proximity to his feet, something alive inside told him to take control. Governed only by instinct, he hurled himself from his chair, shot clean across the room and grabbed Selwyn's throat in one hand, bulldogging him into the opposite wall. He clenched his right fist ready to slug Selwyn's smug expression, but his swing was arrested by a much firmer hand.

"This one belongs to me," Shay objected, forcing Brad to one side to throw a right uppercut. It didn't knock Selwyn cold sober. It was just enough to throw him unsteady on his feet.

Selwyn's eyes widened and the hazel balls of his eyes rolled over. "I should've taken care of you a long time ago," he threatened, seconds before he threw all his weight directly into his Shay's body.

Punches were thrown and ducked in all directions. Arlisa screamed while her sister panted, and Erica rushed out of her chair to the side of her brother. "Get out of the way!" Brad yelled at her, pushing Erica to a safe distance behind him. "This is their fight now."

It certainly was. Each put in as much energy for what it was worth, with as much strength and vigor as any wrestler. When five armed police officers finally rushed the room, Shay brought his foot up sharply, landing it directly into Selwyn's gut, then watched as his enemy woofed and bent double before falling fetal to the ground. Selwyn laughed derisively, a nasty hacking sound as two armed police officers stood statue-still above him, their eyes glued, ready to shoot him at a wink.

"Shay!" Kendra screamed. She stared at his face. He

was nursing a shiner around his left eye. "I'm in labor," she panted, heaving deeply, her hands resting on her tummy, trying to rub and ease away the pain. Shay rushed to Kendra's side instantly, dropping to his knees, placing a bruised hand on her belly.

"You're only seven months," he gasped, concern leveled in his eyes.

"Don't worry," Arlisa buckled in, trying to reassure her sister. "We'll get you to a hospital."

No one saw the move Selwyn made until it was too late. As Shay hugged his wife and Brad held the hand of his sister, Selwyn doubled-up and reached for the pistol on the ground, cutting loose several shots. A passerby would hardly have been distracted by the meager sounds of the reverberating racket that came next.

The noise from the Carnival inside and outside the church drowned them completely as the burst of gunfire destroyed everything at hip level. Splinters of wood flew into the air from holes blown into the chairs. Large holes tracked across the walls, the slugs embedded in powered plaster and brick, spurts of lathe and dust rising like smoke. And as everyone ducked to the floor, holding their heads down, their arms cradled around their ears, a fatal shot was fired.

Arlisa crawled beneath the table and delved quickly into her carry-all, grabbing at the mobile phone Detective Inspector Sullivan had given her. It was Brad's body that she felt at the bottom of her feet as she dialed 999, her voice completely panicked. "Ambulance," she screamed, anxiety racing through her like a wild thing as her gaze caught sight of Shay's body over her sister. "We have an emergency. My sister is having a baby . . ."

Fifteen

"Mad, bad, or sad?" Arlisa remarked crudely as she stared at Brad propped up on two pillows, his bare chest dotted with electrodes while green screens flashed and blipped behind his hospital bed. "That's what the coroner should report as the cause of death after what Selwyn Owens put us all through."

"At least the rest of us are all alive," Brad coughed, the muscles in his stomach clenching involuntarily as he recalled that a stray bullet had caught him in the shoulder.

"Only just," Arlisa shrieked, the horror of their ordeal flashing for an instant through her mind. She held Brad's weak hand and squeezed it tightly, desperately needing to reacquaint the communion that had built up between them. "I was at my wits' end when they wheeled you and Kendra in here, and told me that they had to give you an emergency operation. I still can't believe it all came to this, at the Notting Hill Carnival, too."

"Who signed the consent form for my surgery?" Brad muffled weakly, straining his head to look at Arlisa, seated in the chair by his bed. She had clearly been worried. He could tell from the strain lines embedded on her forehead that what had happened to him affected her dearly.

"Erica," she mocked, nervously curling with one finger the long braids of her hair. "She's outside, smoking a cigarette."

"Your sister . . ." Brad paused to take a slow, ragged breath. "Did she have her baby?"

"Not yet," Arlisa wavered, nervous. "It's been ten hours."

"What time is it?"

"Four o'clock in the morning."

"What?" Brad grew alarmed. "You should be at home, resting."

"I couldn't sleep," Arlisa began, a little weepy. "I had to know that you were all right. Kendra's fine. Shay's with her, and my father. I called him on the way to the hospital."

Brad squeezed her hand, carefully avoiding the wires and electrodes that were on his chest as he gazed at Arlisa. He hated her seeing him like this, chained to his bed by medical science, too weak, too drugged with painkillers to even speak. But in many ways, her being there comforted him. It felt as though Arlisa had become a solid pillar of common sense and virtue, someone to whom he could depend and rely on. He liked that. The thought tugged at his heartstrings. Arlisa hadn't so much blossomed. She had matured.

"Did you tell your father what happened?" he asked.

Arlisa quickly dismissed the scenario that had formed in her head of how she'd quietly planned to relay the story to her father in his car on their way home. "Not yet," she admitted under her breath. "I think I might leave that one to Shay."

Brad smiled weakly, wondering what kind of hell would break loose when his own parents returned from their honeymoon in Venice. He still hadn't been able to bring himself to think of his mother's remarriage to his father, and it bothered him that he might never reconcile their being together in his head either. That would take time, he decided, planting his head deeper into his pillow and sighing heavily. What mattered now was his life. And how he was going to sort himself out with Arlisa.

"What happened after I got shot?" he quavered, closing his eyes slowly to formulate the vision in his head. The last thing he remembered was shouting Arlisa's name, and then he'd felt the sharp, excruciating stab of pain moments before he'd blanked out.

"Detective Inspector Sullivan stormed the room with a platoon of men," Arlisa intoned shakily. "He was furious with Shay apparently. He'd followed us without the inspector knowing, but Shay insists he only did so because he'd seen Selwyn Owens enter the church."

"What about the others . . . the People's Power Party?" Brad croaked.

"Nobody knows where they are," Arlisa rasped in disbelief. "While all the commotion was going on, they managed to slip away."

Brad opened his eyes and then closed them again. "They were smart," he whispered, hardly audible. "They came disguised and left that way with . . ."

"All that top secret, confidential, for-your-eyes-only information," Arlisa finished, looking at Brad. He was tired. Far too sedated to talk to her. In fact, as her gaze deepened, taking in his oval face, the black curly hair trimmed close to his scalp, which was in perfect contrast to the shadow of a moustache that had a much more pronounced stubble on his upper lip, he lapsed into a deep slumber, cut off from the world.

Arlisa placed her head down onto his chest and listened attentively to the beating of his heart. Clasping his hand ever tighter, she raised it to her lips, and planted a soft kiss against Brad's fingers. She felt eternally grateful that he was still alive. Even to sense the thumping coming from his chest told her that blood was circulating normally throughout his veins. The last time she'd felt his heart beat that fast was when they'd made love. It had always been the one trigger she needed to send her pulses racing. And she still remembered the exact day she'd first experienced it beating so strong, too, at Erica's eighteenth birthday party, beneath the stairs when he'd given her that inaugural first kiss of love.

Arlisa sighed heavily and closed her eyes, relieved that their entire ordeal was now truly over. Only now did she feel her own heart could react to the true feelings she'd kept harbored for Brad without guilt or shameful longing. She was his one and only and, in truth, he was hers, too. Had always been hers. However else was she to appeal to her common sense why this one man had been the measure to which she'd compared all other men?

The door behind her silently opened. Arlisa sensed the fresh airy draft and opened her eyes, raising her head instantly. Erica's ragged frame entered meekly and made a slow pursuit toward Brad's bed from across the room. "Is he sleeping?" she inquired, her voice lowered. "I don't want to disturb him."

"He's sleeping," Arlisa acknowledged. She watched as Erica looked over him as though she were an angel overhead passing down sweet blessings, her eyes puffed and reddened from crying and lack of sleep. Arlisa did not need to be a marriage counselor to know that all was not well between Mr. and Mrs. Brown. "Sit down." She motioned to an empty chair across from her, on the opposite side of the bed.

It was a couple of minutes before Erica seated herself and carefully touched her brother's hand. One finger twitched reflexively and she immediately withdrew as though in fear of waking him. "I called our grandfather," she swallowed sadly. "And our parents in Venice," she said, sniffling. "Otis is coming over tomorrow and Mum and Dad are flying back this weekend." She sighed, her tone strenuously taut. "Sounds strange," she began warily. "Saying *mum* and *dad* together. When we were kids, linking them bridged on blasphemy."

"Times have changed, people change," Arlisa said.

"I know," Erica sighed again, her eyes watery. "My husband . . . Tyrone has changed a great deal, only . . . it took me a long time to see it. I should've known . . . I should've questioned exactly what those people he represented were into. But I didn't, and ultimately people's lives were put in danger." Tears fell down her cheeks as she looked at Arlisa in earnest, a certain touch of anger etched in her voice. "I know I'm not wholly to blame," she added vainly, "but . . . I'm a sensible woman. Women like me just don't get caught up in something like this."

"Women like you," Arlisa repeated sardonically, taking a good look at Erica, who was now out of costume. She wore a bright pink Yves Saint Laurent scarf to conceal her lank, curly black hair, which was not in its usual state of careful dishevelment, and a deeper pink linen suit from the sharper end of designer wear clad her helpless limbs. Arlisa could hardly believe that this was the same woman who holidayed in Los Angeles, took lunches with her girlfriends at The Ritz and shopped alone, with her checkbook in St Tropez.

Erica had never been the type to attend auctions held for charity, chair meetings for deserving causes or indulge in conversation about the most needy. Having a caring nature had never been part of her character. In Erica's world, it was all about Erica, the woman who'd catapulted herself to party prominence. "That's your problem," Arlisa reproved with disgust. "Women like you just don't think twice about anything. You live life on a whim, eating Caesar salad and quail's eggs all day."

"I recall you trying to fit into that little habit," Erica bristled under her breath, wounded at Arlisa's correct analysis.

"Once I was prone to long-range fantasies like that," Arlisa mused, pondering all the lessons she'd taken on board. "Now, I'm much more . . . wiser."

Erica chuckled cynically. "I pegged you as being someone quite tasteless; now you're turning the tables on me."

"Erica." Arlisa tried to be kind. "You're a person who would never tell a lie if the truth could do more damage. I can't speak about what is going on in your marriage because I've never met your husband, but for myself, you have interfered to cause so much destruction that I'm personally not surprised that we all got wound up in this . . . this intriguing little mess. Your brother could've been killed."

Erica dipped her head as the truth shook her rigid. "Tyrone's down at New Scotland Yard now, explaining his version of events. I don't know what they're going to do with him, if anything. On all accounts, it's this . . . Selwyn Owens fellow who was at fault. Tyrone was only representing Nico and Claudia, and he still thinks someone high up threw a spanner in his career."

Arlisa didn't want to think about all that now. She looked into Brad's face and squeezed his hand, hoping that in his dreams, he knew she was there. "The only person I care about right now is your brother," she told Erica.

Erica looked at him, too, and rubbed a tear from her cheek. "The last time we spoke, you told me you loved him. Did you really mean what you said?"

Arlisa glanced at Erica, her gaze capturing the deep inquiring interest in Erica's squirrel-brown eyes. "I meant it."

The older woman nodded. To Arlisa, it felt as though Erica had conceded to the inevitable. "Did you read the letter?" she asked.

"The letter?" Arlisa's fawn-brown gaze widened suddenly. "I plan to, when I get a moment." She smiled, returning her gaze to Brad's sleeping profile. "He's already told me what's in it," she added. "But I'd like to read it for myself."

The door opened again. This time it was Shay who put his head through. "Arlisa!" She turned her head quickly, and realizing who it was, immediately left her chair to join Shay in the corridor. "It's a girl," he enthused, pride and joy mirrored in the deepest part of his dusky-brown eyes. "Seven pounds exactly."

"Thank goodness," Arlisa cried. "Seven pounds. Seven must be your lucky number."

"I'd say," Shay cooed in excitement.

"Is Kendra all right?"

"She's fine," Shay laughed. "More than fine. She's already telling the nurses what to do."

Arlisa smiled tearfully. "That sounds like Kendra." Her voice shook and suddenly, the tears spilled from nowhere, plummeting in a mad rush down her cheeks. "Oh, Shay," she sobbed, as he pulled her into his arms, placing comforting arms over her shoulders. "I shouldn't be crying." Arlisa desperately tried to compose herself, but there were too many emotions swirling around inside. "I'm an aunt and Brad's alive. I shouldn't be crying."

"You're having a normal reaction," Shay reassured emotionally. "Look at me." He pulled back and showed Arlisa both hands. "I'm shaking, too."

Arlisa chuckled on a hoarse throat. "It's been . . ." Words failed her.

"We survived it," Shay urged, taking hold of Arlisa's hands, willing her to believe. "Which is more than I can say for Mr. M.P. And how in the hell did those Cuban revolutionaries get away? The police in this country are such ninnies."

"And you are a brash, extroverted American," Arlisa returned, willing herself to smile.

Shay smiled too, and hugged her again. "How is Brad?"

"He's sleeping," she breathed. "Erica's in there with him."

"Sista has a lot to answer for," Shay jabbed.

"Don't even go there," Arlisa warned. "Sista ain't listening."

"Well if it's like that," Shay drawled, becoming excited again. "I'm going back to the ward downstairs to spend more time with my wife and new daughter."

"You do that," Arlisa agreed, patting Shay on the back of his hand. "Tell Kendra I'll come and see her in the morning, after I get some sleep."

"In the morning?" Shay's smile deepened. "You mean later on today. You'll have to come to the house instead because by afternoon, I'm taking Kendra and our new baby home."

Arlisa nodded and returned back to the hospital room Brad was sleeping in. She found Erica still by his bed, rubbing her fingers gently against his. "Your sister?" Erica queried in anticipation.

"A girl. They're both doing fine." She picked up her handbag, which the Detective Inspector had returned to her, and placed it beneath her arms. "I'm just going to use the bathroom," she informed Erica quietly. "Do you want some coffee, tea?"

"No," Erica sighed, still appearing tearful. "I'll see you later."

The bathroom smelled clinically clean as one would expect from a hospital lavatory, everything bleached down to the gray tiling on the floor, when Arlisa entered. She opened the small window and took a breath of night air before she held onto the washbasin, finding herself sobbing again. She tried hard to stop crying, but when she saw her red eyes in the bathroom mirror and the alleviation across her face, she started again. She knew that her tears were ones of overwhelming relief. Her sister was safe and Brad was safe. It was just getting it all out of her system that was bringing on the waterworks.

After a good while, she dried her eyes and washed her face with cold water, patting her eyes dry with a paper towel. She observed herself again in the bathroom mirror, thankful that she was alone. Her tawny-brown complexion seemed paler than usual and there was no doubting that she was in need of sleep, judging by the deep circles around her eyes. Arlisa pinched at her cheeks and then pulled out her tongue in a ruthless gesture to herself that she was behaving weakly, not becoming of a *Hypermega*.

So what, her mind relaxed, uncaring. It was time she put that silly term out of her head. Instantly, Brad's letter flashed through her mind. *I'll read it now,* Arlisa told herself, reaching into the haven of her handbag. *That should cheer me up.*

The seal was easy to break and the half-sized piece of yellow lined paper had been folded several times. Arlisa leaned the small of her back against the washbasin and began to leisurely peruse Brad's handwriting, his long strokes and lazy scrawl coming into focus, clear and precise. The moment the words digested, Arlisa looked disbelieving at them. *This can't be right,* her mind warned in panic.

Thinking maybe she had misread it, she sentenced the words in her head again. It read: *Dear Arlisa. The moment you read this, I will be on my way to the Bahamas. What happened between you and I was an untimely mistake that was neither your fault nor mine. I hope, in time, you find what you are looking for and that when you do, you will know great happiness. I trust that you will keep yourself well and that you receive love, peace and wisdom in abundance. It is what you deserve. Good-bye. Brad Belleville.*

The words blurred. The tears returned, fast and in a flurry, as the paper fell limp from Arlisa's fingers to the floor. She crumbled once more, this time in humiliation. It had all been lies. Brad had led her to believe something that wasn't even written. Had never been written. It hurt. Intolerably. And after all they'd said to one another. She felt irritated, insecure, ugly, all at the same time. What had she been to him exactly? A casual vixen who didn't mind partaking of a few physical recreational activities. *Blah.* Arlisa wanted to wail.

This was too much. It was all simply . . . too much. She couldn't go back into Brad's hospital room. It would be beneath her, especially while Erica was there. She would go right on home, Arlisa decided. That was the best place for her right now. The only place where she could vent out her shame and anguished pain.

The following three days went by in a blur. Refraining from visiting the hospital again to see Brad had added to Arlisa's irritability, though by dodging him it allowed her time to try and erase every facet of him from her memory. If only it could be that easy. She was wretchedly unhappy and couldn't explain the mood swings, where various blunders, misjudgment and misconceptions roiled and festered in her head, making a mountain of a mess. If only things could come the size of mole holes, she'd thought, then she wouldn't feel so bruised and battered.

But she'd been scarred by Brad's lie. In many ways, it felt like being dumped, being passed over for another woman, as Jerome had once done. Only this time there was no other person to plan an offensive attack against. While she'd been able to salvage some pride by seeing Bernadetta Crossland, and realizing that the woman's face was creased and much older than her own, there was no defensive strategy for coming to terms with the fact that she'd been a *nobody* in somebody's life. In her world, she *had* indeed been expendable. And there was a certain core to the whole truth, too. For attempting to love, two men had wounded her. One selfishly. The other needlessly. Both irresponsibly.

Seated at her dressing table, facing the mirror where an almost deranged, yet beautiful face reflected at her, Arlisa looked deeply into her fawn-brown eyes, seeing a somewhat innocent, muzzy-headed romantic looking back at her. *I told you never to believe in fairy tales,* she told herself, aware that throughout the years of knowing Brad, her feet had always been planted nine feet in the air.

Love. Men don't understand what that word means, she reviled herself, thinking of when she'd told Kendra that. It was time she revolved back to the rules of a *Hypermega,* where enlightened women saw men as useful subjects only if they had money. But as she bolted down another glass of whiskey and proceeded to pour herself yet another, Arlisa found herself silently dismissing that option because she'd learned that was not the way to go either. Rich mates don't treat women any better, she surmised. They just have easier and better financial means to manipulate, control and then ditch.

"Oh, Brad," Arlisa cried, her emotions torn and tangled, seeing the yellow lined paper on top of her dressing table through blurred, teary eyes. He'd been kind to let her down gently. By all accounts, the words were considerate and sympathetic, and there was nothing in them one could conceivably rant about, given that it had been written with intentions almost two years old.

Nonetheless, it had broken the spell. She felt as though her guts had been sliced open and pulled out like that of a fish. *How's the trout?* Erica's voice infiltrated suddenly, and Arlisa was taken right back to the time when Brad had first kissed her, when she was fourteen years old. He'd thought then that he was kissing a fish. Maybe to him and Erica, she'd always absurdly been something that could only be found at the fishmongers'.

There was a knock at the bedroom door and Arlisa quickly pulled herself together, aborting all thoughts of insanity where spoils from the sea were concerned. Picking up Brad's letter, she hid it away in her dresser drawer and then wiping the tears that had spilled onto her cheeks, she pulled her bedcoat closer together and bellowed, "Come in, Daddy."

Ramsey Davenport entered, throwing a cautionary glance at his daughter, pausing before he closed the door. He'd been more than aware that Arlisa had sequestered herself in his house since leaving the hospital. And though he was a man who'd grown to enjoying his solitary life, he knew that his daughter could not. Arlisa was a woman of action, of fun and who possessed lively values which over the years had been tamed to wiser ones. Still, he knew she'd always retained a sense of purpose and to him, Arlisa's purpose had always been to come out on top.

"Can I come in?" Ramsey inquired softly in a Jamaican burr, making his way toward the bed. Seating himself there, he looked across at Arlisa. "I'm all ears you know."

Arlisa wanted to beat a hasty retreat, but she knew her father better. He was the man who still hadn't lost his steely-eyed authority from the days when he was editor and proprietor of the *Nubian Chronicle*. And for his near-sixty years, he had always remained fit, his six-feet height formed in a lean body, with a trim waist and hard muscles maintained through regularly joining Kendra whenever she went swimming at the gym.

It kept him alert and insightful. She'd always been unable to hide the truth from him. Abstaining from seeing her father worked better than direct personal confrontation. And if she had to lie, it was done intentionally over the telephone, anything to avoid the direct cutting edge of Ramsey's intuitive gaze, which usually bore into her in a searching, wanton sort of way.

"I'm feeling . . . rejected," she announced with irony.

"From Otis Belleville's grandson?" Ramsey guessed.

Arlisa nodded.

"Well, there's many more fish in the sea," Ramsey encouraged sympathetically. "All you need is a good net and—"

"Don't mention fish," Arlisa rasped sternly.

Ramsey's expression grew bemused. "Were you and him serious?" he asked.

Arlisa nodded again, quite saddened at the revelation.

Ramsey sighed, shaking his head. "You kids today," he muttered uneasily. "When Shay told me what happened, what you two had been through . . . had done to get Kendra, I was . . . perplexed and angry why you both never came to me first. I am your father," he insisted firmly, then paused. "I suppose when girls grow up, they put all their trust in the one man they love."

"I still love you, Daddy," Arlisa reassured, eyeing him through the mirror on her dressing table.

Ramsey nodded, even offered a faint smile. "You've always been reckless, but I love you, too."

Arlisa winced, feeling sorry for herself "You're the only man I know who seems to want to offer me it: that sweet nectar from God, you used to say. I try. I have tried, but . . ."

"Some men don't know a black pearl when they see one," Ramsey retorted. "You know," he began in reminiscence. "When I first saw Merle, your mother, I was twelve years old and I was too frightened to talk to her." Arlisa listened attentively as her father went on, realizing that this was the first time since her mother died that he'd spoken of Merle Davenport. "She was the Reverend's daughter back home in Jamaica, and every Sunday I used to go to church just to pin my eyes on her."

"When did you talk to her, finally?" Arlisa asked, intrigued.

"Years later," Ramsey declared, almost childishly. "Benjamin and she used to go to the same school. Then I heard that he'd started courting her."

"Benjamin Brentwood?" Arlisa was shocked.

"And his father wanted them to get married," Ramsey continued regardless. "Me and Benjamin were partners by then in the *Nubian Chronicle,* which we began back in Jamaica. Even so, I knew I had to tell Merle how I felt about her."

"Which you did, or Kendra and I wouldn't be here," Arlisa smiled warmly.

"I lost Benjamin though," Ramsey added sadly, his eyes straying for a moment as though he'd taken himself back to a time and place where two boys had forged a solid glass friendship, which had cracked and then been broken, but where only time would reveal, and if miracles were possible, them both sharing in the birth of a granddaughter. "There's always going to be casualties in love," Ramsey alerted himself back to the present. "The best thing to do now is pick yourself up and move on."

"But Daddy." Arlisa felt suddenly moved, absorbed by the story of how her father had successfully wooed her mother. "My situation is almost like yours. I've liked Brad from the moment you took me to Otis Belleville's house when I was nine years old. Now I'm in love with him. You knew you wanted Momma, you said so. Well, that's how certain I feel about Brad Belleville."

"Tell him so," Ramsey advised, forthright and simple. "What in the world do you have to lose?"

"My pride, my heart. My integrity," Arlisa whimpered, unsure.

"And what about claiming that other half that will make you whole?" Ramsey rebutted.

Arlisa thought hard and carefully. In his wisdom, her father knew many things. He was telling her all this because he cared about her, and because he was a man, Arlisa felt certain of what he knew. Rising up from her chair, she rushed over to her father and hugged him helplessly. "I'll tell him, Daddy," she enthused mildly. "And if he turns me away, then I'll know for sure that . . . my past can't be my future."

"That's my girl," Ramsey smiled. "And do it soon, because I promised your mother that when you got wed, I'd give you the black pearl necklace I gave to her on our wedding day."

"Oh, Daddy," Arlisa gushed.

Ramsey held his daughter close and hugged her affectionately. He sensed the calming of Arlisa's mood, but what he did not know was that there was one other item Arlisa had to resolve with Brad first.

Sixteen

Brad stared into Arlisa's face and saw the expression of something that had matured from within, something which might probably mark her beautiful face forever. It wasn't sudden or transitory. Perhaps it'd been there for a while and he'd only just noticed it. Whatever it was, it made him realize that Arlisa had come there to see him with matters on her mind she was intent on solving.

He waited until the door closed, even watched as she walked mechanically across the room to seat herself in the chair opposite his hospital bed before he decidedly spoke. "Hello." He injected mirth into his voice. "It's been four days. I've been thinking maybe you've given up on me."

"Should I?" Arlisa threw the two words out slowly and ambivalently, as though afraid of losing either one. She'd dressed that morning in vivid red, the one color that always projected confidence. And she hadn't meant to calculate the collection either, but the Italian shoes, an off-the-rack cashmere and wool dress, the silk scarf, linen jacket and designer handbag, equaled a wardrobe of six hundred and fifty pounds, well below the mark required of a *Hyper-mega.*

Arlisa felt certain she'd now shed that ridiculous habit as she smoothed the knitted line in her dress with steady, controlled fingers. Usually, being in red made her feel more secure. Highly articulate, still a doyenne of her time.

A top-ranking social butterfly, no longer having to feel the need to prove it.

She liked the way she felt. When the autumn sun had risen its head, bringing in the second day of September, she'd made the decision to come and see Brad. Not so much to tell him how she felt, but to discover how he really felt about her. The only way she was going to achieve that was to show Brad the letter he'd written to her some eighteen months ago.

"What's wrong?" Brad said, bemused, smiling weakly at Arlisa, though inside he felt quite well. His wound was healing nicely, the hospital were feeding him adequately and by all counts, his physical condition was more than healthy. But Brad sensed the determination hidden in the depth of Arlisa's eyes.

The last time she'd looked at him like that was when they'd been talking outside the Yaa Asantewaa Art Gallery. She'd been angry. Hurt. And deep down he'd felt some reluctance in losing her. The very thought produced that familiar pain he felt in his heart. He recognized it now and as he thought for a moment, he now knew what it meant, He was afraid to lose Arlisa. His pain was one of fear.

And that fear heightened to its fullest proportion when he watched as she produced a yellow letter from her handbag and placed it, as though it were fragile tissue paper, onto the fresh clean covers of his hospital bed. Brad knew at once what it was. How she came by it never filtered into his mind, only how he was going to explain it.

"You read it?" he asked, recalling the different set of information he'd given her as to its content.

"I thought I'd give you the opportunity to tell me what it means, since I was told something quite different," Arlisa rasped.

Brad watched as the determined set of Arlisa's jaw hardened. He was also very much aware of how attractive she appeared. From the moment she'd entered his room, his heart had begun to sing. She made his pulses dance, aroused his most amorous emotions and something far more solid between his legs was all too in need of her. But all this aside—and it was hard to put it aside—he knew he'd wronged her. He should never have lied about the letter and he'd never thought to ask Erica what she'd done with it, either.

He was laying on his back, but he now turned onto his side and faced her head-on. Seeing her face, braced ready for his reply, almost made a coward out of him. But he was a man, and he was going to deal with this as a man should. "I tried to spare you from being hurt," he began by way of an explanation. "When you told me Erica never gave you a letter, I thought it would be nice for us to start all over again."

"So that's why you lied about what you originally wrote?" Arlisa inquired, calmly. Sensibly.

"I thought, why tell you the truth? They'd be no way of you ever finding out."

"But I have found out," Arlisa responded dryly.

"I know." Brad shook his head. This was not going very well. Again he felt as though he were seventeen and out of his depth when it came to Arlisa Davenport.

"Tell me." Arlisa was curious. So far, she admired the way she was handling everything. Without hysteria, screaming, or behaving like a mad hyena. This ladylike manner was quite appealing. It gave her a certain edge of control. "When you wrote that letter, you weren't intending to see me again, were you?"

"I . . . no," Brad admitted at last. He shifted uncomfortably and uneasily in his bed when he saw how shaken Arlisa had become. Why try and dupe an intuitive woman?

If he were going to mend any fences, everything had to come out into the open once and for all. "It wasn't anything to do with you," he informed nervously. "You were vulnerable and, as for me, I knew that there were things I wanted to do. Your mother had died and, maybe it was immature on my part, but there was too much going on with me to even support you the way you . . . needed. I did not realize I'd left you with residual feelings."

"Is that how you characterize what we had—residual?" Arlisa reproved, absorbing every measure of what Brad was saying.

"I didn't mean it like that." Brad chose his words carefully. "What I should've said is that I rather hoped you had some feelings for me. You see,"—he was not sure whether she would believe him—"when I got to the Bahamas, all I could think about was you."

"Wonders never cease," Arlisa ventured, quite cynical. "You have always been so judgmental of me, I find that rather hard to believe. When I . . ." She shook her head tirelessly. "When I saw you again, I was so determined that we would never get close. But all you could talk about was old times and how our past could be our future, and all I could remember was how you'd left and all the rules I'd devised to live my life by."

"So, what happened?" Brad shrugged.

"You happened." Arlisa wanted to scream the words out, but instead, threw them out haphazardly. "I'm one of those women whose signals gets turned on and tune into a man's wavelength, and I've always been in tune with yours. In many ways, and in not so many ways, you've always been a part of my life."

"That's how I feel, too," Brad wavered majestically.

"Let me finish," Arlisa crooned, regardless of what he'd said. "I need proof that you really want to know me. If you're not sure, then don't. We've been through a lot these past few days and maybe the intensity of it all has clouded everything."

Brad grew alarmed, propping himself up on his pillow. "What are you trying to say, Arlisa?"

Somehow, Arlisa felt like she'd just placed herself into a hole. This wasn't the direction she'd wanted to go in. How on earth did she get here? There was a certain inevitability to what she was saying, as though a conclusion was looming up ahead. Then it dawned on her. She was trying to end her affair with Brad. "I think we should spend some time apart." Even the words spilled out before she could stop herself.

Brad glared at Arlisa, fire banked in his eyes. "You're a hard nut to break," he snapped angrily, displaying a bewildered streak as though he was trying to decipher what was going on in Arlisa's head. He could almost see it now.

Marriage was dead. Love sucked. Affairs were impropriety. Fairy tales were farce. And given that he hadn't played Romeo to her Juliet, she was resuming to the standards set out there by men, where money and beauty went hand in hand. Hadn't their recent lovemaking been proof enough that he deeply pined for her?

Throughout the days he'd spent in his hospital bed, seeing few visitors which had consisted of Erica, Otis and Detective Inspector Sullivan, his thoughts had been only of Arlisa. And he'd quietly dismissed her having not come to see him earlier, knowing that she would probably be offering a helping hand to her sister, but nonetheless looking forward to the day when she would eventually come. Not in his wildest imaginings had he thought she would visit him to end something that had begun to flourish.

"Arlisa!" he protested, feeling himself to blame. "Be reasonable."

"Reasonable?" Arlisa repeated.

"You're overreacting."

"What?" Arlisa found herself on her feet, having levitated from her chair. "I should've seen this coming."

Brad was bemused. "What coming?"

"You behaving like this."

"Like what?"

She stalked toward the door. "This is for the best," she assured him without conviction. It was the last thing Arlisa said before she left the room.

It was a case of cold feet. At least that was what Arlisa decided as she sat at her office desk at the *Nubian Chronicle* three weeks later, thinking back to the day she walked out on Brad. Everything seemed back to normal. The office was buzzing, preparations were being made for Black History Month in October, and there was an uncanny acceptance of her new role as Shay Brentwood's right-hand woman, with her sister being away on maternity leave.

She'd come a long way from the mail room, where she'd first started at the newspaper. A lot had happened since then: the misery of resolving her gambling habit, seeing Brad again, Kendra's kidnapping and the perilous danger they'd all been thrown into at the hands of a deranged maniac. It'd been one hell of a roller-coaster and she'd surmounted unscathed, hardly traumatized, except that her heart was hopelessly in love.

Why couldn't I tell him? Arlisa silently screamed to herself in agony. Fear. That's what it was. Fear. It'd always been at the back of her mind that she could never measure up to what Brad really found wanting in a woman. Hadn't that been the one real motive why she was driven to behaving like a *Hypermega?* She may've invented the word and lived up to its potential, but Brad had always been the root cause behind it. And when she'd tried to banish all the worries and doubts that had plagued her on whether she'd done the right thing or not, uncertainty remained all the same.

A little tremor of shock ran through Arlisa. She might have had her misgivings about what they'd done, but she certainly hadn't expected to react the way she did. She'd walked into that hospital room with every pretext of telling Brad how much she loved him. So what happened exactly? *Cold feet.* That's what. And when her father had jokingly inquired on when they were going to get married, she'd told him that Brad was not planning to be involved in a committed relationship.

She leaned back into her chair and glanced at the Empire Windrush project that had eaten into much of her time recently. Two meetings with the Association of London Local Government, three debates in her office with representatives from the local West Indian community, and she was still no closer to resolving the issue of suggesting a bank holiday date for Windrush Day. And with the new delegated responsibilities Shay had put her way, Arlisa was surprised she found time to think of Brad at all.

By the end of the day she was able, at least for a while, to put him from her thoughts entirely. Their affair was no kismet, not really. More a . . . passing fancy, she told herself on entering her father's house that night. Dinner was spent rather quietly, with Ramsey understanding his daughter's somber mood, knowing that there was nothing he could do about it other than offer her support until she'd healed her broken heart.

In her bedroom that night, Arlisa took a long, soothing bath and decided on a whim that she would go out. Perhaps she would go and visit Kendra. The idea seemed good and she hadn't talked with her sister in a while. Though she knew that their conversation would stray toward diapers, breast feeding and the much finer points of child rearing, it would be far better to listen to that than to have her mind play around thinking about Brad Belleville.

But as she applied eyeshadow to her fawn-brown eyes, blusher to the tawny brown complexion of her skin and marked the defined line of her plucked brows, thoughts of spending time with Kendra began to disappear from Arlisa's mind altogether.

On impulse, she began to dress in something designed for dancing. *I'm still young, free and single,* she told herself. *Life's too short,* came another resounding reminder. Tonight would be the night that she would face up to the fact that her life just had to go on.

Been there, heard it, seen it, done it. These were the words that flew through Arlisa's mind, two hours later, when she found herself on her usual bar stool at La Casa de la Salsa. The Latin groovers were as lively as ever, seething with flair, oozing etiquette and precision in their body movements, reveling in all the majestic, Bacchanalian frenzy that could only be found on a salsa dance floor.

The Afro-Cuban club was kickin'. Delirious bystanders stood by the bar, their gazes fixed with bewildered curiosity as they watched the milling of dancers from all cultures execute their well-bred steps in spectacular style. The attraction did not escape Arlisa either. Though she considered herself to be a good dancer, and was often caught up in the exhibitionism displayed on the dance floor, remarkably, she was not in a mood to join in.

There was a time when doing the salsa was a weekly tradition, a ritual to rub off the stress that had built up throughout the week. While other people preferred to smoke or drink, she instead partook of the regular flirting and flaunting of joyous abandon that came with every practiced step. And when every dance was over, she had enjoyed the sense of surfacing spontaneously, liberated and bursting into the blinding brilliance of ecstatic freedom.

But tonight, Arlisa was not at grips with the intoxicating, effervescent mood of the club. Still in a somber state of mind, she'd ordered her usual Tequila Sunrise and had been sipping it slowly while she looked around, totally bored. The last time she'd been at the club, Mr. Burnt Out, whom she would later know to be Selwyn Owens, had been the intrusive person to infiltrate her boredom. Prior to that, she had been hoping to see Earl Vani, thinking he could inject some sparkle into her night. Nevertheless, she'd experienced an adventure that had spiraled her into the cradle of love. It seemed somehow unnatural to find herself, once again, back among plain mortals, miles away from danger.

Maybe living on the edge as she had done, when finding her sister became imperative, had given her a taste for living another adventure. As Brad had said, there would always be that part of her that liked living on the wild side. She took another sip from her glass of tequila and glanced around again.

The usual crowd was there, their faces familiar, acknowledging her presence with slight inclinations of their heads; the classic Somalis with their good looks and slim figures, the Nigerians repressing their wickedly funny thoughts, the Caribbeans always dressed to kill—always elegant—and the Latinos in a dizzy whirl of conversation and social propriety. Arlisa no longer felt like she fit in. Being there no longer filled the void, hacked away at the stress or made her happy. All Arlisa could think about was Brad Belleville.

Suddenly, his image flew into her mind. She remembered it well, as always. His face had paraded around in her dreams for years. This time, the image was of leaving him as she'd done, though she had not actually said "goodbye." There was a sense of unfinished business about it. The finality was not final, she even thought. *This is for the best,* she'd said. *What was for the best exactly?* Arlisa felt about to scream. Was it cold feet or had she been just plain stupid? Or was it that integrity thing that surfaced every now and again?

Her mind felt so chaotic she hardly noticed the voice that spoke from behind her until she heard it again. "I knew I'd find you in here." It was Kitty Lee and her entourage.

"Hi girlfriend," Arlisa openly announced to the newly married woman who always dressed imaginatively in African print designer shawls to match the single colors she always wore. "How's married life treating you?"

"It's not all that it's cracked up to be," Kitty laughed, as though she were attempting to repress some wickedly funny thought. "Do you know," she began, taking Arlisa by the wrist and gently pulling her from her stool into her fresh circle of friends, "my Nigerian husband told me this morning that he felt it was time I meet prospective wife number two."

"No!" every member of the circle gasped in horror.

"He's not one of those, is he, who believe in having four wives?" another asked in shock.

"It appears so." Kitty smiled, finding the matter totally absurd. "One for his good sex, one for his cheap sex, one to cook and iron his clothes, and another to show off about town."

"Which one are you?" Arlisa found herself asking in disbelief.

"Well," Kitty drawled in irritation. "Tell me what you think? I realized two days ago that the word 'laundry' held no meaning to him. He has no idea whatsoever about the domestic arrangements of our home. Even the words 'washing machine' are a complete mystery. When he couldn't find his polo socks yesterday and I told him that they were probably in the clean-clothes basket, he looked at me as though I were talking Dutch, then asked me in which direction of the house the basket was located."

Arlisa found herself chuckling along with the group of friends, though she knew the situation was not entirely funny. And she thought she had problems simply attempting to be the one woman in one man's life. "What did you tell him?" she inquired, bemused, even as her fawn gaze traveled around the room to find that the dance floor was admitting a new cloudburst of arrivals.

"I told him that I did not appreciate his newly acquired helplessness," Kitty Lee divulged firmly. "And that was when he put the blame on me."

"What?" everyone chorused instantly.

"He said that I was too super-competent," Kitty explained. "You know, the type who can juggle professional, home, social and family life with both hands?"

"Hyperwoman," someone finished.

Hypermega, Arlisa thought.

"That's a moot point when what we're really talking about here is a semiliterate bastard," Kitty harangued. "We've only been married three and a half months. He's supposed to be a successful businessman with a brilliant brain. So why do the words 'shopping list' sound like a six-part symphony to him?"

"I take it you feel like you've been demoted from good

sex to bottle washer and dog's body?" Arlisa finished sympathetically.

"I quail to think," Kitty Lee retorted. "But I'll be damned if he installs some second wife under me. I'll see him in a divorce court first."

"Nigerians," everyone agreed in unison.

Men, Arlisa thought instead.

"So," Kitty hedged, steering the subject swiftly, pointing discreetly in the direction where a raised gazebo was erected for viewers. "You seem to know most people in here, Arlisa. Tell me about the guy over there."

All eyes turned toward the direction Kitty had pointed. Arlisa's breathing suddenly shallowed, her lungs quickly becoming short of breath as she discovered who the man was. Brad Belleville stood within four feet of her—so close, if she were to inch her way forward, she would almost be able to touch that beautifully sculpted body that, even now, paraded through her head. She was so surprised, she hardly knew how to react. Should she go over and talk to him, or should she not?

A few seconds of self-debate and she decided that she would. "Excuse me," she told her bemused friends, her heart pounding like a jackhammer as she departed the circle and began, with unsteady feet, to walk around the bar toward the gazebo. Brad did not see her, and she was glad that he hadn't, until she took the two shallow steps onto the small platform. His head turned and their gazes locked, holding as Brad curtly expelled a breath.

"In God's name, what are you doing here?" Arlisa stuttered quite incredulously.

"God's name has nothing to do with me being here," Brad answered, digging his hands deep into his trouser pockets to silently contemplate her.

"I mean . . ." Arlisa paused, desperately trying to

camouflage the fact that she was thoroughly shaken by Brad's being there. "What are you doing over here?"

"Would you call me selfish if I came over and talked to you?" Brad rebutted, having seen her on his arrival.

"Only to your face," Arlisa offered, half smiling, desperately trying to quell her heart from thumping heavily into her rib cage.

Brad chuckled, gazing sideways as though shrugging off the snub. "I was hoping to find you here," he said quite casually. "I wanted to give you something you've never had."

"A heart attack," Arlisa remarked, just as casually.

Brad laughed again and Arlisa had to admit, she found the sound warming to her soul. Brad looked devastatingly attractive, dressed casually in beige slacks and a deep brown jacket, a cotton Versace shirt with the neck buttons opened to reveal the soft curls of hair on his upper chest. And he was freshly shaven, his hair perfectly groomed, giving the appearance of a successful man who took good care of himself. She found it hard to tear her gaze away from him, even though it somewhat bridged on acrimony. The anger she felt was more against her reaction at seeing him than to do with him actually being within her grasp.

"The only person who may suffer an impending heart attack is me," Brad chided, his honey-brown gaze searching every inch of her body, making Arlisa blatantly aware that he was in full approval of the low-cut, short pink georgette and lace dress she was wearing. "I hope you've got something on underneath that dress."

Arlisa gasped again, this time in recoiling amazement. "Of course, Brad," she insisted in a devilishly sweet tone she knew would rile him. "Chanel Number Five." She felt Brad take ahold of her wrist, but she gingerly pushed his hand away. "Don't," she warned. She meant the order to be obeyed.

Brad's eyes clouded. He knew now it was a mistake to ever come there and try to close the berth between him and Arlisa. "It's been nice seeing you again." He straightened his jacket, and walked away. It was not within his nature to try and force the issue.

"Wait!" Arlisa almost coughed the word out. The warm look of greeting she'd initially seen in Brad's face had now been replaced by silent reproval. Arlisa shivered. She couldn't risk losing Brad again, especially not while he'd come there to give her something. And she didn't want them to argue, not really, but a part of her was still nursing the disappointment he'd put her through. "What was it?"

"What?"

"That you wanted to give me?"

Brad shrugged, throwing an annoyed look across the room. He would've preferred somewhere quieter, more solitary, but this was the one place he knew he would find Arlisa. And it was neutral ground, he reminded himself, because he was not sure how Arlisa would react at seeing him again. At that precise moment, he felt as though he'd wasted his time. She appeared in no mood to hear him out. "I can see it's not important now," he broached, taking one step to the side of her.

"It was important enough for you to come here," Arlisa rasped, slightly irritated, regretting her irrational behavior. "Hoping to find me," she added.

Brad sighed before shaking his head, as though he'd decided to abort the conversation entirely. Following the fiasco of Arlisa walking out on him in his hospital room, thoughts had plagued him about their affair. It would be false to say it hadn't affected him. It had. Only a heartless person could be complacent. And deep down, he more than understood Arlisa's motives. She wasn't sure how seriously he was taking her. She could not see the direction they were going. A woman of her caliber could easily surmise that he was intending to use her. Likewise, he'd thought that she was using him.

But they'd been through so much together that he'd come to see a part of Arlisa that had always smote him. It'd been there from the moment he'd met Arlisa when he was twelve years old. This strong-willed woman who possessed a flair of angelic qualities that had always made him feel so attached to her. He was reminded of that strange, magnetic bonding when he returned home after leaving the hospital and began to steadily wean himself back into his work routine.

While sitting in his living room he remembered the night he and Arlisa had danced the salsa, and the morning that followed when he'd made love to her in the shower. Kissing her then was like kissing her the first time, when he'd been caught up in such a whirl of amorous madness, he'd promised her something. No other woman had ever given him that same fresh taste of sweet nectar. He recalled being so surprised by it that he'd lied to Erica and adolescently told her that kissing Arlisa was like kissing a fish. But as fishes go, Arlisa was the only one in the sea. Brad knew now he could never find another. She was the one he wanted to catch.

"You said something to me once, about what a man would have to do prove his love for a woman."

Arlisa thought back and recollected it well. "He would have to give her something he hadn't thought he would part with," she repeated out loud.

"I remembered it," Brad nodded. "And I want you to have this, for old time's sake." He pulled a small box from his jacket pocket and placed it on the bar.

Arlisa glared at it disbelieving, before she reached out with shaking hands and picked it up. Opening the box, she found inside something she'd seen before. It was the diamond-studded ring Brad always wore on his right middle finger. "This is the ring your father gave you," she said shakily, it also tugging again at a far distant memory.

"I want you to have it," Brad said quite slowly.

"Do you remember," she gulped, almost faint, her mind rushing in all directions. "When I was fourteen, when you kissed me under the stairs, you wanted to give this ring to me then?"

"Yes, I remember," Brad nodded knowingly. "And I've since told you how much it means to me. It seems that you were always the one I've ever meant to give it to."

"Brad . . . I."

"I know what you told me about marriage," Brad interceded quickly. "But because I still believe that your nature will always care for me, I hope some day you will see this ring to be a symbol of how I truly feel about you. Despite everything that has happened between us, Arlisa, past and present, I feel that my confusion . . . our confusion . . . is because, deep down, we really love each other."

"Yes." The word came out suddenly, unexpectedly.

"That's how you feel, too?" Brad wavered.

"Yes." Arlisa nodded her affirmation, again.

"Why didn't you tell me?"

"I . . . cold feet," she rasped.

Brad chuckled amidst the cacophony of laughter and music around them, finding himself gravitating toward her. As their heads came closer, a salsa couple in full swing brushed past them and knocked Arlisa slightly, causing her to topple until she fell off balance, directly into Brad's arms. It was where she wanted to be and it was where he wanted her, too. "Cold feet?" Brad asked, as they immediately embraced in a tender, caressing hug. "That's why when I was in the hospital, you turned things around."

"I didn't intend to," Arlisa breathed, putting her arms around Brad's shoulders, carefully positioning herself back on her feet. "I was scared—"

"I knew you were scared," Brad interrupted. "Because I'd lied to you."

Arlisa glanced at the ring behind Brad's shoulders that remained steadfast in its box. "Are you lying now?" she asked, a little skeptical.

Brad chuckled, though he could hardly blame Arlisa. "No, I'm not. In time, I hope you consider it to be a token of my intention to marry you."

It was Arlisa's turn to chuckle. "Steady on." She refused to take him seriously. "Where did this come from?"

"This comes from a man who is going to prove to you that marriage can be as good for a man as it can for a woman."

Arlisa's arms loosened from around Brad's neck. Deep down, she'd always known that she wanted nothing less than a public expression of her bond between the man she loved. She'd wanted the same kind of love that her parents had shared, that she now saw in Shay and Kendra. But men lied. And Brad had lied. And . . . now he'd given her his most prized sentimental possession. She wanted to think, formulate her thoughts into sentences with words, but numbers rushed her brain instead.

Ninety-one and counting. "I want to believe you," she implored in earnest.

Brad pulled Arlisa's arms from around his neck and clasped her wrists in his hands. "Believe me." His voice was firm as his gaze caught her parted lips, knowledge telling him that her mouth was moist and greedy for him.

The kiss came impulsively. Brad took Arlisa's lips as

though he were tasting honey, filling her mouth with his tongue, twining it with hers until their limbs grew heavy and torpid. All presence of the club was gone, except the most primitive of urges—to hold her to him, to submerge himself in her, to have her bury herself in him. His body stiffened and she arched herself into him. The kiss deepened and both were lost, immediately swept back into the mists of time, teenagers again, this time desperately in love.

For Arlisa, it was like a fairy tale come true to be granted the wish of an intimacy such as this. Her heart became filled with a flurry of expectations as she escaped into Brad's eternal triangle. Everything about the way his lips moved against hers was familiar: pulsing, experienced, and tasting of wine, which left a sweet taste on her tongue. She liked it. It told her everything she needed to know about the mature Brad Belleville.

And her heart began to thud increasingly harder at the ruthless, shameless way in which he was claiming her lips. Gone was the testing feel of which he'd first begun. He was telling her now that he knew what she wanted, that he was the man who was going to give it to her. And what she was getting was sheer, unadulterated familiarity—from when they'd first kissed as teenagers, when Brad still hadn't grown to his full height and she'd had to look down at him then, to the aggressive satisfaction that she herself was now receiving. So immersed was Arlisa in this dream that in her mind's eye, Otis Belleville's face flashed and then, just as quickly, disappeared.

When they both alighted, the déjà vu had her shaking with reaction. Arlisa was stunned. A new top score rebounded in her head, reaching her heart, body and soul. "I believe you." How could she possibly deny what she'd just been plunged into? Every part of her body was protesting that she be submerged yet again.

Brad smiled. It reached both corners of his cheeks. Every sign of love mirrored in his eyes. "Dance?" He raised an inquisitive brow.

Arlisa beamed a huge smile and returned Brad the ring box, which he replaced in his pocket. "Why not."

He held her hand and walked Arlisa to the dance floor, gingerly pulling her into his arms. They began the dance of passion and love, sweeping across the floor in wonderful patterns of artistic originality that went admired by those who saw the vitality and intensity in each step. It was a spontaneous celebration of their having discovered love and as the splendor of it shone in their faces in all its nuances, Arlisa and Brad knew that their journey had just begun, both certain of where it would lead.

ABOUT THE AUTHOR

Sonia Icilyn was born in Sheffield, England where she still lives with her daughter, in a small village which she describes as, "typically British, quiet and where the old money is." She graduated from college with a distinction level Private Secretary's Certificate in business and commerce, and has worked for the City of Sheffield's Education Department. She is currently CEO of her own corporation, The Peacock Company, which manufactures the "Afroderma" skin care line for people of color. *Roses Are Red* was her first title for Arabesque, followed by *Island Romance.*

Sonia would love to hear from her readers:

P.O. Box 438
Sheffield S1 4YX
ENGLAND

E-mail on: SoniaIcilyn@compuserve.com

Coming in January from
Arabesque Books . . .

Celebrate the New Year with Arabesque Romances

__SECRET LOVE by Brenda Jackson
1-58314-073-5 $5.99US/$7.99CAN

__MESMERIZED by Simona Taylor
1-58314-070-0 $5.99US/$7.99CAN

__SAY YOU LOVE ME by Adrianne Byrd
1-58314-071-9 $5.99US/$7.99

__ICE UNDER FIRE by Linda Hudson-Smith
1-58314-072-7 $5.99US/$7.99CAN

Call toll free **1-888-345-BOOK** to order by phone or use this coupon to order by mail.

Name _____
Address _____
City _____ State _____ Zip_____
Please send me the books I have checked above.
I am enclosing $_____
Plus postage and handling* $_____
Sales tax (in NY, TN, and DC) $_____
Total amount enclosed $_____
*Add $2.50 for the first book and $.50 for each additional book.
Send check or money order (no cash or CODs) to: **Arabesque Books, Dept. C.O., 850 Third Avenue, 16th Floor, New York, NY 10022**
Prices and numbers subject to change without notice.
All orders subject to availability.
Visit out our web site at **www.arabesquebooks.com**